D1246602

BLACK EYED
SERAPH

BLACK EYED
SERAPH

MICHAEL KLUG

Charleston, SC
www.PalmettoPublishing.com

Black Eyed Seraph

Copyright © 2021 by Michael Klug

All rights reserved

No portion of this book may be reproduced,
stored in a retrieval system, or transmitted in any form
by any means–electronic, mechanical, photocopy,
recording, or other–except for brief quotations
in printed reviews, without prior permission
of the author.

First Edition

Paperback ISBN: 978-1-63837-299-8
eBook ISBN: 978-1-63837-183-0

For Bob and Jean, with love.

I believe in everything until it's disproved.
So I believe in fairies, the myths, dragons. It all exists,
even if it's in your mind. Who's to say that dreams
and nightmares aren't as real as the here and now.

—John Lennon

PROLOGUE

Jack is running in this dream. Not sprinting, but more like an easy jog. He's wearing an Iowa Hawkeye outfit while barreling down this particular fantasy freeway of his subconscious mind. The old gold hooded sweatshirt emblazoned with a giant black Tigerhawk and black sweats bottoms sporting an old gold "IOWA" in block letters down the left leg were two sizes too big so they made him look skinny. Being a Maize and Blue Michigan man, he likened it to cheating on his favorite school.

And Jack dreams *a lot.* No nightmares, no scary monsters, just regular dreams. Many recur several nights in a row, and it almost seems like he's back in the same scene, just a day (or a week? or a month?) later. And all of them are *extremely* vivid. In one dream series, he's an immigration official of some sort, and he believes he's on Ellis Island because he has glimpsed the Statue of Liberty towering above the harbor a half mile or so away through one of the many windows in the cavernous main hall. The Jack of this dream speaks several languages fluently, especially Slavic dialects, and seems to take great joy in handing out new names and identities to the masses who were coming to America chasing the American Dream. Jack even sometimes thinks about taking a Russian language class at Mott or Kettering just to figure out what the heck he's saying.

In one of the weirdest dreams, he is a logger, hewing tree after tree and dragging them ever further to a building site of the largest sea vessel he'd ever seen. Day after day, he chops down trees and then drags them to the building site. What he would give for a chain saw…or even a decent handsaw. He's chopping and hacking with a stone blade affixed to a piece of wood with a leather strap. The language these people use is even more foreign to him, and he has no idea what anybody is saying. And the people in this dream yell at him all the time.

"Ham!" they often bellow. It's their favorite word, and they use it a lot. What the hell does that even mean? Is he supposed to get them lunch? The person Jack has become in the dream yells an unintelligible litany of throaty syllables right back at them.

"Burger!" Jack shouted back one time, laughing. The two other men in the dream looked confused, and they definitely were not amused.

In this evening's dream, which he has never experienced before, he's not running away from anything—or toward something, for that matter. The landscape is impossibly flat and devoid of scenery, and the lighting is rather dark and eerily pinkish-red. For his effort, he doesn't seem to be getting anywhere or even moving at all. His arms and legs keep pumping, but he doesn't think his feet are even touching the ground. Treading air, he supposes. Jack likened it to what running in space would be like, if that were ever possible.

The pleasant and leisurely jog continues for some time, and all of a sudden, a sense of unease sweeps over Jack, and an odor he can't quite place makes him nauseous. He's also having trouble keeping his pace as his legs are becoming harder to pump, like running through a knee-deep pool of honey. Now he's running to get out of there.

Then the dream takes another peculiar turn. Jack can see his little brother, Jacob, just ahead. Jacob, Jack's only sibling and younger by almost five years, was diagnosed as profoundly autistic and nonverbal at two years of age, though the whole family knew he'd been born that way. But the Jacob in this dream is *different.* He has the same sandy brown curly hair and light blue eyes, but he seems *normal.* The incessant and relentless body posturing and inability to make eye contact, among other symptoms, is not present. Jack feels a wave of emotion envelop him as Jacob gazes back at him. Tears in his eyes, a lump in his throat, Jack would give anything to free Jacob from his personal prison. Deep down, Jack knows there is nothing in this world that can fix Jacob. There is no cure for Jacob's condition.

Now Jack doubles his effort to get to this dream Jacob, his thighs now aching just as much as his heart. He talks at Jacob every day. In this vision he may finally be able to talk *to* his brother. His mind spins with questions: Is he happy? Is he comfortable? As legal guardian and primary caregiver, Jack frequently fears he is somehow failing Jacob regarding his care because Jacob can't precisely convey his desires.

But he just can't get there. The ankle-clasping cesspool is taking its toll, and his pace has slowed considerably. Just lifting his feet is becoming increasingly difficult, and like a spent sprint relay runner, he's ready to pass the baton. And what the hell is that smell? Jack likens the stench to an amalgamation of appalling body odor and rotten eggs mixed with the smell of the Escanaba Paper Company. Jack and his father fished a stretch of the Escanaba for brook and brown trout downwind of the plant five or so years ago, and he will never forget the stench and the resulting stomach cramps that lasted for two full days.

"Jake!" Jack screams at the incarnation before him. Jacob, turning to face a stationary Jack, smiles as he recognizes his brother, and slowly walks toward him. And a simple smile can say so much. Jack, now exhausted from combating the viscous cesspool, correctly reads Jacob's facial expression as adulation, admiration, and gratitude. Jack feels a weight being lifted. This modest yet reassuring gesture means the world to Jack as it validates his loving guardianship of Jacob, even if it is only in a dream.

Jacob, seemingly not affected by the oppressive quagmire and not obviously turned off by the stench, continues his approach. His endearing smile is also transforming into a more serious expression. Jack is again overcome by emotion as he realizes what the autism has robbed Jacob of. The young man before him is absolutely mesmerizing. Adolescents of this sort mature to become the high school quarterback, date the prom queen, pledge for a prestigious fraternity at the university of their choice, and are generally successful in life. Jack finds himself staring, unable and unwilling to take his eyes off him.

It takes little time for Jacob to reach Jack, and he stops at arm's length. The brothers are now face to face, and Jack is captivated, unable to speak. He feels like a small child seeing a mall Santa for the first time: full of ecstasy and awe but also suspicious that something just isn't quite right. Jacob seems relaxed and at ease, and Jack wonders if Jacob dreams like everyone else. Why wouldn't he? Does he have nightmares too?

As Jack is contemplating Jacob's nocturnal escapades, Jacob leans in, cupping his mouth at Jack's ear as if to tell him a secret meant only for him. Jack turns his head slightly to the side, and being several inches taller, stoops down a bit to accommodate him. In the sweetest, most angelic adolescent voice Jack has ever heard, Jacob simply says, "Trust me."

At that moment, Jack hears an odd sound like crackling bacon makes in a hot pan, just a thousand times louder. That doesn't wake him. What does is the resulting thunder report from the lightning superbolt that has just struck outside the front bay window.

Jack had fallen asleep in the Lazy Boy again, as he does many nights while watching whatever is on ESPN. It must be the last few moments of *Pardon the Interruption* because Tony Kornheiser is waving a Canadian flag.

And with that, the dream Jacob is gone.

CHAPTER 1

Silo 9, as it is formally known, was constructed in 1961 and was subsequently outfitted with an SM-65 Atlas Intercontinental Ballistic Missile featuring a single twenty megaton warhead. The only functions of Silo 9, had it been used for its intended purposes, was either to provide the United States the upper hand in a first strike or to ensure mutually assured destruction. Due to Silo 9's distinction of being farthest removed from international borders, it was given top billing when targets were handed out. The preprogrammed destination was 55 45'6"N 37 37'4"E: the Spasskaya Tower of the Great Kremlin Palace, Moscow, USSR.

Missile silos built during the height of the Cold War were for all intents and purposes community projects due to the rural locations and logistical nightmares. They were anything but "secret" to the farmers and townsfolk who lived nearby. Local excavating companies, electricians, and plumbers were closely vetted (along with the farmers and townsfolk) and worked side by side with the specialized government contractors. The typical silo construction went from hole in the ground to weapon of mass destruction abode within six months. The locals took great pride in "their silo," and the projects were generally some of the best kept secrets in America.

Fortunately, Silo 9 was never used for its proposed purpose, or discovered by communist spies, for that matter, as far as anyone knows. When the Cold War ended in the 1980s, most silos were decommissioned, their missiles scrapped, and the land deeded to local government or sold at auction to the highest bidder. Real estate companies specializing in the niche market of rehabilitation and refurbishment of missile silos have turned some into homes many would call works of art.

Except Silo 9. A forward thinker at the Pentagon felt a need to keep the most centrally located of the silos active and off the books, should a need ever arise. The liquid-fueled Atlas was replaced by a solid fueled LGM-118 Peacekeeper tipped with ten separate reentry vehicles, each featuring a three hundred kiloton W87 warhead. The operational range of 8,700 miles effectively made any targets in the Northern Hemisphere accessible. Now instead of wiping out a city, Silo 9 could annihilate a small country.

By 1990, the need for surface-based weapons had also waned. However, Silo 9 would live on once again as an unmanned satellite monitoring station. An array of dishes was inconspicuously erected around the silo in an attempt to hide in plain sight the most intensive and expensive black budget site in the country. Data culled from this clandestine DARPA (The Defense Advanced Research Projects Agency) site played a key role in solving many domestic terrorism cases, including the Oklahoma

City bombing and capture of the Unabomber, among others—all paid for by the Pentagon off the books. The need for the bomb had become secondary to the need for information about nefarious organizations with evil intentions. This technological marvel was capable of listening to any phone, connecting to any computer, and locating and following any person in the continental United States. And the site was fully automated. Any agency in need could remotely access the silo and retrieve their information.

In 2017, the newly formed Office of Temporal Phenomenon launched a satellite, code-named *Icarus*, via Virgin Galactic into geosynchronous orbit designed to detect electromagnetic disturbances caused by as yet to be identified sources. While no one knows for sure, the developing theory is that interdimensional beings of some kind were responsible for the disturbances. Two-person teams were added at Silo 9 to react to the disturbances in real time. These teams were headed by General Rowland Baker, a career military man capable of making tough decisions under duress. General Baker was given carte blanche to recruit his staff and solve the mystery of these "sources."

Four of the five disturbances detected by *Icarus* thus far have been followed within ten minutes by a slightly more powerful temporal anomaly in the same general area. More often than not, a pair of disturbances will be followed several days later by another pair occurring within miles of the first. Most unsettling is that many of the anomalies lead to cases of missing persons being reported in these areas. People are vanishing and turning up days later, either dead from exposure or unable to recall where they have been. These extremely troubling cases, often involving youth, were not a priority for the general.

What interested General Baker were the anomalies not followed up by another. These beings (or whatever they are) either were there for some time and left, or came and are still here. The latter, for obvious reasons, would be the only scenario possibly ending in a capture. The two two-person teams stationed at Silo 9 were trained to use every tracking and tracing tool to their advantage at the outset of an *Icarus* alarm, direct a team to the site and, in theory, swoop in and retrieve the interdimensional bastards without prejudice. Dead or alive, it didn't matter to Baker…though alive was probably better.

Yes, alive would be the superior outcome, Baker thought, *and Silo 9 has never been better prepared.*

CHAPTER 2

This was the day Sebastian had to ask Mikayla out, OCD be damned. Today. It had to be today. The thought was making him physically ill. Mikki, the most beautiful, intelligent, sexy girl he had ever met, had been sitting next to him twelve hours a day, a hundred feet below an Iowa cornfield for the past two months, seemingly oblivious to the intense crush he had on her. Her thick black hair was a stark contrast to her fair complexion and hazel eyes, and it drove him crazy. The last alarm was months ago, and this easy gig they shared could go away at any time. Either one or both of them could be reassigned, and then it would be too late. He would lose her forever.

"Eleven p.m. ping confirmed," Sebastian whimpered out loud. His general lack of enthusiasm was out of character for him. The pings, hourly self-tests of sorts for *Icarus*, had become so habitual they often didn't even notice them.

Mikayla looked above her bank of monitors to see Bass, Sebastian's preferred nickname, slumped in his chair with his head in his hands, his fingers intertwined through his auburn locks. He hadn't been his usual happy-go-lucky self for days, and she was beginning to worry.

"Copy, Bass…ping confirmed. Hey, are you all right?"

"I'm just getting hungry. How does a nice steak dinner sound? I'll cook." His hands were sweating profusely and his right foot was tapping uncontrollably. This was it.

Mikki looked at her right wrist as if a watch were attached. "Yeah, it's about that time. A nice steak dinner sounds delicious. But how would that be different than any other day?" Silo 9 lacked many amenities like fresh air and outside communication, but they sure ate well. As long as Bass cooked, that is.

"I just thought we could have a nice dinner together in my quarters. I picked out a couple of nicely marbled strip steaks, corn on the cob…and I can roast some baby reds in the fresh butter that Baker brought over yesterday…maybe add a little rosemary…and maybe we could watch a movie after…" His voice trailed off to an almost inaudible level.

Oh my God. I can't do this, he thought. Sebastian Parker was a brilliant technician—in the top five in the world probably—but like many people with obsessive-compulsive disorder, he struggled in most social situations, especially with the opposite sex.

Mikayla could see where this was headed.

"Are you asking me out on a date?" Mikki asked, relishing the opportunity to watch Bass squirm a little for a change. Mikayla Wainwright, also technically brilliant, had been gradually falling for Bass, who she would best describe as "nerdy chic," a stark and very welcome departure from the beer-chugging, ass-grabbing men she'd recently dated.

"I guess so." Bass could feel his face flushing. He couldn't take much more of this.

"Well, I guess it's a date then!" Mikki exclaimed. She'd been waiting for Bass to make a move for weeks.

CHAPTER 3

The next forty minutes could not go by fast enough for Sebastian. He'd finally summoned the courage to ask Mikki out and she had accepted—and actually seemed excited. His mind was spinning out of control as the ramifications of his actions were setting in. *What should I wear? Why did she accept so fast? Does she like me? Oh my God, what have I done*, he thought to himself.

"Which movie did you pick?" Mikki asked, looking for information herself. Bass had seemed so uninterested in her sexual innuendos she had all but given up. At one point, she thought he might even be gay.

"Pardon me?" Sebastian asked sheepishly. His eyebrows raised and formed neat peaks above his eyes.

"You said we were going to watch a movie after dinner. What movie did you pick out?"

Think Bass, think fast. "*Room*, have you seen it? I haven't. The review sounded a lot like our situation, seeing how we're being held captive by an evil overlord and all," Bass replied excitedly, not wanting to give away the fact that he hadn't thought that far ahead, and that he indeed had seen the movie.

"Nope, haven't seen it. I think it won a couple of awards so it must be pretty good," Mikki replied, lying herself. She had seen the movie, twice in fact. Brie Larson was one of her favorite actresses. She was Captain Marvel, for Christ's sake. Everyone loves Captain Marvel.

"And the steaks? You said they were strips?" Mikki continued on her data mining expedition.

"Iowa's best. Two inches thick, twenty-five day dry aged. I told General Baker that the meat we've been getting lately was tough and tasted like dog shit. We have ten pounds of prime cuts to share with Sonny and Cher."

Mikki laughed out loud at the pop culture reference. Sonny was actually Steven Silverstein, a nerdy little Jewish blow-hard who thought he knew more than everyone else. He pitched a bitch about pork and kosher when he arrived, so bacon and ribs would never appear on the menu. *Thanks a lot, Steven. His black bowl cut hairdo looked like Sonny Bono's though*, Mikki thought. Cher was Leah Shepherd, the sweetest, kindest soul Mikki had ever met, and she was just as beautiful as the singer/actress. She had been deployed to Silo 9 directly from marine boot camp for reasons unknown to the rest of the group. It seemed a very odd fit because she had very little of the technical training needed to perform her duties properly. What she lacked in knowledge she made up for in determination, so the rest of the group treated her as an equal. Steven had been trying like hell to get his grubby paws on her since the first time the elevator door opened, but to no avail. As long as she stayed away from Bass, they were good. Mikki chuckled to herself at the thought of Steven and Leah singing "I Got You Babe" to each other.

"Cute, Bass, but I think you're giving both of them way too much credit for having talent. Seems to me they're more like Jack and Chrissie from *Three's Company*. Steven has been trying to get into her pants since she arrived."

"Good one, Mick," Bass agreed, laughing heartily himself. "It's hard to watch sometimes. Steven is like a puppy nipping at her heels; then Leah swats him away and says 'No! Get off my leg, *bee-atch!*'" Now they were both doubled over in amusement at the expense of Steven's ongoing futility in his pursuit of Leah.

"She's a little cutie. You ever think about asking her out?" Mikki asked. She thought she knew the answer but wanted to hear him say it.

"I've had my heart set on someone else for a long time."

"Good answer. But why did it take you—" Mikki was interrupted midsentence.

The siren was the first to go off. It wasn't overly loud, but it was extremely annoying. *Whoop…Whoop…Whoop.* It got your attention. Seconds later, the light above Bass's post began swirling its red beam around the station. *Icarus* had detected an anomaly. This is what they were stationed here for.

"Start the clock," Bass directed Mikki. "Let's see if we can figure out what we have here. Could you go over and reset *Icarus*, please?" The closest any two anomalies had presented was less than thirty seconds, so it was very important to conduct a system reset. Bass was already at his post accessing the satellite to pinpoint exactly where the anomaly had presented itself.

"*Icarus* is reset, and the countdown clock is started," Mikki announced. "Do you want me to call General Baker?"

"Not yet. If this is a routine double strike, we can tell him about it later. Can you see if we have a GeoEye or KH-11 over…*Michigan*?" The location surprised Bass. Most of the incidents had been in the Adirondacks or the Mountain West. Evidently, electromagnetic disturbances had no boundaries.

"I have a GeoEye north of Chicago, and another over Milwaukee, both traveling south-by-south-east. Where in Michigan is it?" Mikki asked. The trajectory of each satellite was designed to cover the most populous areas for obvious reasons. They both knew anything north of Detroit was a crapshoot to get any kind of meaningful information.

"Thumb area. Closest town is Bad Axe. Try to get me coverage with a GeoEye." Bass would be able to pinpoint ground zero to within one square meter, given time. "Time check, please."

"Time plus five minutes thirty-five seconds," Mikki replied. They were both expecting and hoping for another episode any second. "The GeoEye near Chicago is closest, but there will be a pretty bad angle. And there is a severe thunderstorm approaching the area…and I mean *severe*. Could the storm have set off *Icarus*?"

"No chance. *Icarus* was designed to pick up one thing, and it found it. Do we have anything in geosync orbit in that area we can use? Like a Misty or a Keyhole?"

"I'm working on it," Mikki replied, all the while poring over satellite trajectory maps and wracking her brain to conjure up any kind of viable intelligence option. She glanced at the countdown clock, giving it a classic double take…and her heart sank.

"Bass…" Her voice was soft and quivering. "We're at time plus ten minutes twenty-five seconds." She knew exactly what that meant.

"OSCAR sends a message to Baker's phone when *Icarus* alerts, so I'm sure he'll be here soon. Call in Sonny and Cher, we'll need their help," Bass muttered dejectedly. This time the reference wasn't nearly as humorous.

The steaks and the date would have to wait.

CHAPTER 4

The early July post-twilight air was calm and dense. Although the approaching thunderstorm was still miles away, the continuous and ominous rolls of thunder in the distance warned of what was soon to come. A small herd of whitetail deer, widespread to the point of nuisance in the Thumb region of mid-Michigan, munched enthusiastically on a nearby farmer's alfalfa crop seemingly laid out before them like an outdoor salad bar. The highly nutritious greens, along with other local crops including soybeans and field corn, led to the subsequent harvest of bucks routinely dressing out at over two hundred pounds in November. Plentiful nourishing fare resulted in monster bucks.

The matriarchal female, or alpha doe, maintained her herd by acting as the lookout, snorting loudly and stomping her front hooves in the face of any perceived danger, and the rest of the herd, especially the fawns, paid close attention to her. The first ten yards or so of the alfalfa crop adjacent to her home woods was especially appealing, as it had a very easy egress should she need it. She was getting rather impatient with the five recently weaned fawns, two of which were her own, and started toward them to end the little game of "not it" they seemed to be playing and get them back to eating. They would thank her this winter for the additional fat reserves when all they had to eat was twigs, stems, and pine bark. It would be a very rude awakening that up to half or more likely would not survive to see spring.

The alpha doe had been raised to avoid the sight and scent of humans at all cost, and she was passing on that critical awareness to the next generation. Her first, and certainly most frightening, experience occurred in the fall of her fawn year. The herd was crossing the *slippery*, and she lingered, her cold hooves taking in the radiant heat, until she was the last of the herd to complete the passage to the safety of the woods. She could see her mother, the previous alpha, pleading with her from the edge of the woods to complete the crossing. But she could also see the bright light approaching, and she was mesmerized, unable to move.

The approaching bright light was getting closer, yet she still could not move! At the very last instant the bright light veered, screeching off the *slippery* just feet from her mother. The ensuing explosion released her from the trance, and she bounded carefully toward her mother and safety. As she ran, she looked back and saw that the bright light had now turned into the flickering light, another of the worldly phenomenon that she was taught to be especially wary of.

The fawn-scolding complete, the Alpha's attention was diverted to the edge of the drainage ditch separating their alfalfa field from the neighboring soybean plot. A ball of light, ever increasing in size and intensity, was forming. The ultraviolet phenomenon transfixed her, as she had never seen anything similar in the past. Its nonthreatening and even welcoming glow drew her toward it. Confused and dazed to the point of forgoing her responsibilities to the herd, she walked toward it. When she reached the bank of the dike, her attention was immediately drawn to the water. The water in the ditch beneath the orb, nearly three feet deep at this time of the year, looked invisible to her. She could see two large and evidently similarly transfixed carp seemingly suspended in midair above the creek bottom.

By then, the rest of the herd, including the frolicking fawns, had made their way toward their matriarch, as following her was all they had ever known. The ball of light, at one time twirling clockwise as it grew in size, had stopped growing. Oddly enough, had any people been in the vicinity of this event, they would not have seen anything out of the ordinary, as the wavelength of light the orb was radiating was about ten nanometers, well below the visible spectrum of the human eye. The show seemed to be directed solely toward the deer herd and the carp.

The waning daylight, the approaching thunderstorm, and the utter stillness of the water-saturated air made the UV orb show quite a spectacle, worthy of an Impressionist's brush, or at least a postcard. That was all about to change. The orb, still stationary and suspended over the water, was fading out. As it was fading, it began swirling again, this time counterclockwise. As the light grew fainter, the swirling increased. Precisely at the point where the light completely blinked out, a mass appeared in its space, suspended as the orb had been. For several seconds, it just hovered, defying the laws of gravity. And then…*sploosh!* The mass fell from its invisible perch and splashed down in the middle of the creek. The alpha doe instinctively snorted two times to alert the herd, and the herd knew exactly what to do: *run!* She had seen this form many times in her past, as now standing before her in the middle of the drainage ditch was a human boy. She directed one final snort at the intruder as if to say, "You don't scare me," turned, and ran after her herd.

CHAPTER 5

"Can we establish and record the exact time *Icarus* alerted?" Bass asked. General Baker would be here soon, and he had better have answers for every question.

"Absolutely," Mikki replied. "Twenty-three oh six and fifteen seconds. That was about twenty minutes ago, and there still hasn't been a second alarm."

"There won't be another alarm, Mikki. These anomalies have been tracked now for almost five years, one way or another. There will eventually be a follow-up single alarm, but it may follow several double alarms. The theory is that someone, or *something*, is invading our land and typically leaving without much delay. Today is the aberration…something came and *stayed*."

"How do we know it's not them leaving from a single alarm in the past?" she asked.

"We don't know for sure. But…even the single events are followed up by another single event within a reasonable amount of time, like a couple of days, or sometimes a week. There hasn't been a single episode in the three months I've been here. In fact, the last time there was a single episode was right before I was assigned here. All

17

three of the techs were reassigned after that, and they brought Steven and me in."

"Don't you find that odd? Why would General Baker turn over the whole staff right after an event?"

"I don't know. You would have to ask him. Do you have any real-time imagery of the alert area yet?" Bass asked, changing the subject.

"What's going on, a-holes?" Steven exclaimed, making his usual brazen and boisterous entrance, Leah at his side. "We're not supposed to come in for another thirty minutes," he protested while leering longingly at Leah, insinuating relations of some kind had been interrupted.

"Never going to happen, Steven," Leah dismissed, shooting him a decidedly loathsome look. She would rather die than sleep with this loudmouthed braggart.

"Hello, Sebastian…" Steven sneered toward Bass in his best Wayne Knight Newman impression. It was terrible, and Bass simply ignored him.

"Look, guys. We've had a single *Icarus* episode, and we all know what that means: all hands on deck. General Baker will be here shortly, and we need to earn our keep," Bass explained. "The incident was in the Thumb region of Michigan, which is very flat topographically, so we should have a good number of satellites that viewed the event. I would like to have at least a basic presentation for the general when he arrives."

"Bass, I have the info uploaded from the Chicago GeoEye," Mikki volunteered. "I'm sending it to the screen now."

The main display in the bunker was a state-of-the-art high-definition computer-aided monitor sixteen feet long and nine feet high. The computer-aided feature was a technological marvel code-named OSCAR (Outsourcing Super Computing and Reviewing), a computer capable of "filling in the blanks" and augmenting any information fed to it. In this case, it would be considerable due to both the distance from the target and the severe thunderstorm it was trying to peer over and through.

"Thank you, Mikki," Bass replied in a tone that sounded sweet and affectionate, a departure from his normal businesslike droning. Leah raised her eyebrows at Mikki as if to say, "What is *that* all about?" Mikki simply shrugged her shoulders and smiled back at Leah.

"Who died and made you God, Bass?" Steven asked indignantly, simply looking to run his mouth. At twenty-three years of age Steven was the oldest crew member, but he unfortunately often acted no more than half of it. Wresting control of this investigation on any level from Sebastian wasn't going to happen, and he knew it.

"That doesn't even make sense, asshole," Mikki snapped. "How could someone die and make Bass God? Even if it was a *really* important person that passed away, I doubt they would have the authority to make Bass *God*. Maybe you should think about your words a little longer before you speak them so you don't sound like an idiot."

Before Steven could rebuke Mikki's punch to the nuts, General Baker thankfully entered through the only easement to or from topside. And he looked rather agitated.

"Get me up to speed quickly, Sebastian," General Baker requested in his trademark raspy yet high-pitched voice. Baker's soft features and somewhat effeminate voice betrayed the fact that he could be a real bastard.

His flat bottom hemmed shirt was untucked, as usual, in an attempt to conceal his protruding gut on one side and ass on the other, and it ticked Bass off because Baker was so adamant that everyone at the silo keep their shirttails in their pants. Baker explained his unkempt civilian look as an integral part of hiding in plain sight.

"Absolutely, General. At approximately 12:06 a.m. local time, *Icarus* detected an anomaly between Bad Axe and Cass City in the Thumb region of Michigan. There has not been a subsequent alarm. We are currently combing the satellite fleet to get eyes on the event and the aftermath. Our best option is a GeoEye that was near Chicago, and it is cued and ready to play."

"Well, let's just see what it got," replied the general as he rubbed the salt-and-pepper stubble on the top of his head. His time to shine in the eyes of his superiors was at hand, and he wasn't going to let any of these little potlickers, including Sebastian, keep him from glory.

The blue screen of the monitor was replaced by an image of what was definitely southern Lake Michigan and Chicago from a considerable altitude. Bass was hoping to see Saginaw Bay or at least the shore of Lake Huron on the far right side of the screen, but neither was there. This was not promising.

"I'm isolating our target zone and will zoom in," Bass stated. The image was moving eastward, and the cities of Kalamazoo and Lansing came into view before giving way to gray and then almost black.

"What am I looking at?" asked the general.

"Severe thunderstorm, sir," Bass replied. "I think our target will be far enough east of the storm, so it shouldn't be in the way." The screen continued rolling, and the city of Flint came into view.

"I'm going to start magnifying," Bass explained. The larger buildings seemed to be tilting considerably to the left. "The angle is going to be a little less than ideal, but we should get a general idea of what happened. Hopefully OSCAR will be able to fill in some of the detail we'll lose because of the distance and pitch," he said, still panning east and magnifying the image.

"Got it," Bass said as a red X entered the image. "Zooming to maximum magnification. What we will see is going to be approximately two thousand square meters." The image continued to enlarge but also started to get very grainy.

"Stop right there, Bass," the general interjected. "If you magnify any more, we won't be able to determine what we are seeing. Go ahead and play it like that."

The image showed what was obviously a deer walking in a field—a very large deer at that. It stopped at the edge of the stream and was apparently looking exactly where the red X was located.

"Deer can see in the UV spectrum," Steven chimed in. "It's why they can see so much better in low light than their predators, especially humans."

"Thank you, Steven," General Baker said, not at all sarcastically. He didn't know that fact, and it made the image make a little more sense.

Suddenly a black mass appeared on the screen next to the X. "Pause the replay, Bass. Can you get that X out of the picture, please?"

"Yes, sir," Bass replied. As he typed on his keyboard, the annoying red X disappeared.

"What *is* that?" Mikki inquired to no one in particular. They were all dumbstruck as to what they were seeing transpire.

"We're about to find out. Roll it, Bass," the general instructed. As the image began playing again, nothing moved for several seconds. All of a sudden, the mass disappeared, and moments later the deer herd bolted.

"What happened?" Leah wondered out loud.

"Keep rolling. I'm pretty sure the mass fell out of the air and into the ditch," General Baker replied. "You can't see the bottom of the ditch due to the acute angle of the image." Moments later, the black mass that had been hanging over the creek appeared on the bank, and it was pretty obvious to everyone what it was.

"Holy shit, it's a person!" Mikki cried out. It was the *very last* thing she expected to crawl out of that ditch. They all watched the being walk in the same direction as the startled deer herd for another two minutes before the image was lost.

"Thunderheads have rolled into our picture, General," Bass said dejectedly.

"Doesn't matter. Great work, everyone. Bass, I need you to lead the team and track this…*kid* wherever it goes by any and all means available. This is now a matter of national security and needs to be treated as such," Baker squeaked as he headed toward the same door he had entered just ten minutes ago. "I'll be in touch. We're in a level one lockdown as of this moment," were the general's final words as the heavy metal door slammed behind him. A lockdown of this type meant absolutely no one in and, more importantly to them, no one out.

"Yes, sir," Bass replied, but the general didn't hear him. He was already gone. "Ok, everyone, you heard the general...where is Steven?" No one had noticed that Steven had slipped out.

"Right here!" Steven shouted as he rounded the corner from the common area. "Had to use the shitter," he explained. What he didn't divulge was the fact that he had also just placed a call with an illicit satellite phone.

CHAPTER 6

A lthough he expected the splashdown, it was a shock all the same. And exhilarating. Now, he had to deal with the distress to his body that traveling caused. He would have to find nourishment, and soon. Standing on the bank of the creek, wet and shivering, he attempted to get his bearings. He never knew *exactly* where he would land when traveling, though it was usually near or over water because water constituted almost sixty percent of a humanoid body's composition. Without obvious landmarks, he really didn't know which way to go from here. Assuming the storm was approaching from the west, north should be toward the woods, and past that he would hopefully find Chapin Road. Once he found Chapin Road, he should be able to find his way from there to his target.

The sounds coming from the forest were compounded by the dead calm of the air. Several different species of birds were chirping, squirrels were barking, and something large, possibly one of the deer he had startled upon his arrival, was walking noisily through the dense brush. Weeds, vines, and other undergrowth, specifically blackberry bushes, would make walking treacherous since his feet were covered by only crude leather-like moccasins. His eyesight would help him avoid the worst of it as even in the low light of the cloud-obscured waning gibbous moon he could still see particularly well. In fact, he could see as well or better in darkness than any animal of this world.

He stopped at the edge of the woods and pondered if passing through to the road here would be better than going around, and he determined that it would. Time was of the essence as he could feel himself weaken with each step. His first step into the woods landed on a brittle oak twig, which snapped easily, announcing his presence. The cacophony that had been soothing to him stopped immediately. The only sound now was the distant and continuous low rumble of thunder. *Got to go*, he thought, as he would have to deal with torrential rainfall soon.

The woods were much thicker than he had anticipated. Vines wrapped around his feet, blackberry bushes attached to his pants and scratched his legs firmly enough to draw blood, and spiderwebs occasionally wrapped around his upper body and face. Wintergreen berries were abundant on the forest floor, and he stopped several times to take advantage of nature's bounty. Raspberry and blackberry plants were also loaded with fruit but they hadn't yet ripened. He thought that somewhat fortunate as he would have lost more blood to the thorns getting to them than the berries would have provided in sustenance.

The rain began just as he exited the woods. Huge drops pummeled his head and torso as he began walking east down Chapin Road. He could see and hear the wind making its way through the forest from the same direction that he had come. The initial gust hit him hard and nearly knocked him over. The rain, once simply a nuisance, was now being thrust at him with such force that it felt like each raindrop was penetrating his skin. There may have even been small hail stones. He had to take cover—*immediately*.

He quickly scampered back to the woods and hunkered down on the east side of the largest tree he could find. What a relief that was. An enormous lightning bolt flashed a mile or so in front of him and was followed about ten seconds later by the crackle and bang of the deafening thunderclap.

"That was close," he said out loud to himself. His voice startled him as it was considerably lower in pitch than the last time he was here. As he cupped his hands out in front of himself to trap a bit of thirst-quenching water, he suddenly realized he knew *exactly* where he was. The mighty bur oak he had taken refuge under still bore the impact scars from the crash, and the rain had released a musty burnt charcoal-like stench from its eternally disfigured trunk. The pain and anguish this unfortunate crash levied upon the survivors caused him to pause, but he quickly put it out of his mind. He had work to do. His makeshift chalice half full, he thought about the last time he had drunk water. It seemed like a lifetime ago, and for good reason. He put his hands to his lips and slurped the cool water. It had never tasted so good, and it gave him the stimulation to move on.

"Re, re, re…mi, mi, mi…do, do, do…" he muttered to himself. He knew many of his body parts, including his vocal cords, would need exercise to get them working properly in this environment again.

"Do, do, do…" he continued, dropping an octave this time. He had now been walking with purpose for almost fifteen minutes, thinking and planning his next moves. He had to start thinking and speaking in English, fortunately one of his stronger languages. Just like riding a bike, which he also knew how to do from past experience. He was ready for this. The time had finally arrived. The people here would say the shit was about to hit the fan, and he laughed out loud at the thought of shit literally hitting a fan and the ensuing mess that would make.

And there it was: *the target.* It was a modest looking, white two-story home with several outbuildings and two identical cylindrical towers, each about fifty feet tall. This was a typical mid-Michigan farm. He paused at end of the driveway, thinking this was the point of no return. His arrival would change many lives, including his own, forever. Thankfully, there were not any other houses nearby in the case ensuing events went sideways.

"Sol, sol, sol…" He finished his five-note tune and strode up the driveway to the front door.

"Here we go," he said to himself, his voice still raspy.

CHAPTER 7

"How long can we keep that GeoEye on the target, and what do we have moving over the area?" Bass asked the group. The silence he received in return provided the unfortunate answer, and he knew General Baker would be calling shortly for this type of information. "Let's divide and conquer so we get all the intel we can. Leah, could you monitor all phone lines for 911 calls? Also find the local police department or the sheriff's office scanner frequency and monitor that."

"On it, Sebastian," she replied. Leah always addressed Bass using his full name. She had been learning quickly but still had a long ways to go. *I can do this*, she thought as she began typing on her keyboard. All she wished for was to be viewed as an equal by her peers. Steven, in spite of his many flaws, had been a pretty good mentor. Leah was well aware that a ten-year-old could process the tasks Bass had given her, but it didn't matter to her.

"Hey, Bass? I took a couple of still shots from the GeoEye and sent them to OSCAR to see if it can clean them up enough to ID the perpetrator," Steven volunteered. The Outsourcing Super Computing and Reviewing system was unique to Silo 9. It was unique to the world, in fact, as it was the first computer of its kind. Constructed by the true geniuses at Oak Ridge National Laboratory, its clock speed came in at right around one hundred petaFLOPS, meaning it could accomplish one hundred quadrillion floating-point operations per second, not to mention the 18 one hundred terabyte Nimbus Exadrives providing generous read only and random access memory, making it the fastest and largest computer on Earth. What made OSCAR unique, though, was its ability to outsource with any other computer hooked up to the Internet in the world. It was the first truly AI computer ever conceived.

"There is a TIRS over New York I could redirect," Mikayla offered. A TIRS satellite with thermographic cameras would work very well for tracking.

"Do it. How long will it take to position it properly?" Bass inquired.

"About thirty minutes. Should I call the NSA first, since it's their satellite?" She knew thirty minutes was optimistic, and she also knew the NSA would not be pleased.

"Get it moving and then notify them. Remember, we have to use *everything* at our disposal. No exceptions. I don't care about bruised egos or hurt feelings right now, and neither should any of you," Bass said, pointing toward each of them as he spoke.

Now that he had each member of his team assigned to a project, Bass sat down and contemplated his next move. As he pored over the Silo 9 security cameras, he noticed that General Baker was still outside, sitting in his car. *Must be on the phone*, he thought. The nagging question on Bass's mind was why Baker referred to the target as a "kid." *Does he know something we don't?* Bass didn't like being in the dark about anything, and asking would surely only get a "you don't need to know" answer.

If he won't tell me, I'm going to find out the easy way, Bass thought as he put on his headphones. Silo 9 was equipped with an outdoor speaker system much like the ones installed in homes. A visitor pushed a button and spoke into the microphone, except this listening device was special. He once directed it at a cow over a mile away and was literally blown out of his chair when it mooed. Bass eased the microphone a couple of clicks to the right to position it in the direction of Baker's car and turned up the volume a bit.

"Yes, sir. Yes, sir," Bass heard the general say. Unfortunately he could only pick up General Baker's end of the conversation.

"All they know is that *Icarus* picked up an anomaly, and they are currently tracking it. These four techs are the best in the business, you know that. You helped me identify and groom them. We can't track the kid without their help," Bass overheard the general saying. Bass was starting to feel like it was a bad idea snooping like this. It was too late now, and the proverbial cat was about to jump right out of the bag.

"I know they did, and that was my fault," Baker continued. "Yes, I *know* where the body bags are, but I assure you it will not come to that again."

Bass was really confused now. What was the general talking about? And who the hell was he talking *to*?

"I give you my word. If any or all of them compromise our mission, I will personally eliminate them. Yes, sir, *all* of them."

CHAPTER 8

The last thing Jack was expecting at midnight was someone knocking on the front door. Everyone who knew him also knew that he *never* locked his doors, and they were welcome to walk right in any time, day or night. Except Uncle Pete. That piece of shit could stand on the front step until hell froze over. The only reason he still let him visit was because Jacob really liked him, likely due to Pete's uncanny resemblance to his brother, Jacob's father.

Good old Uncle Pete tried to steal Jacob away from him after their parents died in a single car crash on Chapin Road almost two years ago. Zach and Rebecca Wheaton were headed home from their weekly bowling league at Longshot Lanes in Bad Axe that fateful Friday night in November and never made it. The car skidded then rolled three times before smashing roof first into the largest tree for miles. If the impact injuries didn't kill them, the resulting fireball surely did. The sheriff and coroner both had their theories as to what *really* happened that night (murder/suicide? double suicide?), and the investigation was actually still open. Jack knew in his heart it was simply a tragic accident.

Uncle Pete, ever the martyr, put the Beefeater down long enough to attend the probate hearings. He presented himself well and had a good job—that wasn't the issue. At the time, he'd been the midnight watchman at Miller's Tool and Die for almost ten years and made pretty good money. Pete didn't give two shits about the boys or the house. He wanted *the land*. When Jack testified to the fact that Pete was a womanizer and alcoholic looking to make a quick buck, he convinced Judge Haller to deny Pete's request to usurp the family farm despite the fact that Zach and Rebecca had never taken the time to put their wishes in writing.

Jack subsequently had to petition the court twice, first to become an emancipated minor at sixteen, then to persuade the judge (thankfully Haller again) that he could handle being Jacob's legal guardian. Uncle Pete put up a contentious argument, claiming he should be the boys' guardian, but the judge ultimately sided with Jack, and Uncle Pete, for all his trouble, "got jack."

The summer had been remarkable, and the brothers had bonded more than they ever had in the past. Jack outfitted the John Deere 4640 with a side seat so Jacob could ride along while seeding and tilling the fields, and he loved it. Jack would outfit the harvester in the same manner that fall.

The second round of knocks was a little louder and seemed much more urgent, jolting Jack out of his reminisce. "I'm coming!" Jack blurted out, not so loud as to wake Jacob. He had almost fallen back to sleep on the recliner before he was so rudely interrupted. He tugged on the recliner's lever and pulled his legs toward him until the leg rest snapped backward with a *thud*. As he stood, he could feel all the blood rushing to his head to the point that he had to sit back down rather than risk possibly falling down.

His moment of lightheadedness cleared, and he made his way down the hallway to the front door. He noticed the door was still unlocked, so a slight pang of fear began to surface. It was not someone he knew as they would have walked in on their own. He gripped the handle and froze as the slight pang turned up a notch into full fledged fear. The door didn't have a peek hole, so he couldn't see who was out there.

"Just open the door, you pussy," he whispered to himself. And he did. Standing before him was a dark-haired boy of eleven or twelve who couldn't weigh a hundred pounds soaking wet, which he most definitely was. The boy's curly black hair was matted to his head and was a stark contrast to his pasty white skin tone. A combination of water and likely sweat was beading down his ashy cheeks and dripping off his chin. Jack's relief was palpable as he let out the breath he had been holding. *Not a thing to fear here*, he thought.

"Hey, buddy. Are you all right?" Jack asked the trespasser. "What are you doing in the middle of nowhere, in the middle of the night, no less?" This was the point at which the odor hit him. This poor kid smelled as if he had just drug himself out of a sewer.

"Can I enter your home?" the boy asked. His voice was soft and gentle yet somewhat hoarse. He simply stood there staring at his feet as if in embarrassment, which looked to be covered by leather moccasins. He wore a long sleeve shirt and long pants, and both seemed to be a couple of sizes too small for his frame. "High-water pants" is what the bullies in school called them. While the clothing was still utile, Jack was sure this poor kid was wearing hand-me-downs.

"Where are your parents? Are you hurt? Are they hurt?" Jack's mind was swirling. He'd never had a random kid show up at his door in the middle of the night, soaking wet, wearing his big brother's clothes that fit him last year, so there was little to reference the situation to.

There must have been an accident, he thought. This poor kid was probably just a little slow, or in shock, or even possibly on the spectrum, like Jacob. Living and caring for a special needs person gave one perspective others didn't have. The smell was really bothering Jack, though. He intended to have words with the boy's parents. *Special needs kids require special attention, and bathing and cleanliness are of the utmost importance*, he would scold them.

"I must enter your home," the boy declared boldly, still looking at his plain leather foot coverings. This time it was a statement, not a question of permission, and Jack could feel the hair on his neck rise. His fear factor ratcheted back up to the level it had been at before he opened the door. Jack took comfort in the fact that he could take him if it came down to it—at least he hoped he could. He had never been in a fight with a crazy sixth grader before, so he didn't really know for sure.

"You're confusing what you 'must' do with what I'm going to 'allow' you to do, kid," Jack explained. "If you don't tell me what happened to your parents, I'm going to close the door. You can try the next house a couple of miles down the road." *I told him. Youth these days think they're owed everything. There is a proper way to ask, and this little boy is going to learn it.*

"No. I must enter *this* home," the boy stated, even more forcefully this time. As he talked, he raised his chin to make eye contact with Jack. What Jack saw terrorized him. This boy's eyes were totally and completely black. The pupils (if he even had them), iris, cornea, sclera... everything. *All black.* Jack thought it looked as if the boy had no eyes at all, just two black chasms in his head. Jack's fight or flight sympathetic nervous system was telling him to *fly*—now.

As Jack moved back from the entryway, he grabbed the inside door handle with his left hand. Once out of the way, he attempted to swing the door shut with all his might and as quickly as possible. He had no problem slamming the door in this black-eyed kid's face. But the door was stuck.

It was Jacob! He had somehow snuck up from behind him and grabbed the door above the handle with both hands.

"Jacob, stop!" Jack screamed. "Go back to bed!" Jacob did not let up on his grip of the door. And he was particularly strong for a thirteen-year-old boy. Not only was the door not closing, it was actually opening wider. At that point, both of their attentions redirected to the black-eyed boy, for he was now down on his knees with his head lowered once again.

"*Enke, Ishk elsai mahore, Elohim,*" the black-eyed boy stated reverentially. Both Jack and Jacob eased their grip on the door. Jack's heart was beating rapidly, and his mind was once again racing in several directions at once. What did he just say? Something about a hanky, a sycamore, and a yellow meme?

Jacob, not fazed a bit by the unknown interloper, simply took a step forward, closed his eyes, and placed his right hand on the black-eyed boy's damp head.

What the fuck is going on? thought Jack.

CHAPTER 9

*W*hat had General Baker meant when he said he would *eliminate us?* Bass asked himself. *Send us all to a remote outpost in Alaska or the South Pole? Kill all of us?* They had no means to defend themselves other than a lockdown, but even that could be overridden from the outside with a proper pass key, and such a pass key was owned by none other than General Baker. They didn't have guns, or any other weapons short of steak knives for that matter, in the silo. Bass was hereby determined to gather all of the information he could to keep the staff useful to Baker. And he would keep the elimination declaration to himself. *And what did he mean when he said he groomed us? Sounds like something a sexual predator does. And what had happened to the previous staff? So many questions…it's time to get some answers.*

"Hey, Steven, what do you know about the previous staff?" Bass asked. Steven had been stationed there before Bass arrived, so he would be the only one here who may have met them.

"Never saw them. They were gone when I got here. Baker said I just missed them. Why do you ask?" *Why the hell is Sebastian asking stupid questions?* thought Steven.

"Just curious. It might be advantageous to ask them their protocol when they had *Icarus* alarms. I've never been too proud to ask for help."

So they were gone before we arrived, they were never mentioned by General Baker, and they could all be dead for all we know, Bass thought.

"I'm sure they had their fair share of them," Bass presumed. He didn't trust Steven. He would lie about trivial matters like using his razor and drinking milk straight from the jug, and it bothered Bass immensely.

"Do you guys talk about what we do here when you call home?" Bass asked, addressing the question to all three of them. Bass didn't notice that Steven flinched reflexively.

"I don't really have anyone to call," Mikki replied. "I was tossed from foster home to foster home my whole childhood and never made any real connection with any of them. The day I turned eighteen I joined the air force."

"I don't have anyone to call either, Sebastian," Leah added. She had been estranged from her parents since the day they tried to trade her body for heroin when she was fourteen. She stayed with her grandmother until she finished high school and, like Mikayla, also joined the armed forces on her eighteenth birthday as an escape and a fresh start.

"Neither do I, really," Steven confirmed half-heartedly. *Does Bass know I made a phone call?* Steven thought to himself. *Is that what he's fishing for?* "What are you getting at, Bass? Are you accusing us of something?"

"No, nothing like that. I would just caution each of you to not divulge the true nature of our work here. To *anyone.*"

They all knew that, of course.

That bastard Baker groomed people who wouldn't be missed, Bass thought. *Each and every one of us could fall off the face of the Earth and no one would miss us. Ever.*

"We just need to be careful about what we say and to whom we say it, that's all. I'll go put on a fresh pot of coffee," Bass explained, trying to allay their fears. "We're all going to be here a while," he added, more as an actor's aside than a statement to the group.

Now he wasn't so sure they would be.

CHAPTER 10

The look in Jacob's eyes was one he'd seen before in the dream. It was a knowing look, pleading for Jack to trust him. For whatever reason, Jack did trust him. He still wasn't so sure about this kid, though.

"May I enter your home?" the black-eyed boy stated now for the third time. "I must have nourishment."

"And I must have some answers, now!" Jack demanded. "Who are you, where did you come from, where are your parents, what is wrong with your eyes, and most of all, *how in the hell do you know my little brother?*" Jack could tell his blood pressure was rising because he could feel his pulse in both of his temples. His paternal instinct to protect his child was going full throttle despite the fact that he wasn't even Jacob's father.

"Jackson Wheaton, I will answer all of your questions in time. At this moment I must have nourishment. Please!"

Well, at least the kid had some manners after all. But it only brought forth more questions. *Has this kid been stalking us? What is his angle? Why is he wearing those freaky contact lenses?* Jack still couldn't get past the kid's messed-up eyes.

"I'm not going to argue with you anymore. Come in out of the rain," Jack conceded as he backed away and stood to the side, holding the door open. This whole time Jacob had been standing attentively, or so it seemed. Jack never knew if Jacob understood what was going on around him, but he hoped he did.

As the boy passed him and entered the hallway, the stench that had only been a mild annoyance when he was outside blossomed into an all-out reek, and the kid seemed to know it.

"May I also clean myself? I realize I have a certain odor that you find unpleasant."

It was at this point that Jack recognized the smell. It was the same stench he had the displeasure of experiencing in the dream: body odor/rotten egg/paper mill. Same smell, same look from Jacob. It was as if parts of the dream were coming to pass, piece by piece and bit by bit.

"You're not from around here, are you?" Jack asked. It was becoming clear to him that the boy didn't show up here by accident. And his parents' car hadn't broken down, if he even had parents. It was also Jack's impression that the boy intended to stay for a while, for a reason that he would surely find out soon. He seemed harmless enough—other than the onyx eyes, of course.

"No, Jackson. I am not from around here."

"Please call me Jack. What do *you* think, Jacob?" Jack asked his younger brother more rhetorically than actually, as Jacob had never spoken a word in his life.

Jacob looked at Jack, then at the boy, then back at Jack. *He doesn't have to say anything,* Jack thought. Jacob's demeanor, his aura, said more than any words could. Jacob approved of the boy entering their home, and he seemed to know a lot more in relation to the situation than Jack did. That was all Jack needed.

"Welcome to our home," Jack stated apprehensively while throwing his hands in the air. *This is going to be quite a night,* he thought.

He had no idea.

CHAPTER 11

"Your boy in Iowa has a lead for you," the tall man with an abnormally long face said to the much older, slightly overweight, balding man. This is exactly what they had been waiting for.

"The kid in the bunker? You don't say. I had all but given up on him. Where exactly was the crossing?" the balding man asked as he poured himself a neat Balvenie, distilled when he was a second-year Eli.

"Michigan. He said it looked like a boy. Do you think it could be *our* boy?" the equine-faced man asked.

"It doesn't matter. We need to get someone out there immediately," the bald man growled. "Last time was a fiasco. We must learn from our past mistakes so we don't repeat them. Do you understand?"

"Completely, sir. I plan on handling this myself. My plane leaves within the hour. My flight plan has me landing at Bishop Airport, in Flint, at 4:35 a.m. I will be at the scene within five hours," the long-faced man explained.

"Fine. Take the Nordic with you. He may be able to diffuse situations that you cannot."

"I would rather not. He will shoot first and ask questions later...and he makes me uncomfortable," the long-faced man retorted. He had worked with the Nordic before and was afraid of him. Terrified, actually.

"It is not a request. Our Nordic friend knows the results I will be satisfied with. I trust him, and so should you," the balding man explained.

"Yes, sir. I...*we* will not fail this time," the long-faced man replied. *This was going to be quite a trip*, he thought, *like carrying around a ticking time bomb*.

CHAPTER 12

"What is your name?" Jack asked the boy as they walked down the hall. Jack's guard was still up, though the full-on flight mode with the accompanying jolt of adrenaline had subsided somewhat.

"You can call me Noah," the boy replied. *Noah is just one of the names I've had, but now is not the time for that discussion*, the boy thought.

"Ok, Noah. You nailed it right on the head. You smell *really* bad. Why don't you clean yourself up and get out of those wet clothes. The bathroom is up the stairs and down the hall on the left," Jack told him, pointing out the path. "I'm sure Jacob has something that will fit you. What would you like to eat?"

"Toast, jam, honey," Noah replied, walking up the stairwell toward the bathroom as Jack followed. "Thank you."

Jack was starting to feel sorry for Noah. It seemed obvious that he has been neglected, at least by deprivation of the ability to keep himself and his clothes clean. *A call to social services is an option*, he thought. Get the boy out of what must be a very bad situation. When all was said and done, social services really got it right regarding Jack and Jacob's case. It could have very easily gone the other way, and they could both be living with Uncle Pete. His blood pressure started its throbbing assault on his temples again at the mere thought of it.

"I have toast, I have jam, and I have honey. Get yourself cleaned up and come down to the kitchen," Jack offered as he was putting together an outfit of Jacob's clothes. "Here are some clean clothes. Towels are in the cabinet above the toilet." Jack handed the clothes to Noah and walked back down the hall toward the stairway.

"I'm sure you know exactly what's going on here, don't you?" Jack asked Jacob once he had reached the kitchen. Jacob was sitting in his chair by the window staring back at Jack, but of course he gave no response. Jack again thought back to the dream he'd had earlier in which Jacob was not autistic, about the smells, and about the inability to run in the cesspool. Was it all connected somehow? Jack didn't know, but he would surely find out.

"You want some toast, buddy?" Jack asked Jacob. Jack always talked to Jacob in this manner even though the questions were always rhetorical and could never be answered. Jack liked to think Jacob understood everything but simply lacked the ability to answer. "I'll make a couple of slices for you," Jack answered for him. If Jacob didn't want them, he would eat them himself.

Jack placed the two slices with butter and honey on the table on top of the two slices with strawberry jam that had popped up a few minutes ago. Jacob didn't seem to be interested in the snack but was patiently waiting for Noah.

Noah tells me three times that he's hungry, that he just has to have nourishment, and then takes a twenty-minute shower? Nothing is making sense tonight, thought Jack as he walked back up the stairs. That took Jack back to the long showers he took when he was twelve, and he snickered quietly to himself, shaking his head back and forth as he walked down the hall to the bathroom.

"Are you ok in there?" Jack asked while rapping softly on the bathroom door. He could hear the shower water running, but there was no response. "Hey, are you all right, Noah?" he asked again, this time opening the door a crack. The bathroom was saturated with water vapor to the point that visibility was only a foot or two at best. As the open door began to clear the air, he could see Noah standing in the tub with his back to the spout, his eyes closed.

"Noah!" Jack shrieked as he rushed over and turned the hot water spigot off. The cold water tap had not been opened. The upper part of Noah's back was beet red and looked extremely irritated. He was definitely burned to the point blisters would form, possibly worse. Jack put his left arm around Noah's shoulders just as the boy was falling backward, and he positioned his right arm behind Noah's knees to pick him up. Noah's body was limp, and he was utterly unconscious.

"Jesus Christ, now what?" Jack moaned out loud. He could see the headline in *The Flint Journal* now: "Unknown naked kid dies on Wheaton bathroom floor from third-degree burns." Jack would spend the rest of his life in prison, and Jacob would be sent to live with Uncle Fucking Pete.

"I'm all right. I need food now," Noah whispered as he regained consciousness. Jack let out an audible sigh of relief. Jack sat Noah up and slid him backward so his back rested on the side of the tub, and then he grabbed a towel from the cabinet and began patting him dry.

"What happened? You scared the shit out of me, Noah," Jack said with more than a little contrition. *Every shower is different*, Jack thought. *I should have started the water for him.* As he was drying him off, Jack could not help but notice how *white* Noah was. Every part of his body was the same color of white, completely lacking any pigment, like an albino.

Tell me what twelve-year-old doesn't have tan lines on his thighs and arms, or at least his neck, Jack thought. *Has this boy been captive in a dungeon or something? Is that why he was wandering around, smelling to high heaven no less, on a dark and stormy night? Is he an escapee from a house of horrors?*

Jack also noticed that Noah was physically fit. *Very* fit. His abdominals protruded from his stomach area like they would on a body builder. His biceps, triceps, laterals, and pectorals were in perfect condition and proportion for his small body. Even his thighs and calves demonstrated phenomenal definition. Some boys in their mid to late teens could develop such musculature, but that was with the aid of testosterone coursing through their veins for at least a couple of years. Noah hadn't yet matured to that point as evidenced by his completely hairless body and other characteristics suggesting he hadn't yet reached puberty.

"I am so sorry. I am very weak," Noah sighed.

"Don't worry about it, buddy. You're going to have a sore back for a few days, though, if not longer. Let's get you dressed…your toast is ready in the kitchen," Jack informed him, hoping against all hope a sore back would be the extent of the boy's injuries. Jack grabbed the shirt he had picked out for Noah and scrunched it up to the armpit seams. Noah turned his back and lifted his arms to facilitate.

"What the…" Jack asked quizzically. Noah's back, moments ago the color of a fire engine, was now miraculously the same opaque milky white as the rest of his body.

CHAPTER 13

"My apologies for the late-night teleconference, gentlemen. General Baker has reported an illicit crossing in Michigan," Beau Trusdale, the Secretary of Homeland Security, announced to the group, using a laser to point out the intruder on the screen. "Time is of the essence if we wish to intercept the interloper this time."

"Is it the same boy? It looks like him," Matthew Nastally, the Secretary of Temporal Phenomenon, asked.

"It's too early to tell. General Baker referred to the individual as a boy, not *the* boy," Trusdale replied.

"I vote to immediately mobilize with the intent to capture without prejudice. I'm sick and tired of playing grab ass with these kids," Donovan Childress, the Secretary of the Joint Chiefs, offered. "And keep POTUS out of the loop. He needs plausible deniability in the event this goes public. Those fucking TMZ cameras are everywhere."

"I agree. This needs to end now, but not that way. You kill this kid and you risk starting a war you likely have no chance of winning. We all know exactly what he is capable of," Nastally emphasized. "I can place a small

SEAL team there within the hour, and we can pick him up the right way."

"I don't think we should do anything. To my knowledge, these kids have never hurt anybody and we have no idea what one may do if cornered," Jameson McBride, the attorney general of the United States, countered. "What are you going to do with him if you catch him anyways? Lock him up? Dissect him?"

"We have solid data suggesting people have disappeared in the vicinity of the electromagnetic anomaly incidents on federal land too many times to count. There are crimes being committed," Childress stated. "The public pays us to protect them, to keep them safe. It would be a dereliction of our sworn duty to turn the other cheek."

He made a good case. People had been mysteriously disappearing from North American forests for hundreds of years all the way back to the American Indians. Young children, doctors, scientists, and hunters of all races and ethnicities simply vanished into thin air. Sometimes they came back alive, but most of the time they did not. The young children, many barely able to walk, were often found miles away from the disappearance site, across terrain and at elevations they simply could not have reached on their own.

"I think we all agree that we need more information, and the only way to get it is by capturing one of these things," Nastally declared. "I can direct my team to capture alive. If there is any possibility of loss of life, I will order them to stand down," he emphasized, noticing everyone on his monitor was nodding.

"I think we are all in agreement, then, Matthew. Does anyone disagree?" Trusdale asked. There were no dissentions from the group. "Good. Nastally, get your team to Michigan immediately."

"Done. If you will excuse me, gentlemen," Nastally said as he flicked off his monitor. *Those pussies don't have the balls to do what needs to be done*, he thought. He then placed a call to Lieutenant Brady Gumper, leader of the black ops Temporal Anomaly SEAL team, of which there were three elite members.

"We're a go. Kill or capture without prejudice," Nastally told Gumper.

CHAPTER 14

"The toast is good!" Noah exclaimed. Those were his first words since his miraculous recovery.

What in the world is he even doing here? Jack thought. Noah's eyes, earlier one-hundred-percent pupil, were now, thankfully, returning to a more non-demonic look. At least part of the sclera was visible now. No iris yet, though. Jack really wanted to look at his back again. He knew what he saw—it was burned, and there should be blisters. The boy had been fed, now it was time for some answers.

"I'm glad you approve," Jack said somewhat sarcastically. *Does he even know how preposterous it is to knock on a stranger's door at midnight and ask for something to eat?* Jack thought. "How is your back?" he asked, trying to sound empathetic, but in actuality he was still simply curious.

"It's fine. I heal fast," Noah replied.

"No shit. You should be on your way to the hospital right now. I'm just going to get right to the point, Noah. Who are you, and why are you here?" Jack demanded. Jacob, who had been sitting quietly at the other end of the table, sat up straight and peered directly at Noah.

Jack once again felt like the least informed person in the room.

"Isaiah coined the word *Seraphim* in his chapter of the Bible to describe beings like myself. I would describe myself less like a Seraph and more like a Watcher Angel, or simply a Watcher. I'm from another world and I am here for Jacob. You could say we're old friends," Noah explained.

Jack once again felt the hair on the back of his neck stiffen significantly. He could also feel his patience wearing thinner and thinner.

"In case you didn't notice, Jacob is autistic. He can't talk. He can't do a lot of things normal people do," Jack explained.

"I know. I was there when it happened. You were holding him," Noah admitted nonchalantly between bites, displaying absolutely no emotion.

Jack's mind drifted back to that dreadful day thirteen years ago. Jacob was a mere ten minutes old, and Jack's father held out the newborn to Jack, asking if he would like to hold his little brother. Jack accepted. As the tiny package was slipped into his arms, Jack whispered to Jacob that he would be the best big brother in the world, and he would go to the ends of the earth to protect him. After only a minute or so, Jack looked down at baby Jacob, who was for some reason now blue and not breathing. He also began to convulse uncontrollably.

"Dad…" Little Jack quivered as he offered his baby brother back to his father.

"What have you done!" Jack's father screamed accusingly. He grabbed Jacob from a stunned Jack's arms and began screaming for a doctor. "My son is not breathing! My baby is dying!" his father yelled over and over. A nurse had swept the baby from his father's arms and taken him to the ICU, where they were thankfully able to revive him. For many years, Jack thought he was the reason Jacob was different, that he had somehow harmed Jacob, and only his mother's constant reassurance to the contrary eased his fears.

"It wasn't your fault, Jackson," his mother would say. "God gave him to us this way."

Jack's father, however, was never the same to him. He blamed him, and Jack knew it. Now this little freak was bringing it up all over again. *Why?*

"You had better explain yourself, Noah. How could you possibly have been there when Jacob is obviously older than you?" Jack was seething. He was standing now, leaning over the table and hovering mere inches above Noah.

"I'm older than you think I am, Jack, and I *was* there," Noah retorted. "Remember?" Noah hissed at Jack as he grabbed him by the arm and focused his still ghoulish eyes directly into Jack's.

And suddenly Jack was back in the hospital cradling little Jacob, who had his head turned toward the lobby as if he was looking there for someone or something. And who was sitting there staring right back? *Noah*, and he had his right hand wrapped around his own throat. Jack shook his head violently, releasing himself from the vision.

"No!" Jack screamed. "You did it! You caused Jacob to be autistic!"

"No, Jack. I was there to warn Jacob and to protect him. He did it to himself. Jacob simply stopped breathing until he passed out. He intentionally put himself into a coma, effectively killing a sizable portion of his brain, Jack. He knew the ramifications of being discovered by the wrong people. He had to shut down what he was broadcasting. His ability to speak and many of his motor functions were collateral damage. That act, and that act alone, caused his autism, not you," Noah clarified. Noah and Jack both looked at Jacob at the same time. He was still sitting attentively and peacefully like he had been for some time now.

The only difference was the lone tear streaming down his right cheek.

CHAPTER 15

"The hijacked TIRS is in place, Bass," Mikayla offered. "I can put the real-time images on the screen if you would like." *Ever since Baker left, Bass has been acting really strange*, she thought, *like he's seen a ghost*.

"Not necessary, thanks, Mikki," Bass replied. "I don't know what were even looking for. My plan is to throw everything we have at it and let OSCAR do his thing." He'd decided that the previous Silo 9 staff must have seen something or heard something not meant for their eyes or ears, so the less they knew, the better. Baker could execute OSCAR then. He snickered to himself at the image in his mind of Baker shooting the computer.

"Did you find any interesting phone calls, Leah?" Bass asked.

"Nothing, Sebastian. No 911 calls, no calls about UFOs, nothing," Leah replied. She was happy she could help but really wished something juicy would develop so she could prove her worth.

"Good job, Leah. Keep at it. Steven…where is Steven?" Bass asked. It was just like him to be screwing around.

"He said something about the 'shitter' again and walked out a few minutes ago," Leah replied. "He must be having issues with his bowels."

Bass made his way to the only bathroom in the complex. At the time it was built, there had never been an issue. Now, with two women on staff, it seemed like it was always occupied, especially when someone really needed to use it. As Bass approached the door, he could hear Steven talking but couldn't make out the words. The only telephone in the complex was located in the main control room, and it was corded. It was probably left over from the sixties, Bass had joked. So who the hell was he talking to and why? He needed to find out.

"Who are you talking to?" Bass blurted out as he stormed through the door. Steven immediately flipped shut the satellite phone he had been talking on. "A satellite phone? Why do you have a satellite phone? Who are you talking to, Steven?" Bass demanded.

"My friend Thomas in La Jolla. What business is it of yours?" Steven calmly replied, lying of course. He was scared shitless right now. *What had Bass heard?* he wondered.

"Bullshit! You know sat-phones are prohibited here. Give it to me right now," Bass demanded. Protocol dictated that any outgoing phone calls had to be made using the hard line in the bunker—for security reasons, Baker had told them. Bass was starting to see the whole picture now. The Silo 9 phone was undoubtedly tapped to ensure sensitive information wasn't leaked. Bass started to think that they hadn't been told the whole story concerning exactly what they were tracking in the first place. He was also starting to wish he had never agreed to come here.

"It's not a big deal, Bass," Steven pleaded. "There are times when I just want a little privacy, that's all. You know they're listening."

"Then tell me who you were talking to and what the conversation was about, and I will determine if it is a big deal." Steven was going to get both of them—make that all four of them—killed.

"I can't. I know we haven't seen eye to eye all of the time, and we're not good buddies, but you have to trust me on this, Sebastian. Please," Steven begged.

"I'm trying to protect all of us, and you lying to me is making that particularly hard. But I will let this go this time only. You cannot tell the girls you've been making clandestine calls either." He was done arguing with Steven. Since he used a satellite phone, there would be no record of the call anyway. He also couldn't figure how calling anyone would jeopardize the work they were involved in.

"And next time, lock the door," Bass warned.

"Thank you. I owe you one." The phone call Steven had just made, Bass would find out later, would end up changing all of their lives forever.

CHAPTER 16

"Tell me why a ten-minute-old child attempts suicide," Jack sarcastically asked Noah. This ought to be good. *This kid is so full of shit his eyes literally turned black*, Jack thought.

"It's a long story, and it's complicated."

"I have all the time in the world. Speak!" Jack sharply demanded.

"All right. Do you believe in God, Jack? Or more importantly, do you believe in life after death…or reincarnation?" Noah asked.

"I suppose so. I've sworn at God my fair share of times for what he did to Jacob," Jack answered. The fair share was a bit of an understatement, though. Jack blamed God incessantly for smiting Jacob. He also had a fair share of survivor's guilt, to the point that he often deprived himself of his own happiness out of his perceived shame. It was a heavy burden for a teenager to bear by himself. "I've never really thought about reincarnation. I'm just trying to get through this life."

"Well, the soul is, in essence, what makes a human being *human*. The souls of this universe have always been, and they always will be. A soul cannot be created, nor can it be destroyed. It *is*, and it contains the knowledge of the universe, called the Akashic records, along with the memories of all the past lives it has lived. And you could also say it learns as it grows. Do you understand what I am saying?"

"I suppose so. You're saying all the souls of the universe were created in the Big Bang billions of years ago, and they never die, right?" Jack replied.

"Correct, but it wasn't a Big Bang, though…that's another story. So a soul attaches to a future being at the moment of fertilization. It is the way of the universe. The only stipulation is that the being must be evolved to the point best summed up by René Descartes when he stated '*Cogito, ergo sum*,' I think, therefore I am. Jacob's soul, your soul, and every other human soul, even my soul for that matter, are all the same in that respect," Noah explained. "Are you still with me?"

Jack nodded his head that he was. "Yeah, still with you."

"Ok, good. Jacob is not supposed to be human. He is an Anunnakan Watcher like me and we reside on the planet Niburu. Jacob therefore has, also like me, an Annunaki soul that should only inhabit an Anunnakan's body. He, meaning his soul, was accidentally and irrevocably inserted into the developing fetus of your mother and father," Noah continued. "The human soul gradually loses its knowledge of the universe and with it all of its past lives as the fetus develops until there is, in essence, a blank slate at birth. Jacob's soul did not lose this knowledge as it should have because he is an Anunnaki, and our souls do not ever lose this knowledge…we live with this information from conception to death."

"Why is that?" Jack asked with much more skepticism than he intended. Jacob was still at his side taking it all in.

"It doesn't matter to me if you believe what I'm saying, Jack. You asked, and I'm telling you the truth. It wasn't always that way. We, the Anunnaki, came to Earth for the one thing we needed for our ailing planet: gold. The population of this planet at the time was soulless and unable to help in their present state of development, so we genetically modified them, giving them speech, a greater ability to reason, and most importantly, a soul, among other advantages."

"So you're telling me you gave us a bigger brain and made yourself some slaves?" Jack asked. He had some knowledge of Niburu, the Anunnaki and Zacharia Sitchin's theories of how and why they came here. It seemed as though it may not be a theory after all.

"No. You humans were not slaves. We sped up your development by millions of years in exchange for work in the mines. That's why your archeologists will never find the 'missing link' in your evolution. We were your gods and you were our servants. It was an equitable exchange that both benefited from."

"What about the soul? Why did you make the soul different?" Jack asked.

"They are not different. Your soul is just like mine, except my soul—and Jacob's—will only pair with an Anunnaki host. In fact, every soul in the universe is equal in every way, although some have led many more lives than others. The human being was originally enhanced as an equal to the Anunnaki in every way. Like the Bible says, you were made in God's image. Adam and subsequently Eve were awarded the fruits of the earth and were crowned king of this domain. They even had thousand-year life spans just like us. Humans, however, did quite poorly knowing the reality of the universe and remembering past lives…so they, along with other unsavory beings such as the Nephilim, were later mostly exterminated in the Great Flood, save a select few: Noah and his family. The human genome was again manipulated to limit humanity to lives of eighty or so years, and the Akashic record became inaccessible during the life of the host."

"So what happened to Jacob? Why wasn't his record wiped clean?" This was getting stranger and stranger, and Jack's head was starting to hurt. "And why would he try to kill himself?"

"He was in danger. There are groups that hunt for infants like Jacob. These searchers possess an extrasensory perception they can attune to the unique rhythm of an unencumbered Anunnaki soul. How it's done is much less important than why it's done. Imagine having a child that is knowledgeable about the universe and the mechanics of the soul. He was in danger, and I led them away," Noah explained.

"That doesn't answer my question. Why wasn't Jacob's record wiped clean?" Jack demanded.

"It seems Jacob is the reunion of the descendants of a pair of siblings split up long ago, each of whom ultimately passed on to your parents the gene trait responsible for wiping, or more correctly not wiping, the human Akashic record clean. It was literally a fifty-fifty chance in the offspring of your parents. You didn't get it, and Jacob did. It has been a very long time since any human being was born with this gene turned on."

"How long? Who was the last person to have this… affliction?" Jack asked.

"Over two millennium. The last person born on the earth with this Anunnaki-type gene was the father of those two siblings: Jesus of Nazareth," Noah revealed. "Jacob, whether he likes it or not, is, in essence, the second coming of Jesus Christ."

CHAPTER 17

"Balthasar! We must stop for the night. Gaspar and I need food and rest, and I am sure you do too," Melchior pleaded. They were all sweaty and tired, but Balthasar was the leader of their group and he would decide where and when they would stop.

"We must keep moving. I am sure our destination is near. I can practically hear the Lord whispering in my ear, 'Balthasar…believe in me and you shall live forever, in my kingdom…follow the light to the east…everlasting life is yours…' I cannot get it out of my head!" Balthasar replied. He had been hearing these whispers and having vivid dreams for months.

"But all we do is wander aimlessly around the countryside! Where are we going?" Gaspar asked. Their food and water supplies had dwindled to drastically low amounts, they were all weary, and it was getting dark.

"Let's stop here for the night. Tie up the camels and pitch the tent, Gaspar," Balthasar directed. As Balthasar grabbed his sleeping roll from the pack on the camel, a shriek—a child's scream—startled him, and he fell to his knees and raised his hands in the air.

"Lord! Show me a sign! I cannot endure this wretched wandering much longer!" Balthasar implored. Immediately a ten-meter-wide beam of light, originating from the heavens, bathed the three men in its golden glow. Melchior and Gaspar fell to their knees and raised their hands to the sky as well.

"It is a sign! The Lord shines his light upon us!" Gaspar declared. What the men couldn't know was that the beam of light actually originated from a near-Earth artificial satellite, its reflective panels perfectly positioned to reflect the sun's rays precisely on the men. The intense and beautiful beam began moving slowly toward the east.

"Quick! Grab the gifts for the King of Kings and let us follow this heavenly light! Leave the camels…we shall go on foot!" Balthasar eagerly shouted. The men grabbed their meager belongings, including the special gifts, and followed Balthasar and the heavenly sign. They traveled well into the night until they came upon a small town named Bethlehem. The beam had now stopped moving, and it was squarely fixed upon a small farm building.

Protect the child, Balthasar…protect the King of Kings, Balthasar heard in his head, and he knew exactly what he had to do. If he could hear this child, surely other less pious individuals could too. Balthasar directed Gaspar to dig a hole at the edge of town away from roads and buildings. Once Gaspar departed, Balthasar instructed Melchior to find a suckling pig, sacrifice it, and bring it to him. Balthasar then entered the barn, where he met a man and a woman holding a child.

"I am the Magi Balthasar, and my friends and I have traveled from lands to the west to protect you and your newborn child. Please do as I say and no harm shall come to any of you," Balthasar explained.

"I am Joseph, and this is my wife Mary, and she has recently given birth to our child, a boy," Joseph stated. He was clearly nervous and leery of this stranger showing up in the middle of the night.

"You must do exactly as I say. The child is in danger," Balthasar declared. Now that he was next to the infant, he knew the spiritual messages had originated from him. The moment of the boy's birth was the scream that had dropped Balthasar and his friends to their knees. "Joseph, apply this frankincense to the boy's body and leave town at once. Do not tell anyone where you are going, not even Mary. You will find each other again in time. Also, place these gold coins, all of them, within the child's swaddling. It will keep the child's soul hidden from the searchers. Leave at once!" Balthasar demanded. Moments after Joseph exited the barn with the baby, Melchior entered with the dead pig.

"Excellent, Melchior! Swathe the pig with myrrh and wrap it with the swaddling from the manger." Melchior did as he was instructed until the pig was wrapped tight. It oddly had the size and general shape of a human baby. Balthasar noticed he could no longer hear the voice in his head, and he was relieved. The gold was working. "Mary, we must find Gaspar and bury this *child*. Melchior, head immediately back to our camp and speak to no one." Mary and Balthasar walked to the edge of town where they found Gaspar, who had just finished digging the hole as previously told.

"Good work, Gaspar. Unfortunately, the child was stillborn. Put him in the hole and cover it up so he is properly buried," Balthasar instructed. As he was tamping down the last of the dirt, a towering, ginger-haired beast of a man walked up and asked if they knew of any babies being born in the area. Gaspar, thinking he had just buried a baby, spoke up.

"We've just buried a stillborn baby, sir, as you can clearly see." Gaspar replied. The brute, easily nine feet tall and certainly clairvoyant himself, studied Gaspar intently for several minutes before turning his attention to the makeshift grave. The man gripped his spear tightly with his six-fingered hands, raised it above his head, and thrust it with his considerable strength into the grave, easily penetrating the "child." The man brought the spear tip to his mouth and licked the tip with his split tongue.

"Blood and embalming oil…I'm sorry for your loss," he grunted as he walked away in the direction from which he had come. Balthasar let out the breath he had been holding.

"The Nephilim will not bother you, your husband, or your child again, Mary," Balthasar said. "By the way, what is the name of your child?"

"We are going to name him Jesus," she replied.

CHAPTER 18

Simon Dobbs had been a pleaser his whole life. His fondest memories of childhood, though few and far between, all involved pleasing his mother. Getting straight As made her happy, so he would get straight As.

"Run to Leroy's and get me a pack of Pall Malls and a fifth of Popov, Simon," his mother would ask, and Simon would make the three-mile round trip on his bicycle in less than fifteen minutes—and that included the three minutes spent convincing Leroy that the goods were for his mother. Simon would simply reason with him. "What would an eight-year-old do with a pack of smokes and a bottle of liquor, Mr. Leroy?" Simon would ask. He wouldn't realize until years later that pleasing his mother in this way also led to her premature death from emphysema and liver cancer.

As a teen, Simon was bullied incessantly due to his appearance. "Why the long face, Simon?" they would ask. "Hey, Citation, too bad your prick's not as big as a horse's!" If ripping on him made them happy, he didn't care.

Simon answered a help wanted ad for a driver in 1976, and he had served Dr. Carrington since. It was more like a marriage than many marriages. Simon was Hollis's gopher, basically. He was there to please him like a maid or butler would. Hollis paid handsomely for this arrangement, although Simon had little want or need for money. No wife, no living family, hence no real need for money. Dr. Carrington paid for everything, and Simon was grateful to finally have a purpose in life.

That was exactly the reason he wanted to succeed in this current endeavor. Hollis *needed* this boy, or whatever it was, very badly. Life or death badly. Simon felt as though his success would validate his usefulness to Dr. Carrington.

Simon looked across the Gulfstream G650 at the only thing that could screw this up for him: the Nordic. Dr. Carrington's hired heavy hand and bodyguard. His fixer. And he'd been busy lately. With what, Simon had no clue. The only thing either would say about their "business" together was that it was above Simon's pay grade and that he probably didn't want to know.

"Why don't you get some sleep?" Simon asked. The Nordic turned his head and stared at him with those steely dead eyes but said nothing. After what seemed like an eternity, he simply turned his head back and continued staring at the head rest in front of him.

This is going to be a blast, thought Simon.

CHAPTER 19

This was all a bit much for Jack to digest. In a little over two hours, a diminutive, albeit chiseled, black-eyed little alien boy showed up at his house, severely burned his back, subsequently healed himself, and then delivered the bombshell that his little brother may be about to start the *Rapture*. Funny thing, though, Jack somehow believed him.

"Say all of this is true. You still haven't told me why you are here," Jack stated.

"I have already told you. I am here for Jacob," Noah replied indifferently.

"Let me make myself clear. Jacob isn't going anywhere with you or anybody else. End of discussion." His blood pressure was starting to rise again. *This little shit isn't taking Jacob anywhere*, Jack thought.

"And let me make myself clear. Jacob *is* coming with me whether you like it or not. You are more than welcome to join us. In fact, it's probably a good idea because neither of us can drive."

Jack laughed at the prospect of either of these two boys driving a car, although he'd put money on Jacob being the better driver of the two.

"I just can't drop everything and cart you two who knows where. I have fields to till to keep this roof over our heads." It was only kind of true. While the money made from the crops covered the taxes on the land and house, it was the insurance proceeds from their parents' accident, along with Jacob's Social Security and SSI, which was more than enough to sustain the two of them for the rest of their lives. The fields simply kept them both busy, and the fact that Jacob enjoyed doing it was an added bonus.

"Sure you can. My arrival here has not gone unnoticed, either. There will be a point in the very near future where it will not be safe here."

"More riddles. What is it with you, anyways? You come in here making demands and now you say we're in danger? Who is after you?" Jack asked. His temples were throbbing again. Jack could see the sky just starting to brighten in the northeastern sky. He looked at the clock above the breakfast nook window, and it was a quarter past four. Had they really been sitting at this table for two hours?

"It doesn't matter. The less you know now, the better. I promise you no harm will come to the three of you."

Before Jack could point out to Noah that he couldn't count, Abbie walked through the front door carrying an over-stuffed paper grocery bag, and she was as full of joy as ever. *Oh shit*, Jack thought. Abigail Cooke was a former high school study buddy Jack could count on and trust to watch Jacob in their home when he had errands to run sans Jacob. Jacob adored her and always pepped up when she came over to watch him. Jack had plenty of misgivings concerning Jacob's care, but thankfully leaving him with Abbie was not one of them.

"Jack, Jake. You guys are up awfully early. I wanted to surprise you guys with a big country breakfast." Abbie excitedly chirped. She was always happy. Then she took notice of Noah skeptically, thinking he may be a new babysitter, but he looked younger than Jacob. "Who's your friend?" she asked solemnly. Thankfully, Noah's eyes were almost normal now.

"This is Noah. He's a friend…of Jacob's." Jack couldn't take his eyes off Noah. He was so mad right now he could explode. The little bastard somehow knew she was coming, and he was just sitting there with a smug look on his face. If Noah had showed up any other day of the week, Abbie wouldn't be involved in this madness.

"Say, Abbie, I'm not going to need you today after all. All of my appointments have canceled," he lied. Jack had to get rid of her immediately. The last thing he wanted was to get her mixed up in this foolishness.

"Actually, we're all going on a little adventure. Would you like to join us?" Noah interjected before Abbie could respond.

What the hell is Noah doing? Jack wondered.

Jack then looked at Jacob, still sitting silently with his elbows on the table and his chin resting in his cupped palms. It was something in Jacob's eyes, something Jack had seen before, that simply said *"trust me"* again, just like in the dream. Jack would, so he remained silent after Noah made his offer, but his look of disdain as he glared at Noah was palpable.

"It's a date!" Abbie exclaimed with excitement. She really liked Jack, and she hoped spending time together would bring them together as a couple. *A girl can always hope*, she thought. "Where are we going?" she asked.

"Yeah, Noah. Where are we going?"

CHAPTER 20

The phone was ringing, and Bass knew exactly who it was and what he wanted. He named it the "shat" phone because it didn't have the ability to dial out to anyone other than General Baker, like the Bat Phone with Commissioner Gordon, only shittier because it was always merely Baker that called. Hence the "shat" phone. An answering machine would come in handy about now too: "Hi! You've reached Silo Nine! We can't come to the phone right now, but your call is very important to us! Leave your name and number at the tone, and we'll call you back at our earliest convenience!" Unfortunately it would just ring and ring until Baker got so pissed off he would hang up and call again. There was no avoiding this one.

"Hello," Bass spoke into the receiver after picking it up midway through the fifth ring. *Keep it simple*, he thought.

"Bass, General Baker," Baker said as if he thought Bass was waiting for another call for some reason. "I have a team headed to the site. I need you to send everything OSCAR has to the IP address 31.415.926. What did you come up with?" he asked. Bass couldn't get past Baker's raspy, effeminate voice. On a call last month, Bass actually replied, "Yes, ma'am—sir" by accident to a question Baker had asked. If Bass had had a gun, he would have shot himself in the temple right then, but Baker didn't say anything. Maybe he didn't hear him, or maybe he didn't care. He surely realized he had an "old-lady-two-pack-a-day" voice, Bass figured.

"We hijacked a TIRS from the NSA, but the area was clear before we had eyes on the scene. OSCAR is still working through all the data, although he estimates the subject to be five foot five and weigh about a hundred pounds. There hasn't been any unusual chatter in the area, but we are monitoring." Bass was expecting Baker to go on a tirade because this wasn't much more info than they had when Baker was there.

"Good job. Keep working it, Bass. Remember, this is what we are here for, all of us. Get the info to the IP I gave you and continue pumping data into OSCAR."

"Yes, sir, thank you, sir. I'm sending the data myself as we speak." The other end of the line clicked off before Bass could add any regards. Sebastian wasn't the type to make excuses but had several at the ready, like "the weather was disruptive" and "the TIRS wasn't taking coordinate commands." Thank God he didn't need them. But was Baker really ok with the work they'd done, or was it simply lip service with a side of execution?

"Bass? OSCAR has something," Steven exclaimed, arousing Bass from his self-doubt journey. "Based upon the initial direction of travel and the time interval between the initial sighting and the TIRS satellite arriving, OSCAR has narrowed down his destination to six houses, unless he hitched a ride or is hiding in the woods."

"That's awesome, Steven," Bass commended. *We finally get a break*, he thought. "I want to know everything about the occupants of those homes. Names, ages, photos, anything you can find. This is now the priority."

Now Bass couldn't wait for the "shat" phone to ring.

CHAPTER 21

The Boeing CH-47F Chinook was steadily gaining altitude and would soon be screaming over Lake Michigan at over two hundred miles per hour. It was a stroke of luck that Lt. Brady Gumper and his team were at Naval Station Great Lakes working with a brand-new class of navy SEAL candidates. Information was now coming across each of the team's face shields concerning the exact landing site, along with a physical description: 5′5″ and a hundred pounds, gender uncertain, probably male. *Not exactly your typical terrorist*, Gump thought. Brady and his boys would complete their mission just the same. Locate and neutralize the subject, this time without prejudice. Nastally stated the subject was extremely dangerous, so he and his team would proceed with the necessary caution.

Shiva, the canine member of the team, was lying down on the seat next to Gump. "Going after a real badass, boy," Gump said sarcastically to his furry friend. Shiva's ears perked at the mention of his name, and he offered a little yip in reply.

"Hey, Gump…couldn't they have sent someone else on this one, like a Girl Scout den mother or something?" one of his men asked. That got the whole crew grinning, and Shiva added another little yip himself.

"That's enough. You all know this unit handles the shit no one else will touch. The target may be small, but there is a reason why we were called. Nastally said it came from off-world, so it might not even be human," Gump explained. He had to get them in the proper frame of mind. Overconfidence led to underestimating, and that led more often than not to failure.

"Sorry, Gump. This just doesn't reek of our typical mission," the soldier countered. "It just kind of sounds like we're going up against a middle schooler, that's all."

"Hitler wasn't much bigger, you know? Just think how many lives would have been saved if we'd taken him out in 1939? The bottom line is: we get orders, we carry out orders. And remember, this mission is without prejudice on American soil. We have the authority to eliminate anyone that stands in the way of completing this mission. Nastally is taking this mission very seriously, and so will we." Even Shiva set his head down on his outstretched paws in perceived ignominy.

"Yes, sir," the others mumbled in unison. *Gump is right*, they thought. *We get paid to complete missions, not question them.*

What they didn't know was this "middle schooler" would give them all they could handle and then some.

CHAPTER 22

Hollis had just received a text stating the team had arrived in Flint. *I should have gone with them*, he thought. His frail health had made plane travel particularly troublesome, even with all the amenities of the Gulfstream. He said a silent prayer that Simon and the Nordic would be successful.

Hollis has been looking for this kid, or at least one from the same mold, for over fifty years. One of these "kids" had infiltrated one of the most top secret black budget government endeavors ever: the Montauk Project. The activities took place at the Montauk Air Force Station/ Camp Hero in Montauk, New York, between 1962 and 1967. The work Hollis had spearheaded involved time travel and mind control using ancient and/or alien technology.

Dr. Hollis Carrington had been the director of the portion of the project that used, and often unfortunately abused, children in the pursuit of their goals. The children, nicknamed the Montauk Boys, were boys between the ages of nine and thirteen. Carrington used a test he created and administered through the public school system to glean the most psychically gifted children from a nine-state area. If a child was deemed gifted enough, he would be placed in the Montauk chair wearing an ancient crystal relic on his head that allowed the most exceptional of the boys to travel through time and even manifest an object from their thoughts.

The chair was believed to work by reading the thoughts of the occupants via electrodes placed on the skull and the bowl-shaped crystal relic placed over the electrodes. The relic somehow read the user's thoughts and promptly manifested the object being thought of. Girls of any age and boys over the age of thirteen or so were unable to get any meaningful results from the chair for reasons unknown.

Carrington had found the most gifted of the group while checking out at the Stop & Shop on Lakewood in Toms River, New Jersey, in July of 1967.

"Your total is $5.74, sir," the cashier directed Hollis. Hollis had made a quick stop on his way back to the base for a carton of Lucky Strikes. He knew he would be stuck on base for at least the next five days and had considered buying two cartons. Hollis pulled out his billfold and handed the cashier a five-dollar bill. He reached into the front left pocket of his slacks to retrieve his blue and silver air force logoed coin pouch, the plastic type that you squeeze the sides to open, when a small black-haired boy behind him in line interrupted.

"You will have to give her another single, mister. You only have sixty-three cents in your little coin purse," the boy posited.

"It's a pouch, not a purse, and how do you know that? Are you psychic or something?" Hollis asked. The boy seemed to be about ten or eleven years old and had all of the trademarks of mid-Sixties youth: Beatles-inspired curly black mop top hairdo, red short-sleeve horizontally lined shirt, and denim jeans. He could be anyone's son or grandson. But was he gifted?

"I don't think so. Something in my head just tells me things," the boy explained.

"I see. Something in your head tells you. What does your head tell you about the Yankees this year?" Hollis asked, smiling at the clerk while he counted out the change in the plastic pouch. Exactly sixty-three cents. That didn't necessarily mean the boy was gifted; he could just as easily be lucky. "You hit it right on the button, boy! Sixty-three cents in the pouch!"

As Hollis reached back into his billfold to retrieve a single to complete his purchase, his mind was spinning. How was he going to get this kid tested? How would he explain it to the parents? He had four boys at the moment who were not extraordinary. Hell, they were barely ordinary. He felt as though he needed this boy.

"Unfortunately, the Dodgers are going to sweep the Yankees in the World Series. As for my parents minding, that won't be a problem…and you should definitely buy another carton."

Holy shit, the kid is reading my mind, thought Hollis as he put his arm over the boy's shoulder and walked him out the door.

"What's your name, son?" Hollis asked the boy as he opened the front passenger side door of his '58

Bel Air Impala. The child paused for a moment before answering.

"You can call me Noah."

CHAPTER 23

"We're going out of town to visit some people," Noah explained, cryptic as usual. Getting details out of the kid was like pulling teeth. "Time is of the essence, and we must leave immediately."

"Do I need to pack anything for Jacob? He is very regimented and gets agitated if his schedule is interrupted." That was an understatement. Jacob once threw a fit at Meijer's Thrifty Acres because he would miss the beginning of *Judge Judy*. Nothing could be planned between 4:00 and 5:00 p.m. weekdays because Jacob had to be glued to the television to view the latest cases.

"We can pick up most of what we need as we go. Throw some juice boxes in Jacob's backpack, and let's get started while it's still dark."

This was the first time Jack could read tension in Noah. Everything to this point was almost as if he was reading a script. But now, he seemed scared. In the distance, the faint yet ominous whir of a helicopter rotor could be heard. As it increased in intensity, they all paused and instinctively looked in that direction. They followed the sound anxiously until it was virtually directly overhead, then, thankfully, continued on. Everyone subsequently focused their attention to Noah—even Abbie, who really didn't have a clue about what was happening.

"Is that about you?" Jack asked Noah accusingly. "I'm pretty sure that wasn't a news helicopter looking for a scoop on the five a.m. milking at old man Barnes's farm."

"Yes. They are searching for me. That is why time is of the essence. We must leave now." The fear in his voice was conspicuous, but there was also a resolve to get his mission started, whatever that was.

"I swear to God, if anything happens to Jacob or Abbie, I will hand you over to the police myself. If I was in my right mind, I would call 911 and do it right now. I have a bad feeling about this," Jack said. He was trying to listen to his gut, but it was giving him conflicting messages. Weird kid, cryptic messages, and the like would make any sane person leery. But there was also the fact he was here, and he had to be here for a good reason, whatever it was. So Jack would trust him for now.

"As I explained earlier, I will do everything in my power to see that no harm comes to any of you. But we have to leave *now*," Noah promised with a bit of annoyance and a lot of urgency.

"Ok. Ok. Let's go." Jacob, who had been sitting at the dining room table for hours taking it all in, had slipped away and was standing at the front door. Evidently, he was more than ready.

"I'll raid my 'fun money' fund so I can pay for this little excursion of yours," Jack said as he was walking toward the stairs leading to his bedroom. "How much do you think we'll need? The Suburban doesn't get good mileage, and food for four people can get expensive."

"There is no need for money, but I do need a handful of change: two quarters, two nickels, and three pennies. There is a transfer waiting through Western Union—just log in and claim it. You can put it directly into your checking account. Now let's go."

"All right, you're the boss. Let's go," Jack said as he was pulling up the Western Union app on his phone. A couple of identity questions and prompts later, and the transfer was successful. "Five thousand dollars? Do you think that will be enough to get us out of town?" Jack asked facetiously. This kid had a surprise around every corner.

"Yes, Jack. I have friends here that are very interested in my success. Let's go!" Noah stated with even more aggression.

"Let's go then." As they all headed toward the door, Jack's heart sank as Jacob was no longer standing there. He opened the door, and before he could call out his name, he saw him. Jacob was sitting, head down as if in prayer, in the back seat of the Suburban. He was ready to go.

CHAPTER 24

G eneral Baker was sitting in his car just outside his favorite liquor store, Super Spirits, enjoying his Stoli straight from the bottle and contemplating his next move. *The team should be at the site about now*, he thought. *What if he's captured alive? Where should I have them take him?* Transport to Silo 9 made the most sense. Baker could have his way with him before the scientists swooped in. And if he was dead? He didn't want to think about that. He knew now that all this would be for naught if they killed the boy.

Rowland Stanley Baker was born December 7th, 1955 to naturalized parents who had their only child later in life. One could almost call him an accident, as his mother was forty-six at the time of his birth, his father three years older. His parents incongruously met at Ellis Island in May of 1921 and shared fourteen days of quarantine together as children. Young Ukrainian-born Stanislov and Russian-born Marissa made an oath that they would find each other at all costs, eventually get married, have a gaggle of children, and live happily ever after in the Land of Opportunity. The fairy tale didn't exactly unfold that way, though both remained steadfastly true to their pledge.

The difficulty finding each other after detention was compounded when Gustav Kollektivnyy, Stanislov's father, opted (at *great* urging from immigration officials) to change his surname to reflect his occupation, thus becoming Gus Baker, father to Stanley Baker. Marissa Preobrazhensky would become Mary Mason for similar reasons, and the youngsters would hence not meet again for almost nineteen years by happenstance at an open market in the Bronx, though they lived less than ten miles apart. It was an embrace that rivaled the VJ day in Times Square kiss photographed by Alfred Eisenstaedt in 1945, and Stanley and Mary were inseparable until the day they died.

Young Rowland was born a full fifteen years later, though not for a lack of trying. Stanley and Mary had for some time resigned themselves to a childless union, and they were at peace with that. Money was always tight for the Baker family as the American Dream had at times become a nightmare for the couple. The Great Depression had wreaked havoc on the Baker finances, and the couple never fully recovered.

So it was largely for monetary reasons that Stanley and Mary decided to send their bright (and often misunderstood) twelve-year-old boy, Rowland, off to a military school in the summer of 1967. Not only was it one less mouth to feed, but the military also would pay a $200 stipend each month, a significant amount at the time. The couple saw young Rowland off on June 1, 1967, incidentally the first day of the Summer of Love. It would also be the last time they ever saw their son.

Yes, Baker reflected. *It was high time for some payback.*

CHAPTER 25

The main screen showing the TIRS satellite image hijacked from the NSA to help with tracking, which had been virtually void of movement for over two hours, suddenly showed a flurry of activity as the Chinook landed in the alfalfa field twenty yards from the anomaly presentation location.

Bass and the rest of the Silo 9 staff took a break from their assigned activities to watch as the operation unfolded in real time. It was apparent the three soldiers, probably SEALs or other special forces, had been sent along with one canine on this particular mission.

"What are they expecting to find there? Nothing has moved in quite some time," Leah asked.

"Start at the point of entry and track from there, I suppose," Bass replied. "They have a dog with them."

"A dog's nose can pick up a scent as little as one or two parts per trillion, which is hundreds of times better than a human's sense of smell," Steven chimed in, always at the ready with trivia tidbits nobody cared about.

"Well, it looks like this one is pissed off or something. He's just lying there," Mikayla said to no one in particular.

"Yeah, it does seem like that's the case," Bass replied. Mikki was right. The dog eagerly jumped out of the Chinook, stuck its nose in the air, and promptly laid down right there in the field. The two soldiers who had originally fanned out to clear the site and establish a perimeter now returned to where the unenthusiastic dog laid down. The men were obviously at a loss as to why the canine member of the unit was acting so strangely.

"Enough of that, we have work to do. What do we have on the six addresses OSCAR gave us?" Bass asked in the general direction of Steven and Leah. *We're going to have to help that SEAL team*, Bass thought. *Why would the dog, specifically trained to track, be so uninterested in following the trail of the kid?* The reason would alarm Bass—or anyone else—to their core. Multidimensional beings (grays, elves, and cryptids of all kinds, including Bigfoot) had been scratching, seizing, and otherwise terrorizing all inhabitants of the earth, both human and animal, for millennia. Their smell, or aura, had been instinctively passed for generations in the animal world as a sign of warning, of danger. The SEALs at the site could coax their canine with a two-pound T-bone or a slab of bacon and the result will always be the same: the dog would just lay there, scared and confused.

"Address number one: white male, white female, both retired and in their seventies, own twenty acres and have a small pond behind their home and a Winnebago in the driveway," Steven offered.

"Address number two: family of five, two boys, one girl, ages five to eleven, father an elementary school teacher, mother unemployed, own their home, own two cars," Leah continued.

"Address number three: two males, one thirteen, and the other an emancipated eighteen-year-old, own several hundred acres, which they both lease out and farm themselves. One registered transportation vehicle, a Suburban, and two tractors. The younger boy receives Social Security and SSI, so he must have a disability of some kind," Steven explained.

"Stop there. Mikki, bring that address up on the screen," Bass requested. He didn't know how or why, call it a gut feeling, but Bass felt like this is where the boy was headed. As Mikki manipulated the satellite's image, the men with the uninspired pooch got smaller and the image crawled to the north. "Good, Mikki. Now zoom in a little bit." The house and surrounding property gained size until it filled the screen.

"Looks like a nice place to live," Leah speculated, and it did. Nice large Victorian, big yard, a couple of oversized outbuildings. It looked like the typical farm.

"I don't see the Suburban…only a small sedan. Can you rewind it, Mick?" Bass asked. *There isn't anything out of the ordinary here*, Bass thought. They could have the truck parked in the barn, and Mee-Maw and Pop-Pop could be visiting their grandchildren.

"I'll go as far back as I can, but I don't have much, Bass. The satellite hasn't been in place for very long," Mikayla warned as the time stamp in the upper left corner started to roll backward. The missing Suburban suddenly appeared on the screen.

"Stop! Ease it back verrrrry slowly," Bass screamed, startling everyone in the bunker. They all watched as the truck crept up the driveway and came to a stop near the house. Three people then exited the vehicle and were walking backward up toward the house. "Keep it going," Bass asked of Mikayla. One minute after the group of three entered the home, another person exited the vehicle, walked backwards toward the house, and also went inside.

"Who goes for a drive at four in the morning?" Leah asked. She had a point. This didn't seem like typical behavior.

"Farmers, Leah. Cows have to be milked in twelve-hour intervals for peak production. If the farmer milks his herd at 4:00 a.m., he can milk them again right before dinner," Steven explained, once again showing off his overabundance of banal trivia.

"Play it forward now, Mick," Bass asked. The scene unfolded once again, this time in the way in which it actually happened. A boy came outside, probably the one on SSI due to his odd gait, and sat in the rear seat on the driver's side. One minute later, the rest came out and made their way to the truck, one to the driver's seat, one to rear passenger side, and one to the…

"Stop!" Bass startled them all again. The person getting into the front passenger seat paused before getting in and sitting down. *That figure is our target*, Bass determined.

The target did something that unsettled all of them. He had turned slightly to the southeast and looked up, staring directly at the satellite. And it looked like he was *waving*.

CHAPTER 26

"We're coming up on the coordinates…slow down," Simon instructed the Nordic. The Nordic, or Sven, as he liked to be called, had an array of surveillance devices at his disposal any gumshoe would be downright envious of. Night vision goggles, night vision binoculars, heat-detecting equipment, even a dish-shaped contraption used for eavesdropping from extreme distances, among other tools. Simon grabbed the night vision binoculars from the backseat and started surveying the area.

"Stop! Goddammit, we're too late to the party," Simon grumbled. In the field ahead was a military helicopter parked exactly at their destination. It seemed the men were just standing in a circle, perhaps establishing a plan. Nope, there was a dog there also, just lying on the ground between them.

"No…this is good!" the Nordic stated in his staccato broken English. "Let them do the tracking. Then we follow the soldiers."

That actually isn't a bad plan, Simon thought as they really had no way of tracking the boy.

"Nice to see you actually talk, Sven. I was starting to think you went mute. So how are we going to get the boy away from these guys if they get to him first?" Simon asked. Another valid point as the military squad had them outnumbered three to two and surely had considerably more firepower.

"Let me worry about that," Sven answered. "I am the best at what I do. You're just along for the ride, so don't get in my way."

"You realize Mr. Carrington needs this one alive, right? You just can't go out and kill shit and then drag it home like you're on some big game hunt. And you are going up against the United States Armed Forces, probably SEALs or Berets."

"They're all pussies. I get my man, one way or another. Like I said, just stay out of my way, Mr. Ed," Sven chided.

"Fuck you, you pasty white Nordic son of a whore. And call me that again, I dare you!" Simon bellowed, his cheeks getting flush. *I knew this was a bad idea*, he thought. Both men had been keeping an eye on the landing site while they exchanged insults, so both perked up when the movement started. One of the men literally picked up the dog and placed him in the helicopter. The other two raced around to the other side before jumping in themselves. The helicopter's rotors began turning, and soon after, the machine ascended into the early dawn sky.

"They're bugging out…but why?" Simon asked, not expecting an answer.

"They must have some kind of new intel. Otherwise they would track; at least that's what I would do," Sven replied.

"So what do we do?" They didn't seem to have too many options, at least not good ones.

"We follow the chopper," Sven said. What the two men didn't realize was that several minutes ago, while approaching the site, they had actually passed a non-descript blue Suburban. No one in either vehicle had noticed the other, in fact, except one. The boy in the driver's side back seat had taken notice. He had taken great notice.

CHAPTER 27

"Yes, sir. I already sent the home address and GPS coordinates to the team. Yes, sir. We're trying to locate the vehicle now. Yes, sir, I will keep in touch. Thank you, sir. Goodbye." Bass was thankful the general was still in a good mood, and the conversation concerning new intel on the target's initial destination could not have gone better. *If we can continue to provide the team on the ground useful information, it just may save our lives,* Bass thought.

"General Baker wants you and me to get some rest, Mikki. He's right; we've been on for almost eighteen hours now. I'll cook us up some grub too," Bass said. They had split an apple several hours ago but hadn't had anything substantial to eat since lunch yesterday. The steaks, the date, and the movie were all distant, foggy memories. *Mikki knows how I feel, though, and I think she feels the same way,* Bass thought.

"Good, I am starving. Lead the way and I will help you cook," Mikki replied, getting up from her station and heading toward the galley. "Hey, Bass, I just want you to know that I thought you were great today," she added, causing Bass to blush a bit as they made their way down the hallway. "When we do have that date night, it is going to be special." She took the opportunity to squeeze his hand tenderly as they turned the corner to the kitchen. She had wanted to take him in her arms and more several times over the course of the night.

"Thank you, Mick. That means more to me than you'll ever know." Her loving caress on his hand had caused uncontrollable physiological stimulation in his head, his heart, and, unfortunately, his groin. He turned away, but it was too late: she noticed. "I'm sorry. I want to tell you right now that I have never been with a woman, never really even kissed a girl. And I like you. I mean, I *really* like you," Bass clarified. He really liked this girl and didn't want his inexperience to be a deal breaker. He might even be in love with her.

"Are you kidding me? That's adorable! Bass, I've been dreaming about you, about us, since the day I arrived. I have had a few relationships, I mean a few bad relationships, and I kept telling myself that you were out of my league, that you were too good for me," Mikki admitted.

Bass, taking advantage of the moment, cupped Mikki's face in his hands and went in for a kiss. As his lips met hers, months of longing and anticipation fell away. The kiss deepened, and Mikki grabbed him around the waist and pulled him in tight. His ever expanding and notably adequate bulge was pressed tight against her midsection and sent shivers up Mikki's spine.

"Well, now I'm impressed again. And too bad for the rest of the women of the world that you're a virgin," Mikki offered as she felt his bulge from the outside of his jeans. She fought the temptation to take him right then and there on the kitchen island, but there would be a time and a place for that. She vowed to herself to make his first time *special*.

"We can't right now, Mick, but I want to more than anything in this world. We have to get through this ordeal first. Let's get some food, get some rest, and finish this mission. There are plenty of MRE's in the cupboard. What'll it be…meatloaf or macaroni and cheese?" Bass asked, his erection abating as he got back to the business at hand.

"Mac and cheese, please, and a side of you some time in the future," Mikki replied, smiling sweetly. *He is right*, she thought. There was plenty of time to build a relationship. They were trapped down here together, after all. She just wished she had made a move on him sooner.

"Coming right up!" *I've done it*, he thought. Sebastian Parker and Mikayla Wainright were officially a couple. He had a girlfriend for the first time in his life. And though he wasn't positive, he was pretty sure he was in love, and so was she.

CHAPTER 28

"So tell me, Noah, how is it that you are so physically fit? You look like a mini body builder," Jack asked as they sped down Chapin Road toward Flint. There were still a couple of major issues he had with Noah, so he thought he would break the ice with a simple question.

"Due to perfect nutrition and genetics, mostly. Where I come from, we don't physically eat or drink. We get the sustenance we need through our respiratory system. It's the same way the Hebrews survived on manna during the Exodus. Manna is more than ninety-nine percent pure nutrients, so there is little to excrete. Combine perfect nutrition with gravity that is almost twice that of Earth and you…Oh, and, of course, the perfect genetics, and you get me. That is why I had to eat something right away. You could say my lifeline had been severed," Noah explained.

"So you've never taken a crap before?" Abbie asked incredulously.

"No, I have," Noah answered matter-of-factly. Jack admired the fact that he seemed very humble and had absolutely no modesty concerning his bodily functions or even being naked. He hadn't tried to cover up any bits or pieces after regaining consciousness in the bathroom earlier like most young boys would.

"I said it was ninety-nine percent pure. That other one percent has to go somewhere, and I have been to this world before—several times actually. When I am here, I must ingest and excrete food and water like everyone else on this planet," Noah disclosed.

"So when were you here before?" Jack asked. *Since the kid is talking, I might as well get everything I can out of him*, he thought.

"I was here for a couple of months in the late 1960s. In a way, I am here now to finish what I started back then. And, of course, I was here when Jacob was born. There were a few times in between and since, but they were mostly inconsequential," Noah explained.

He would give just enough detail to answer the question and nothing more, Jack thought.

"So what year were you born?" Jack asked. Noah had already said his lifespan was different from theirs. Jack was about to find out just how different.

"I was born on February 3rd, 1907, and I expect to live about nine hundred years. My age right now, in human years, is about twelve," Noah revealed. Jack had been slowly and subconsciously shaking his head side to side for the past five minutes, and when Noah revealed he was over a hundred years old, the shaking sped up considerably.

"How long will it take to get through puberty, twenty or thirty years?" Abbie asked, genuinely interested. She wasn't at all fazed by this extraterrestrial being. *But what if she had seen his eyes?* Jack pondered.

"Oh, heavens no. My body will soon start showing signs of becoming an adult, and then I will have the ability to procreate, but the Anunnaki as a species don't do that. Within a year or so, I will resemble a thirteen- or fourteen-year-old human boy. The Anunnaki were also prey during our evolution, much like humans were. For example, I wasn't a helpless infant for twenty years. After I was born, I grew quickly and became a toddler and then a child much like you did, Abbie. I just stayed that way for a much longer time. Now I will go from a boy's body to a man's body like you did, Jack, but again I will seem to stay in my teens for a very long time," Noah stated.

"How did your back heal so fast? Scalding water was pelting your back for who knows how long. You should be in the hospital," Jack asked. He was also curious about how Noah's people propagated their species without having sex, so he filed that one away in his mind for later.

"We're just different, Jack. My metabolism is much higher than yours, and I heal faster than you. Is that so hard to believe? I can probably dunk a basketball, too, and run a hundred meters in eight seconds. Once again, my genetics and nutrition are unsurpassed compared to yours, so I can do things you can't," Noah explained. "Our first stop is just ahead," Noah directed, changing the subject again. He didn't want to reveal that the perfect genes were drawn from kidnapped humans, as he didn't think Jack and Abbie would understand.

"Pull into the parking garage, Jack," Noah urged. Noah leaned backward, braced himself, and closed his eyes when Jack made the right turn on the entrance ramp as if he was bracing himself for a collision.

"Are you all right?" Jack asked.

"Fine, thank you. I just get a little nervous around enclosed buildings. Fortunately for me this structure is open air." Jack himself could feel claustrophobic at times so he didn't press Noah for details.

It seemed as though they were going to a hospital after all, Hurley Medical Center, the birthplace of both Jack and Jacob. There was a certain tension in his voice again.

"What are we doing here?" Abbie asked. It was a valid point. Noah certainly did not need medical attention with the way he healed.

"Jack, we must swap rides. Drive up to the second deck. We have to find a certain vehicle, and then Abbie will drive the Suburban north on I-75. Abbie, you will be stopped, but you will not be harmed. Cooperate with the soldiers and tell them everything you know," Noah stated nonchalantly, and Jack started to think about the plan. There really wasn't a plan, so Abbie wouldn't be able to tell them much, but this whole excursion now sounded dangerous.

"You mean you are going to steal a car? I'm out. We're all out. I was playing along with this little game you're playing, but I draw the line at felonies," Jack stated as he pulled the Suburban into a parking space, actually two parking spaces, on the second deck. *The kid has lost his mind if he thinks I'm going to aid and abet a crime spree.* There was simply too much to lose, namely Jacob.

Just then, Jacob set his hand on Jack's shoulder and a wave of calm enveloped Jack. It was like Jacob was speaking to him and reassuring him without using words. The sensation was very relaxing, and Jack knew what he had to do.

"We're not stealing anything, Jack. I told you before that I have friends here. A vehicle was left in this structure for me. I just don't know which one it is," Noah explained.

"I really want to go with you guys!" Abbie wailed. What she really wanted was to connect with Jack, but that wasn't going to happen if she had to drive the bait car.

"Abbie, you are a fine human being. You can help me, Jack, and Jacob the most by driving this vehicle north on I-75, and you must leave right now," Noah reiterated, as he opened the door and stepped out. "Jack, go withdraw as much cash as you can from the ATM just inside the double doors. Jacob can help me find the vehicle that was left for us. Abbie must leave right now."

"Fine. Will you call me when this is all over, Jack?" Abbie asked. It was right then that Jack realized her ulterior motives. It was something in her voice, or maybe her body language. Unfortunately, Jack didn't have any romantic feelings to reciprocate.

"Sure, Abbie. Jacob and I will stop by when this is finished." He didn't have the heart to hurt her feelings right this minute by explaining his lack of any romantic attraction toward her.

"Give your phone to Abbie, Jack," Noah ordered.

Jack was pretty sure it was the government chasing this kid, so tracking a phone would be child's play for them. As Jack eased over to the window, he could envision Abbie closing her eyes and puckering her lips for a sweet goodbye kiss. It wasn't going to happen, not today, probably not ever.

"Here you go, Abbie. Take good care of the truck," Jack instructed. "Hey, can you also grab me the Cusco CD's from the glove box? We'll need them if Jacob gets restless." As Abbie handed Jack the discs, she actually did lean toward him a bit. No lip puckering, though.

"Bye, guys. I hope you find what you're looking for, Noah, and take good care of my boys," Abbie said as she drove off into the dim light of the morning sunrise. She would drive north for nearly two hours before the Chinook would land on the highway in front of her.

CHAPTER 29

General Rowland Baker, having finished his breakfast pint of Stoli, tilted the backrest of the sedan to a more reclining position and closed his eyes. *Mission is going fine*, he thought. *The boys should be picking up the little shit right now.* He envisioned the boy surrounded by the tactical team with his arms raised high in surrender. He knew of three different black-eyed kids, or BEKs, as they were called by the government, and he wondered which one it was.

As he drifted off, he thought back to that fateful day in June of 1967 when Dr. Carrington promised young Rowland and his parents the finest military education in the world. On top of that, Rowland would be able to contribute substantially to the household given the large stipend his parents would receive. He was so excited. All he ever wanted was to be a soldier. He frequently even dreamed of being an officer, fighting for the Union in the Civil War.

"He will be in my custody one hundred percent of the time, and I will personally see to it that he is well cared for. Unfortunately, phone calls are not allowed, but we encourage writing to each other. Part of Rowland's training will entail drafting letters, so it will be excellent practice," Hollis explained.

The real reason was a bit more sinister. He would personally intercept correspondence from both parties, edit and rewrite to suit, then deliver. You never knew what was going through a young boy's head, and Hollis needed results no matter what.

"We always knew Rowland was special, Doctor, and we are just so proud of him," Mary gushed. "Please take good care of my boy," she added as Hollis walked to the front door of the Baker home with young Rowland under his wing.

"I will treat him as my own, ma'am. Here is the first stipend check." Hollis handed the check to Stanley as the boy hugged his mother goodbye.

"I love you so much, Rowie. I know you will make your mother and me so proud," Stanley told the boy as he gave him a warm embrace himself. "Behave yourself, and do what they tell you," Stanley warned, almost scolded, as he thought about how incorrigible Rowland could be at times. Mr. Baker didn't want a sassy mouth to screw up a stipend that was almost as much as his own monthly salary.

"I will, Papa," Rowland replied.

"You two don't worry about a thing. From what I have seen, Rowland is a very well-behaved young man. This camp will be an invaluable asset for his development," Hollis assured the parents one final time.

Once Dr. Carrington and young Rowland were headed down Route 3 toward the Montauk Air Force

Base, Rowland turned and asked Hollis what exactly he would be doing at Camp Hero to earn two hundred dollars per month.

"Well, Rowland, you know how to sit in a chair, don't you?"

CHAPTER 30

Nikola Tesla was a Serbian-born inventor and engineer best known for the development of the alternating current electricity supply system. Without it, the world would quite possibly have Edison's brainchild of placing direct current electricity-producing substations approximately every two hundred yards or so. He was also the holder of over three hundred patents, most of which dealt with electricity.

In March of 1923, Tesla received a small, nondescript package from none other than Howard Carter, the discoverer of King Tutankhamun's tomb in the Valley of the Kings, Egypt. Inside the package, Tesla found a personalized note from Carter and a solid crystal semicircular bowl-shaped apparatus that Carter described in the letter as a "dream catcher" due to the experience one of his men had when he placed it upon his head.

The man claimed the device virtually transported him to what must have been the past as the characters in the vision wore period attire. The man also claimed to have dreamed several times of the mental picture he experienced while wearing the crystal helmet.

Intrigued, Tesla performed numerous tests on the crystal artifact with less than tantalizing results. On one occasion while testing the item (on his own head, of course), he thought he smelled the aroma of baking bread and cracked black pepper but later convinced himself it was a delusion.

Certain the crystal relic was void of any particular power and convinced the object would not allow the wearer any added clairvoyance, Tesla placed the item on a bookshelf in his study, where it rested until the time of his death in 1943. At that time, proxies of the federal government swooped in and collected anything and everything of value from Tesla's home and office. The item from Tutankhamun's tomb was used as a basket to carry many of the smaller items out.

The contents of Tesla's office were then confined to a ten foot by ten foot storage closet in the basement of the Smithsonian. Seventeen years later, while conducting an inventory of the contents of the room, Smithsonian employee John Atchison noticed the peculiar piece was not on the manifest and surreptitiously took the piece home as a gift for his wife, Susan. She used it as a fruit basket for several years.

One day, the Atchisons' young son, Carl, was playing in the family's backyard as he was often known to do. The boy regularly dreamed of having been Baron Manfred von Richthofen, a German fighter pilot in The Great War, World War I. Donning the fruit basket as a helmet and using a bungee cord as a strap, young Carl began having visions of airplanes darting left and dodging right. Carl was the leader of a whole squadron, himself in a bright red biplane at the head of the sortie. It was almost as if he were sitting in the cockpit himself.

"Manfred, the enemy is just ahead!" the man in the biplane to his right shouted over the cacophony of the engines and wind.

"They only have us outnumbered three to one! Too bad for them!" Carl screamed back as he piloted his crimson Fokker. This was so real for the young boy he could even smell the exhaust from the rotary engine. Suddenly, a barrage of bullets tore through the fuselage with a flurry of fury, and Carl banked to the right. Moments later, a Jenny entered his crosshairs, and the boy squeezed the twin triggers simultaneously.

"*Nimm das du Yankee Bastard*!" Carl yelled in German, a language he personally had never been exposed to, as the salvo hit its mark, and the enemy plane first smoked heavily then nosedived. The boy was centering another enemy plane when he could feel hands wrap around his shoulders. It was his father who, unbeknownst to Carl, had witnessed this airborne battle.

"What on earth are you doing, son?" John asked his boy. Both parents were well aware of young Carl's dreams of past lives, which they always explained as the overactive imagination of a very bright boy. Carl enthusiastically replayed his aerial escapade to his father. John held the makeshift helmet responsible for the visions, and he cursed himself for ever bringing it home. John and Mary were downright terrified of it now.

The next day, John phoned the only scientist he knew, Dr. Hollis Carrington, and offered the crystal bowl to him after embarrassingly describing the circumstances in which he had taken custody. Dr. Carrington picked up the alien technology used centuries ago for entertainment, to transport twenty-ton blocks and, more importantly, to transport *gold*.

Consequently, the Red Baron was, for at least the remainder of Carl Atchison's lifetime, now grounded.

CHAPTER 31

"Do you want me to catch up to them?" the pilot asked Gump.

"No. Not yet, anyways. The dispatch stated they were tracking them heading north in a Suburban. I want to go to the house and see if we can get some intel," Gumper replied. Something about this mission was making him nervous. The way Shiva was acting was just amplifying things.

"You got it, Gump," the pilot replied. They were at the farm in less than a minute.

"Dispatch is stating the house is vacant at present, but use hostile combatant protocols, boys," Gump said through the microphone in his helmet. The team exited the Chinook together, minus Shiva. Gump felt as though he was done for the day. Something about this situation had overwritten years of canine obedience training. Shiva had never acted in this manner, and Gump was going to find out why.

"Johnny, you go to the back; Joe and I will take the front," Gump directed. Once the men were in place, they simply opened the doors, which were unlocked, and entered. As the dispatch had stated, the house was deserted.

"Look around and see what you can find. We're look-ing for anything out of the ordinary," Gump ordered. The home was very well-kept, at least by young bachelor standards. There were a few dirty dishes in the sink, but the furniture and décor were nice. Nothing jumped out at the team saying "evil maniacal warlord" or anything else they had become accustomed to seeing.

"Up here, Gump!" one of the men yelled out. He was obviously upstairs, so Gump took the steps two at a time and then took a right down the hallway. His man was in a room on the left. As he neared the door, the noticeable odor became more and more pungent.

"What the fuck is that smell?" Gump asked. The soldier explained that it seemed to be coming from the clothes on the floor. Gump was trying to put the scenario together in his head. An interdimensional something-or-other knocks on these folks' door, they offer him a bath, and then they all leave together a couple of hours later? Something wasn't quite adding up, unless, of course, the people who lived here knew the visitor.

"Do you think those are his clothes?" the soldier asked.

"Sure seems that way," Gump replied as he picked up the shirt with his gloved hand. The shirt was very soft, like cotton, but much less flexible. Gump looked for a tag behind the collar, but there wasn't one. The shirt seemed to be about a boys' size fourteen, so it would be a little big on Brady's own son, who had recently turned nine. Upon closer inspection, it didn't appear to even

115

have seams, just one continuous piece of fabric formed into a shirt.

Closer inspection of the pants yielded the same observations: soft yet sturdy fabric but no seams. It was all one piece, just like the shirt. Gump checked the front pockets and found a small handful of change in the left one. The slacks had no back pockets. That was the extent of the clothing, so unless their perpetrator put back on some *really* stinky underwear, he had come here going commando.

"Bag it. We'll take it with us," Gump instructed the soldier. He would later be informed that both articles of clothing were constructed of an unknown material that could withstand incredible heat and radiation, and was impenetrable even by bullets.

"Let's head out!" Gump yelled as he took the stairs two at a time again. "Let's go take this motherfucker down!" The men were all back outside and headed for the Chinook when Shiva jumped to his feet, raised his hackles, and began to bark incessantly.

"Calm down, boy. We're getting out of here," Gump tried to reassure him. As the man holding the bag of clothes neared, Shiva bared his teeth and began to growl fiercely toward him.

"Throw the bag in the front with the pilot," Gump instructed the man. *Shiva does not like this thing, whatever it is*, Gump thought. He liked it less and less himself.

Gump and his men were supposed to start leave tomorrow. He was going back to Rock Hill, South Carolina, to finalize wedding plans with his fiancé, Ginny. The other two men had plans also…he knew Johnny was going to visit his recently windowed mother in Alexandria, Louisiana, and Joe was to travel to Denver, Colorado, to hang out with some of his millennial friends. The tryst with Ginny, he was sure, would have to be canceled. He knew she would understand, as she always did. He would have to use much more tact with his men.

The manhunt for the diminutive intruder would no doubt revoke their leave, and the boys were going to be pissed.

CHAPTER 32

It was Jacob who actually found the truck: a like-new 2017 metallic mint-green Dodge Durango in brand new condition. The keys were under the visor, right where Noah had said they would be. He had also said there would be an envelope with one thousand dollars enclosed in the glove box, and there was. It was enough to convince Jack that this car *had* been left for Noah.

"Pretty sweet ride, huh, Jacob?" Jack asked, rhetorically as always. It wasn't exactly the vehicle one wished for when attempting to operate under the radar, but Jack was thankful it wasn't a PT Cruiser or something equally as tasteless. *Too bad it isn't a Tesla, though*, he thought.

"We have a long drive ahead of us, so let's get moving. Take I-69 South to I-94 West," Noah instructed.

"Are you going to tell me where we're going yet?" Jack asked. He wasn't nearly as perturbed as he was back at the house, but he sure was curious. He also felt this was at least mildly dangerous. Jack was pretty sure the helicopter that flew over the roof had guns and missiles attached with people inside who knew exactly how to use them.

"We are driving to Ames, Iowa," Noah stated.

"What the hell, Noah! *Iowa?* You have got to be kidding me. We are not going to Iowa, Noah!" Jack screamed as he was about to back the truck out of its space. It was one thing to go on a little adventure, but quite another to drive halfway across the country for no good reason.

"Calm down, Jack. Put the truck in reverse, and let's get out of here. We are driving to Iowa with a couple of stops in between and that's about all I can, or want, to tell you right now. We have plenty of cash for gas and food, so the only thing you will have invested is time."

"You have to look at this from my perspective. You show up in the middle of night, claim you are some alien from Timbuktu, then say that you're here for my brother, who, by the way, can't even talk…should I go on?" Jack angrily chastised Noah. When he spoke the words, it sounded even more ludicrous.

"I'm from Niburu; Timbuktu is in Africa," Noah corrected Jack. "You have to believe what I'm doing is important, and I'm sure you know Jacob is a vital part of the plan. I just can't tell you what that plan is at this time." If Jack was having doubts now, the future would have him crying for his mother.

Jack looked in the rearview mirror and saw Jacob sitting silently and patiently as usual. Their eyes met, and Jack got the feeling once again that Jacob knew exactly what was going on. It was as if Jacob was pleading with Jack to believe Noah, to get over himself and his misgivings, and to get moving.

"Goddamnit," Jack said exasperatedly as he put the Durango into reverse and began backing up. "All right, you win. I-69 South to I-94 West. Ames, Iowa, here we come. You have to tell me just one more thing: who are we going to meet?" Jack asked in resignation.

"We're going to see the people tracking us," Noah replied in a hushed, matter-of-fact tone. Jack rolled his eyes and placed the gear shift lever in "D."

"Of course we are," was all Jack could muster.

CHAPTER 33

"How much change was in his pocket?" General Baker asked Lt. Gumper. Gump was giving Baker the rundown of the raid on the suspect's most recent location: the home of Jack and Jacob Wheaton. What the hell did he want with these kids anyways? What was his angle, his mission?

"Are you still there, Lieutenant Gumper?"

"Yes, sir. I put the change back in the pocket and sealed the bag. The clothes smelled like shit, if you'll pardon my language. My canine doesn't want anything to do with this whole operation, and I think the stench has something to do with it. Here it is…let's see…there is a total of sixty-three cents, sir."

The total was like a punch to the gut. Sixty-three cents. *Sixty-three fucking cents!* Rowland first heard the story about the psychic boy who could guess your pocket change the day the new boy arrived with Dr. Carrington. It was definitely Noah, and Rowland didn't know if this was good news or bad news.

Rowland had always been friendly toward Noah, but they had never really been friends. Rowland saw Noah's arrival as a threat. For almost two months, Rowland had Dr. Carrington at his beck and call. Now there was a shiny new toy for Carrington to play with, and Rowland did not like that one bit.

Rowland had been time traveling to two distinct eras during expeditions using the Montauk chair: 1835 to 1885 and 1910 to 1945. The former was the era the doctor was most interested in. When he traveled, it was as if Rowland was there in the scene, moving and interacting with people, places, and things. Everything Rowland experienced in the journeys was superimposed via the crystalline headpiece onto a large display for anyone in the room to see—except the occupant of the chair, of course, who was so heavily dosed with a cocktail of barbiturates including PCP, LSD, and sodium pentothal that he typically slept for twenty-four hours or more after each excursion.

The most interesting scene Rowland could conjure occurred on April 14th, 1865, at Ford's Theater in Washington D.C. Rowland had access to all areas of the theater and could freely walk among the patrons. On each successive trip, he would be given instructions to focus on certain attendees, especially those just outside the presidential box. If the images Rowland evoked were the actual events of the evening, there was most definitely a conspiracy to kill Lincoln, as evidenced by the indifference and ambivalence shown toward Booth as he made his way unencumbered to carry out the plot. The man who could have saved Lincoln actually held the curtain back to allow Booth entry to the presidential box. Lincoln never had a chance.

Dr. Carrington and the other "scientists" on the Camp Hero staff thought they were witnessing true time travel. They were convinced these special boys could peel back the layers of time, using the device, of course, and witness history. They couldn't have known the truth: these boys were simply reliving past experiences from their own past lives, like echoes in a canyon. The earlier the life lived and the further away from their own most recent birth, the fainter the echo. Carrington erroneously thought the onset of adulthood provided the final barrier for this type of time travel and had already been contemplating what to do with Rowland, who was now twelve-and-a-half years old, should his abilities start to decline.

The emergence of Noah changed everything. Noah could not only travel freely within the time frames that Rowland could, but could also go as far back as biblical times and beyond. And he could make things appear out of thin air! It began with an apple, then an ear of corn. Dr. Carrington once asked Noah to think about a puppy, and moments later, a cute little fur ball appeared on the screen. Carrington went on to describe it as a mongrel mutt nobody could love with mangy fur and a hairless tail and cataract-infected eyes. It had fleas. It was emaciated. Rowland watched as the image on the screen morphed from a cute and playful bundle of love to an abomination as Carrington added the sordid characteristics. Once he finished, the animal simply appeared right in Noah's lap. The hideous creature fortunately died several minutes later. The burial was officiated by Noah himself, and he seemed genuinely heartbroken.

Noah was now the wonder child, and Rowland saw less and less of the chair. When he did get his chance, he strained to reach further back, and one time he did. He was aboard a ship out in the open ocean, the seas rough and the weather nasty. Carrington thought it to be some time in the seventeenth century based on the clothing and type of ship. The man who was obviously the captain was constantly barking orders in French to the scurrying crew. Rowland had trouble keeping his balance in spite of the fact that it was only a vision, and Carrington thought that most interesting. The approaching rogue wave was awe-inspiring, and it moved many of the men to drop to their knees in prayer despite orders from the captain.

The ship was simply enveloped by the wall of water. Once the wave passed over, the ship, now split in half, began its slow journey to the bottom of the ocean. Rowland, feeling calm and serene as he was suspended below the surface, watched in wonder as crates, barrels, personal trunks, and even men slowly descended before him. Then Rowland began convulsing, both in his image and real life. At first, it looked like an occasional hiccup, but progressed to violent spasms. Dr. Carrington slapped Rowland's face several times in an attempt to awaken him from the trance without success. The quick-thinking doctor then plunged a syringe containing three milligrams of adrenaline directly into young Rowland's heart, which fortunately did the trick. Rowland awoke and promptly ejected what seemed like gallons of actual seawater from his lungs. Rowland never wanted to visit that ship again, and he never did.

CHAPTER 34

As Bass began to awaken, he just laid there in that realm between dreamland and real life. *Did I really kiss Mikayla? Did she really feel my erection through my pants? Am I really in love?* The longer he lay there, the surer he was: yes to all of the above. It was the best day of Sebastian Parker's life by a long shot. There was work to do, though, as the memories of the intruder, Baker's threat, and all the bullshit that went with them came back too.

As Bass made his way down the hallway toward the kitchen, he could hear hushed voices, *women's* voices, and stopped short of the door to see if he could make out what they were saying. Unfortunately, he could not.

"Good morning, ladies!" Bass announced as he faked rounding the corner. Leah was her normal good-looking self, but Mikayla looked striking. Bass could definitely see himself waking up next to her every morning.

"Good morning, *Baaass*," the girls replied in unison, drawing out his name coyly.

"What are you two talking about?" A pang of fear went through him, up his spine and into his head, making him a little dizzy. Was Mikki telling Leah about last night? Were they making fun of him because he was inexperienced? Was Mikki really not into him?

"Gotta run. You two lovebirds behave yourselves!" Leah exclaimed as she walked out with a piece of turkey bacon hanging out of her mouth. Bass's fears were instantly allayed as Mikki stared at him with longing eyes, the kind of look one gets only from someone who truly loves them.

"What were you two talking about?" Bass asked. Mikki could hear the trepidation, the fear, in Bass's voice. She knew she would have to proceed cautiously.

"Just girl stuff, sweetie. Hey, about last night, I just want to tell you I truly meant everything I said and did. I think you are the best, and I want nothing more than to be with you." Bass could feel tears welling up in his eyes. No one had ever talked to him this way, not even his mother (when she was in the picture, anyway). He wanted to tell Mikki he loved her, and he was sure he did, but thankfully fought off the urge. He didn't want to chase her off by using *the* "L-word" after only getting to first base.

"Me too. I can't wait to go out on a real date, away from this place. You are a special person, Mikki, and I want to be with you too. Now, can I have a piece of your bacon?"

"You're going to be disappointed, because it's turkey bacon. Faux bacon, thanks to Steven's anti-pork crusade. You help yourself, though," Mikki replied. Bass grabbed two pieces and headed for the door.

"Come down to the command center when you're finished here. I want to catch this…*thing* today so we can start the rest of our lives together."

"Wait, I'm coming!" Mikki shrieked as she scurried to catch up with her man. When she did, she took his hand in hers so their fingers interlocked. "Let's go together. Leah knows, so Steven probably knows now too."

"Ok." Her gentle touch affected him again to the point he wished he hadn't tucked his shirt in. They were both smiling as they entered the control room.

"What's the latest, Steven?" Bass asked. It was just after 7:00 a.m. so they had both slept about four hours. *A lot can happen in four hours though*, Bass thought.

"The SUV is headed north on I-75, and it is currently near…Standish. It gets pretty desolate a bit further north, so the team is coordinating with the Michigan State Police to block both lanes and take it down with the Chinook shortly," Steven replied as he glanced at his monitor to get the SUV's current location. "Baker called about an hour ago wanting to congratulate us on a 'job well done.' He said he would stop by after the mission was over."

"Thank you, Steven. He's right. All of you have done an exceptional job. Let's stay on guard, though, as anything can happen."

Why was Baker going to stop by after the mission? *Is that how he took care of the last staff? Stop by after an alarm and kill all of them? I have to come up with a plan to keep us valuable and keep all of us alive*, Bass thought. *Then, if it comes down to it, we have to be able to defend ourselves against Baker. We will either need weapons of our own or a plan to keep sidearm-packing generals out.*

"Mick, can you see if it is possible to deactivate all entrance and elevator pass keys?" Bass whispered to Mikki so only she could hear.

"Uh, yes. But why would I?" She recognized the trepidation in Bass's voice once again. *What does he know that he's not telling us?* she wondered. *Why would we block access to our superior?* The one thing she did know was that she could trust Bass. "Never mind. If you think it's important, I'll find a way."

"Thank you, Mikki." *If General Baker can't get in, he can't possibly kill us now, could he?* Bass had a satisfied look on his face as he felt he'd found the answer. *We could hunker down here for a month,* he thought, *and we have a satellite phone.*

CHAPTER 35

"You want me to buy what?" Jack asked Noah. "It sounded like you said an ounce of gold." *Why on Earth would he need an ounce of gold? This is getting weirder and weirder*, Jack thought.

"Yes, one ounce of gold, *pure* gold. It has to be twenty-four carat gold, so you can't just buy a coin. Pure gold is sold in one-ounce bars. We need one of them. Can you handle that?" Noah asked somewhat sarcastically. This little boy was beginning to wear Jack down.

"If you want it so bad, why don't you go buy it yourself? Here's two grand, which should cover it," Jack replied as he tried to hand a wad of money to Noah. Jack just happened to look in the rearview mirror again, and there was Jacob, staring right back at him with a certain admonishment. *Jesus Christ*, Jack thought, *this is two against one.*

"I can't. I cannot go certain places in your world, Jack. If I break the rule, I'll simply vanish, and it may take some time for me to get back. I would rather that not happen, so would you please go buy one ounce of pure gold?" Noah asked again, clarifying the matter…kind of.

"You tell me why you can't go into that pawn shop, the *real* reason, and I will buy your ounce of gold for you," Jack demanded. Maybe he could get some answers by bargaining with Noah.

Noah paused for a moment. "Deal. I cannot enter any building, any vehicle, any structure or fully enclosed area of any kind on Earth, without being clearly invited by an occupant, if there is one. It has been this way forever, even before the Flood. The reason has never been completely understood by us, but we live with it. We're sure it has something to do with the soul and the free will of humans. I know one thing for certain: I walk into that store uninvited, I will disappear and find myself back somewhere on Niburu."

Jack thought he was telling the truth, but he had a few questions. *It's time to make the little shit squirm.*

"So you're like a vampire then?" Jack asked, trying not to smile.

"Actually, yes, like your historical vampire. Your vampires were simply visiting seraphs like me that were exposed by humans. Vlad the Impaler was the most recognized vampire in your history. People make things up to explain what they see. Vlad III was an Anunnaki searching for pure blood, blood like Jacob's, and he thought he could find it in Romania."

"Yeah, right, and he could turn into a bat," Jack added, doubt registering strongly in his voice.

"I just said people make things up to explain what they see, didn't I? Vlad could disappear at will, or jump dimensions, just as I can. If a bat flew by as he disappeared or a wolf ran for the hills, what do you think people would believe happened?" Noah asked in his uniquely condescending manner. "Your government has kept the truth from you, Jack, about a number of things, like aliens, the Mothman, even Sasquatch. They are all watchers of a sort, like me."

Jack was numb. Could he possibly be telling the truth? He really had no reason to lie. *I've done everything he has asked of me*, Jack thought. If this was just some random kid pulling a prank, which had occurred to him, he had gone to great expense to pull it off. There's no way… all of this *had* to be real.

"Ok, I believe you, Noah, and I apologize for questioning you and for being so stubborn. I just need to know one more thing before I go any further: why are you *really* here?"

"All right, Jack. You deserve the truth. I'm here for Jacob, and I am here for gold. Where we come from, Jacob is a very important being, the glue that holds everything together, so to speak, and he was taken from us. There is a man, a very bad man with a very bad soul, who has something that belongs to me and my people, and he needs to be stopped. Jacob is one of the keys to stopping him and returning to us that which is rightfully ours," Noah admitted. This sounded very foreboding to Jack.

"So Jacob is going to leave me?" Jack asked as tears began to well up in his eyes. He couldn't tolerate the thought of losing Jacob. He was all Jack had left in this world.

"No, Jacob is not going to leave you. He will make the trip to Niburu with me to liberate his soul and then return to Earth to help me complete my mission. When we are finished, he is free to live out his human life," Noah declared. That still didn't answer Jack's question, but it would do for now, he supposed. He trusted Noah now, and he knew Noah would not lie to him.

"Oh, and one more thing. I have a score to settle with this very bad man, and if all goes as planned, it will end poorly for him," Noah added in a matter of fact fashion.

"You said you are here for gold too. You mean to tell me you came all this way for this piddly one ounce of gold I'm about to buy?" Jack asked incredulously.

"No, not *that* gold. I came for the gold that was stolen from Fort Knox in 1967. It was right around one hundred million ounces, if I recall correctly."

Jack's jaw dropped at the immensity of the robbery. "Who in the world could have stolen that much gold?" he asked.

"I did," Noah replied with a wry smile on his face. *Of course he did*, Jack thought as he exited the vehicle and headed toward the door of the pawn shop to buy Noah his one ounce of pure gold.

What else could he do?

CHAPTER 36

No one would ever accuse Hollis Carrington of being a patient man. In fact, people surrounding him had paid dearly for not being able to produce the timely results he commanded. Simon and the Nordic hadn't sent an update in more than three hours, and his patience was wearing very thin.

When Hollis was seven years old, he and a younger boy, Jimmy Watkins, were shooting steel ball bearings with Jimmy's brand-new slingshot. Hollis, eager to take his turn, begged Jimmy to hand it over immediately.

"Just one more. I want to hit the bird feeder!" Jimmy gleefully exclaimed. Hollis, unwilling to abide by those terms, delivered a karate chop so hard to the left arm as Jimmy was taking aim that it fractured the ulna. The slingshot flung backward with such ferocity it knocked out two teeth and bloodied both Jimmy's upper and lower lips.

"*Thesith Crithe, Hollith!*" young Jimmy wailed, falling to the ground writhing in pain. Hollis simply picked up the bloody slingshot, placed a steelie in the leather band, pulled the rubbers taut, and fired the projectile at the bird feeder. The thud a moment later confirmed the target had been hit.

"That's how you do it, Jimmy. You should have handed it over when I asked," Hollis stated with more than a little admonishment.

"Yer a pfucker, Hollith! My momths gonna *kill* me!" Jimmie complained as he looked for the second of his two missing teeth, which were thankfully both primaries. Jimmy's mother had warned him about dangerous weapons, and hell hath nowhere near the fury she would if he hurt himself or anyone else using it, she had told him.

"I'll give you two dollars for it," Hollis offered. That seemed more than reasonable to him. It was used now and covered in blood. When Hollis first saw Jimmy pull it from his back pocket, he thought he would have to give at least five. *In light of recent events, the value has experienced some heavy depreciation*, thought Hollis.

"But it coths theven! I uthed my allowanth!" Jimmy wailed. This was a battle he knew he wouldn't win. If he took the slingshot home, his mother would probably bury it in his head. His father had returned just six months ago from battling the Germans at Normandy, so Jimmy wouldn't get much sympathy for a little bloody lip. Either way, he would never be able to use the slingshot again anyways.

"Fine, thithead. I'll take two dallarths," Jimmy conceded. Hollis Carrington *always* got what he wanted.

CHAPTER 37

The entire vehicle was shaking as the helicopter hovered just twenty feet in front of the Suburban. Abbie could see several soldiers pointing machine guns in her direction, and they looked as if they weren't afraid to use them.

"Put the vehicle in park and step out of the vehicle!" the voice on the bullhorn commanded. She didn't have much choice but to obey.

"Please don't shoot me!" Abbie pleaded as she opened the door and exited. The helicopter backed off several yards and thankfully landed. Three of the heavily armed men jumped out of the Chinook and stormed the Suburban with guns raised.

"Where are the rest of them?" the man who was obviously the leader asked. Abbie had been practicing her story since she left Flint.

"If you're talking about my friends, they're at the hospital. Jacob has physical therapy on Tuesdays and Thursdays. I'm heading to St. Ignace to visit my grandmother." That wasn't entirely a lie. Jacob did have biweekly therapy sessions, but they didn't take place at the hospital. Abbie helped Jack with them at the house. "Am I under arrest?"

"Who is the other boy with them, and where is he?" the lead soldier asked. His demeanor changed when he saw that the truck was empty, and he seemed much more relaxed now.

"Georgie? That's Jack and Jacob's cousin Georgie from Derry," Abbie explained while trying not to laugh. *This is fun*, she thought. She knew her rights as an American on American soil. She didn't even care if they threw her in jail. Jack would owe her big time for this one either way.

"This Georgie from Derry, he's extremely dangerous and is a fugitive from the federal government," the soldier stated, not getting the *It* reference until one of his buddies evidently explained it through his earpiece.

"Look, bitch, you're going to tell me where this kid is right now or things are going to get ugly really fast," the soldier warned, his demeanor changing yet again. Abbie felt he was under a lot of pressure to find Noah. She didn't care.

"Eat shit, asshole! You can't just fly your helicopter around stopping people on the highway. I have rights!"

"Not with me you don't. I'm above the law. I can put a bullet between your eyes right now if I wanted to," the soldier bragged.

"Make sure you smile while you're doing it because all of this is streaming live from my dash cam!" Abbie yelled back, laughing. She wasn't streaming the encounter, but he didn't know that. "Now I'm going to get back in my truck and continue my trip to see my Bubbe, and you idiots are going to get back in your big bad chopper and go back to where you came from," Abbie chortled as she walked back to the truck, got in, and sat down. All three of the men had their heads down and tilted to the side. They were obviously informing someone of the situation. After a few moments, one of the other men came to the door and asked her to roll down the window.

"Look, Abigail. Maybe we handled this wrong, and for that I apologize. That kid with your friends is responsible for the deaths of many people. He may not look dangerous, but believe me, he is. Your friends are not safe," the obvious "good cop" stated. It wasn't going to work on Abbie, though. She trusted Jack.

"Your boss should drink decaf," Abbie suggested. "I don't know what to tell you. I don't know the boy, I don't know why he's here, and I don't know where they're going." It was true; all of the plans had been made out of her presence.

"Well, we can't let you go. You are going to have to come with us," the good cop demanded.

"No, I don't. I'm leaving now, and if you feel you have to stop me, then you stop me. Tell your boss I said to go screw himself too," Abbie replied as she started the truck and put it in drive.

"Goodbye!" she yelled as she drove by the lead soldier. He was still talking into his headset but thankfully had lowered his weapon. *That went better than I expected*, thought Abbie. As she drove off, she wondered if Noah really was a murderer like they said. *Nah, he's a little creepy, but he's definitely not a murderer.* Abbie, normally a very good judge of character, had never been more wrong about a person in her life.

CHAPTER 38

J ack had the cruise control set at seventy-five, so they were hurtling down the highway at a pretty good clip. If he had had his phone, he could have routed the trip on MapQuest. The extended adrenaline infusion Noah had elicited had thankfully ceased. A little more needling seemed to be in order.

"I wonder if Abbie is all right," Jack wondered out loud. She was a good girl and a great friend, but now she apparently wanted something more, something Jack could not give her. He would hate himself if anything bad happened to her though.

"She's fine, Jack," Noah replied. Jack sensed that he wasn't just saying the words; somehow Noah knew Abbie was out of danger.

"How do you know? Do you have psychic abilities or something?" Jack asked.

"I suppose you could say that. I told you I was a Watcher, so it's kind of my area of expertise," Noah explained as cryptically as ever.

This kid wouldn't know a straight answer if it bit him on the ass. "So you sit around watching people all day, even when they're on the shitter?" Jack asked while trying to keep his composure. Jack happened to glance in the rearview mirror at Jacob and swore he saw him smile.

"Of course not. I don't physically watch people. A better, more descriptive name would have been *senser*. I sense souls. I know when someone dies or even when they've had a trauma that bares the soul," Noah explained. Jack couldn't quite wrap his head around it yet.

"So how many people are in the group you watch? Kind of sounds like Santa Claus with his list of naughty and nice kids."

"I sense all of them, and so will you when you're released from your human body. You will have the knowledge of the universe. You have to remember my soul, and yours and Jacob's, and every other soul in the universe has been in existence for billions of years. There are literally trillions of them, and they have been around for a very long time. Although I don't necessarily know all of the souls, I can definitely feel them."

"Imagine this, Jack. You are sitting in your rocking chair on your porch and there are a million bottle rockets set up in the cornfield across the road. You don't notice any one particular rocket, but you can see them all. Now suppose one of them is fired off. You can see just that rocket. Or, if one were to explode in its bottle, you would notice that one too. The rocket that is Abbie hasn't been launched, and it hasn't exploded on the pad," Noah explained.

"Well, I can't wait to die then. I want answers!" Jack excitedly exclaimed. Noah was making life sound so trivial. Maybe Jacob would even enjoy life better in the spirit world. God knows they had both suffered enough here.

"Don't say that! *Do not ever fucking say that, Jack!*" Noah screamed. This was a side of the usually calm and reserved Noah that Jack didn't think existed, and the *F*-word sounded funny coming out of his mouth. His outburst even caused Jacob to sit up straight. "Life is sacred. Life is priceless. I would give anything to be human, to be rid of this knowledge for just one lifetime. To not have to breathe my dinner or to simply be able to close my eyes and sleep in peace," Noah confided, finally settling back down.

"I'm sorry, Noah. I would never…I mean, I would never harm myself or Jacob. You just make it sound so appealing to have the answers to questions mankind has pondered over for thousands of years," Jack declared as Noah wiped tears from his eyes.

"Well, it's not."

Jack was certain both he and Jacob would be old and gray when the time came for them to learn the secrets of the universe. In fact, he would see to it.

"Stop the car!" Noah screamed for no apparent reason.

CHAPTER 39

Bass could hear the shat phone ringing as he made his way down the corridor to the control room. *Just what I need*, Bass thought. Thankfully, Steven had picked up, so maybe he wouldn't have to talk to the general after all.

"Yes, sir. Ok, sir. We're on it, sir. OSCAR will find them, sir. Ok, yes. Goodbye," Steven muttered softly as he was obviously being dressed down by General Baker.

What the hell happened in here while I was sleeping? thought Bass.

"The Suburban only had the girl in it and the phone we were also tracking. The girl's name is Abigail Cooke and she is the owner of the sedan we saw in the driveway. When they stopped at the hospital parking garage in Flint they must have changed vehicles. The girl kept going as a decoy," Steven stated dejectedly. Bass looked over at Leah for any information she may have discovered.

"Abigail wasn't at the hospital very long at all, maybe five minutes. Jack Wheaton used the ATM and it seemed as if they all left together in the Suburban. No reports of car alarms, 911 calls, or stolen vehicles. Unfortunately, we don't have continuous coverage of Flint either," Leah reported.

"Steven, set up OSCAR to trace every vehicle that has exited the structure from the point the Suburban entered it forward. For all we know, they are still there. What did General Baker have to say?" Bass asked. He didn't care nearly as much about finding this kid as he did about keeping everyone at Silo 9 alive. *Do we already know too much about this mission?* Bass asked himself.

"Baker didn't seem mad. He just sounded really disappointed. He said this could be a marathon and not a sprint and for us to stay focused. And he'll be here tonight," Steven offered.

That's just great, Bass thought. He also wondered if Mikki had any luck locking out every access code to the only entrance. He'd hoped so as they may have to test it out soon.

"Ok, Steven. I want every image in every city, town, highway, ATM, and traffic light sent to OSCAR. Use every satellite we have access to. He should be able to sort through all of it and find our perps. The sheer volume of information can be vetted by only one computer in the world, and we have it, so let's use it." Sebastian's little pep talk seemed to rekindle everyone's spirit.

"Steven, once you get the image and video feeds directed to OSCAR, why don't you go get some food and rest. Leah, you too," Bass directed. Steven raised an eyebrow at Leah, suggesting some extracurricular activities, and she promptly and elegantly flipped him the bird.

"Are you two going to be able to keep your hands off each other long enough to get any work done?" Steven asked, directing the question toward both Bass and Mikki. Mikayla didn't have any problem answering.

"Maybe if you weren't such an asshole and treated women with respect instead of viewing us as sexual possessions, you might just grab the attention of one of us," Mikki blurted out. Mikki was just as sick of his sexual harassment of Leah as she was.

"Screw you, Mikayla. I would rather date my right hand than go out with you."

"Well, I feel sorry for your hand, then. Touching your dick every day must give it a good deal of humiliation."

"Enough! This isn't helping, you guys," Bass interjected. These two would go at it all day if Bass allowed it. He had actually seen it firsthand, several times in fact, and Mikki always came out on top to the extent that Steven began stuttering. Once she even made him tear up.

"I'm out of here. You guys do it yourself! Bass, you better teach your woman some manners," Steven stammered as he walked toward the corridor. "Come on, Leah. I'll make us some breakfast."

"I'll go calm him down. That was worth the price of admission, Mikayla!" Leah exclaimed as she followed after Steven. Mikayla and Bass were alone again.

"That wasn't very nice, Mick. You know he's harmless, don't you?" He didn't particularly like Steven, but he also knew what it was like to be teased by a bully.

"Don't defend him, Bass. The way he treats and talks about women is reprehensible. People like that have to be put in their place. Steven is a pig."

"I agree, he is a sexist pig, but at the end of the day he would do anything to protect you, me, and Leah. I know he's insecure because I am too. So you can't take his words and actions at face value all the time," Bass explained. While Steven would display his insecurities by acting and lashing out, Bass would simply internalize.

"Ok. You're insecure and adorable, and he's insecure and gross, but I'll give him the benefit of the doubt for you, but you're going to owe me big time."

"Thank you. What did you have in mind?" Bass asked. He could feel himself already blushing.

"We can start with that steak dinner, then the movie. After that you're all mine to do with as I please."

We have to find this kid, thought Bass.

CHAPTER 40

General Rowland Baker sat outside his home contemplating his next move, and he did not seem to have any viable options. He knew the deception he pulled on the Office of Temporal Phenomenon, and in essence, the Secretary of Defense, couldn't be safely continued much longer. He was technically running his own black site, funneling funds from another black site, Silo 9. That was how badly he wanted to find and destroy the man who ruined his life: Dr. Hollis Carrington.

On March 15th of this year, the three-person staff at the Silo 9 black site, there since its inception, was witness to the strangest and most disturbing temporal phenomenon to date. The three technicians responded to the *Icarus* alarm exactly as they had been trained. It occurred in the Coconino National Forest near Flagstaff, Arizona.

A five-year-old boy named Luca Wagner had wandered momentarily from his vacationing family's campsite and simply vanished. Two Keyhole-class satellites were in perfect position the view the scene, and the Silo 9 team was astonished and horrified by what they saw.

The team, with the help of OSCAR's ability to enhance satellite imagery, witnessed an eight-to-ten-foot-tall being covered in shaggy-brown hair appear on the shore of Ashurst Lake about ten feet from the boy, who undoubtedly was the monster's target. As he approached the boy from behind, it wrapped a hairy hand around his mouth, picked up the startled youngster, and carried him around the edge of the lake for about a hundred yards or so. The beast then entered the water that was approximately waist deep and simply disappeared. The boy was not moving during the kidnapping, so it was unclear at the time if he was dead or alive.

The two Keyholes recorded everything, and OSCAR was able to enhance the video, making it three dimensional and almost to the point of a decent quality black-and-white movie. The boy had vanished before his parents, vacationing from Germany, even knew he was gone. Once the report of a missing boy was filed, a manhunt of mammoth proportions was conducted. The National Guard was called in with helicopters, and over two hundred volunteers scoured the park for seven days but found not so much as a trace of young Luca.

The Silo 9 team was dumbstruck and was told that under no circumstances were they to get involved.

"We have information that could help them, General. Can we at least tell them that the boy is gone?" Tom Stack, the leader of the team, asked Baker on day three of the search. They all felt so helpless.

"We can't do that, son. Our orders are to stand down. It's not why we're here. We're here for the interlopers that come and stay. This event is extremely unfortunate, not to mention unsettling, but we can't do anything about it," General Baker explained.

"Yes, sir. I understand, sir," Tom replied, but he just couldn't follow the order. If that was his son, he would want to know what happened to him. The hard-line telephone in the bunker was used only to communicate with General Baker while he was out, but at that time, it still had a viable outside line. Tom called the tip line that had been established and reported that a hairy monster had snatched the boy, walked north along the beach, entered the water to his waist, and promptly disappeared with the boy.

Word of the report, not taken seriously of course, made its rounds among the National Guardsmen and volunteers, and they all got a much needed laugh. A news crew actually mentioned it on air, much to the interest of Matthew Nastally, the Temporal Phenomenon secretary, who subsequently had the call traced. And where could an absurd (and absolutely accurate) call like this one originate from? Why, no other place than a cornfield in the middle of Iowa.

At that point Baker was given two choices: one, eliminate the Silo 9 crew and operate the center himself, or two, eliminate the Silo 9 crew and replace the staff with certain conditions. No outside phone lines or Internet access, no leaving the silo without a chaperone, and no viewing of the back-to-back anomalies. Baker took option two.

The outcome of the Coconino kidnapping actually had a happy ending. On day nine, a passing motorist just happened to glance out into the desert and saw what he thought looked like a young boy. Curious, he stopped his car and made his way out to see exactly what it was. It was young Luca, barefoot, hypothermic (despite the 102-degree desert heat), and dehydrated, but in otherwise decent health approximately twenty-three miles from the point of abduction. He unfortunately had no recall of the events of the past week other than remembering a very bad odor and being "helped" by a very large and hairy man. The mother and father praised the Lord for his safe return and called it a miracle.

The Silo 9 staff, alerted by the *Icarus* alarm and enhancement by OSCAR, saw Luca appear suddenly in the arms of a small boy near an enormous boulder in the middle of the desert. The boy carried Luca for almost a mile toward the highway, set the boy down, and disappeared. The staff subsequently witnessed the Good Samaritan's discovery of Luca, and there wasn't a dry eye in the bunker.

Two days later, Dr. Eugene MacIntosh arrived at Silo 9 to deliver routine immunizations, or at least that is what they were told.

"How long will the sedative take to knock them out?" Baker asked Dr. MacIntosh. They had already devised a plan, but much of it depended upon the amount of time between the injection and unconsciousness. It couldn't be too long, but it had to be long enough.

"About three minutes, so I will need them all in the infirmary at the same time so they're not staggering around and passing out in front of one another. After they're out, I'll inject the Propofol that will cause them to stop breathing. Believe me, they won't feel a thing," the doctor answered loudly and clearly. Baker had sought out these recruits because they had very few or no ties to the outside world and would not be missed. Black sites were purposely staffed with "lone wolves" to lessen outside communication and restrict the number of people with knowledge of the site, among other reasons.

"Ok then. I'll round them up. Let's get this over with." Once the injections were administered, the three technicians began to get drowsy and subsequently passed out, just as the doctor had promised. As Dr. MacIntosh readied the first Propofol injection, Baked slipped behind him, unholstered his weapon, and promptly shot the doctor in the back of the head with his .22 caliber sidearm at point-blank range.

"I'm sorry, Dr. MacIntosh," Baker muttered out loud, looking and speaking directly at the infirmary's inside doorknob. He proceeded to inject each of the young technicians with the saline solution the doctor had prepared in the Propofol vial. After he'd finished he placed a call.

"It's done, Mr. Secretary," Baker said into his phone. Baker then swung the phone camera in an arc to display the carnage he'd caused.

"So I've been told. That's a pretty messy scene you've got there, Baker. Clean it up and get rid of the bodies. This is your last chance, Baker, so don't fuck this next one up," the secretary warned. It was clear to Rowland that his own life would be in serious danger if there was any kind of breach with the next group.

Aware of the extensive network of cameras and microphones in and around the complex, General Baker needed to make it look and sound like he was removing bodies, just in case someone was watching. He rolled each of the bodies into blankets, took them topside via the elevator, and loaded each one into the transport van there for the occupants use.

Once out of the line of sight of the silo, Rowland stopped the van and unrolled each of the techs so he could tie them up—for their own good, of course. He didn't have to tie up the doctor because he was helping Baker with the charade of executing the entire staff of Silo 9. Rowland then proceeded to his home in Dubuque. Once there, Rowland patiently waited for the drugs to wear off. They all regained consciousness within minutes of each other.

"What the hell are we doing here, General, and why are we tied up?" Tom asked, still somewhat groggy from the sedation. At that point, General Baker told them the truth, the whole truth, and nothing but the truth, at least his version of it. They were given the option of taking new identities and disappearing, or taking new identities and working for Baker from his home, which was now equipped with a vast array of computers and monitors that held the best skip tracing software stolen black budget money could buy. The new mission: *find Hollis Carrington*.

One of the techs, a young soldier named Trisha, decided to move to Alaska. The other two, Tom and Angela, decided to stay on and help Baker locate the elusive Hollis Carrington.

Roland put the car in park and reached under the driver's seat for any remnants of his breakfast. The two fingers that remained in the Stoli bottle was exactly what he needed to take the edge off and he promptly drained it in one long draw. As Roland walked to the front door, he hoped—no, *prayed*—the team had good news for him.

CHAPTER 41

"What the hell, Noah!" Jack screamed back as he slammed on the brakes. "You don't yell 'stop the car' at the driver of said car when said car is traveling seventy-five miles an hour down the turnpike! In traffic and in a tunnel to boot! Shit!" The vehicle had almost stopped, and Jack was trying to find the toggle switch for the hazard lights when he turned to Noah and just stared at him. He looked like a little boy who was about to cry.

"Look, I'm sorry I yelled at you, but don't ever do that again. Now what is so important that we have to stop right now in this tunnel?" Jack asked in a much less harsh manner. He was still pissed off at him, though.

"I have to get in the back seat," Noah stated as he unbuckled his seat belt and climbed over the hump to sit with Jacob. Jack's anger was starting to boil over again.

"Jesus Christ. This couldn't wait until the next rest stop?"

"No. Satellites are trying to find our location. I would rather they not know at this point of the trip," Noah replied, insinuating that there would be a time and place for them to show their hand.

"All right, that makes sense," Jack responded, calming back down again. This trip—make that the whole ordeal from the moment Noah entered the house—had been a roller coaster ride. "What are you going to do, sit in his lap?" Jack asked, dumbfounded.

"Yes. They have a satellite that detects heat signatures. When it detects only two people in the vehicle, it will hopefully throw them off the scent, at least for a little while."

"Have they been monitoring us the whole way? Why haven't they tried to stop us?"

"They lost us; they are looking at every vehicle in a three-state area and will use algorithms to decide which one is us. Eventually they will find us, but it will hopefully be too late."

"That's impossible. There isn't a computer in the world that could possibly calculate all that information," Jack retorted.

"There is exactly one, and it is in Iowa. It's the whole reason we're going to Iowa at all. I need to use that computer, and I need the person's help who is most familiar with it," Noah explained.

Finally getting some answers from the kid anyway, Jack figured.

"Are you ready to go now?" Jack asked rather sardonically. *This kid is not only in control of our destiny, but he also knows how to push my buttons*, Jack thought. It also made him think of all the "arguments" he and Jacob would have had over the years, and it was heartrending.

"Yes, sir! All buckled in and ready to go!" Noah yelled louder than what was necessary. Jack looked at them in the rearview mirror, and it looked like Jacob was having the time of his life, smiling ear to ear. Noah was literally sitting in Jacob's lap, and the seatbelt was extended about as far as it could go. Simply seeing the two children having fun caused the melancholy feelings of moments ago to fade quickly. Jacob was happy, so Jack was happy.

"All right then. Off we go!"

CHAPTER 42

Baker considered knocking before he entered just in case Tom and Angela were indecent. One time, they had obviously been going at it before he arrived, but at least they did it in their bedroom and covered themselves when they came out. Baker didn't mind. Hell, part of grooming the techs was trying to find a compatible mate. Baker was pretty sure Tom and Angela would hook up eventually, and they did. He was also sure Sebastian and Mikayla would unite, but either they hadn't yet or hid it really well. Rowland actually envied the youngsters and got satisfaction from giving them a good love life in exchange for screwing up the rest of their lives.

Baker knocked anyway. Three raps and then he entered. Both Tom and Angela looked hard at work at their stations, and Tom turned to him with a big smile. It seemed they had long forgotten about their near-death experience and subsequent kidnapping.

"General Baker! We're glad you're here. I think we've found something!" Tom squawked excitedly. "There was a satellite phone transmission from the silo to an unlisted number in the suburbs of Atlanta. We didn't think much of it, but we really haven't had anything else to follow up on." Tom was correct. They had been looking for Hollis Carrington for almost three months with nothing to show for it. Both Tom and Angie had come to the conclusion that Carrington was most likely dead.

"That little rat fink bastard Steven," Baker muttered. He knew Sebastian or either of the girls would never use an unauthorized phone.

"Excuse me, sir?" Tom replied. He didn't hear exactly what Baker said. *Was it something about a mink and plaster?*

"Never mind. What do you have for me, Thomas?" Baker said, much louder and better enunciated. Rowland hated the fact that he couldn't whisper. When his diaphragm wasn't forcing air through his vocal cords, his voice went up *another* octave. *One of the bullets I deposit into Carrington's ass will be for my voice*, thought Rowland.

"Well, like I said, there was a sat-phone call to an unlisted number. We traced all of the phone numbers that the phone has had contact with, and we found that one of the numbers belongs to a Simon Dobbs. Mr. Dobbs works for a man that fits the age requirements of Hollis Carrington," Tom stated. "And…one of the incoming calls to the unlisted number originated from the site of the most recent anomaly early this morning," he continued, smiling and generally pleased with himself. "And that's not all. There is another number *that* phone calls that travels all over the country and sometimes Europe. I wish I could get the times and locations loaded into OSCAR to see if he can make any other correlations."

"That's great, Thomas. Keep at it and see if you can get me an address for the unlisted number. And give me the dates and times of the calls to that other number. I'll try to get them loaded into OSCAR tonight when I'm there," Baker replied. There's no doubt Steven tipped off someone about the anomaly, probably for money, but what would Carrington want with a BEK? The last time they were all together at Camp Hero, Noah left suddenly without a trace.

"I'm one step ahead of you, General. The address is 16 Parkside Lane in Buckhead, North Atlanta, Georgia, and here is a list of the places and times," Thomas offered, still smiling as he handed the paperwork to Baker.

"I think you two have done a great job here and, regardless the outcome of this address, your time here is over," Baker dryly stated. Baker could see their demeanor instantly change as Thomas's smile vanished and Angela moved back and behind Thomas. Holy shit, were these kids jumpy, but Baker figured they had good reason to be. Just then his phone started to ring, but he sent it to voicemail as quickly as he could.

"I'm not going to hurt you. Look, I got you guys into this and I'm going to get you out of it. Take the new identities and start new lives somewhere. I can even give you ten grand or so to get you started," Baker promised as he opened the wall safe in the living room to retrieve some money and the prepared new identity documents. "You can never talk about what you did or saw at Silo 9, and don't ever get fingerprinted." These were good kids, and Baker knew they would keep quiet.

"Yes, sir," Tom replied. Angela began to cry as she walked over to Baker and hugged him dearly.

"Thank you for everything, sir. You've taught me a lot, and I'll remember you forever," Angela declared. Although they had only known each other a short time, Baker was the closest thing to a father she'd ever had.

"You're welcome, Angela. It's just not safe for you two to be here any longer. I'm pretty sure this address in Atlanta will house my target, so my quest is just about finished as well. I hope to be sipping margaritas in Aruba at this time next week." All the secrecy and all the drama had taken its toll on Rowland as much as anyone, and he was tired.

"It's settled then. You two disappear before I get back, and I wish you well. Please do not ever try to contact me," Baker insisted as he headed back out the door he entered. He had what he wanted: the address of Dr. Hollis Carrington.

CHAPTER 43

"He's not picking up, Gump," Joe stated as he tossed his phone on the seat of the Chinook after leaving a short message. Gump did not like losing, and they were definitely losing. The boy was still at large, the bitch in the truck had gotten the better of him, and Shiva was still as nervous as ever. It'd been a bad day so far.

"We're just going to have to wait for General Baker for new intelligence. They're supposed to have this super computer there, so they'll find the kid. We just have to hang tight," Gump explained. He figured the Chinook could catch up with any vehicle in no time at all once it was located, so they were still in the ball game. It was the eighth inning and they were down a couple runs, but they were still in it. After the failed Suburban takedown, they had flown south and parked the Chinook in a field north of Jackson, hoping their quarry had also headed south.

"Baker is quite a character. Sounds like a woman on the phone," Joe offered. Sometimes Joe made statements without thinking them over, and this was one of them.

"Seriously? Don't talk about a general like that. You know, you sound like a pussy when you talk to your mom," Gump retorted. He hated people that hated on people. *Why can't everyone just be accepting?* he thought as the phone on the seat began to vibrate.

"Gumper." It could only be one of two people, and he listened intently as General Baker gave the leader of the squad instructions. Gump even jotted down a few notes.

"Aye, aye, sir, we'll be there for you. We can overnight at Dobbins and hang out there for a couple of days. If you think your boy will turn up in Atlanta eventually, we'll stay as long as it takes. We'll be about five minutes from your address." Dobbins was one of the nicer air force bases, so he had no issues with laying low there for a couple of days. Gump fought off a smile thinking about what Joe said about the general's voice. It was quite feminine sounding, but he couldn't, and wouldn't, legitimatize Joe's comment by acknowledging it.

"Absolutely, sir…no problem…yes, sir…goodbye." Gump responded to each query Baker had made directly and concisely. "Ok, boys. We're off to Dobbins for a couple of days. General Baker believes the boy to be on his way to Atlanta, so we're going there to await further orders. I may be able to get us a little R & R, particularly tonight," Gump explained. It took about twelve hours to get from Flint to Atlanta by car, so they could technically get there sometime tonight. *Traveling with a special needs boy will certainly slow them down, though*, he thought.

"All right, Gump. Let's get the hell out of here!" Johnny burst out. Shiva, who had been lying patiently behind the seats, barked twice in approval. He definitely wanted to get the hell out of Michigan and not look back.

"Maybe we'll try to find a bitch for you at Dobbins, Shiva. Get you out of your funk," Gump said to the German shepherd, who barked two more times in approval.

CHAPTER 44

"All right, Noah, we're now in the great state of Iowa. Where exactly are we headed?" Jack asked as they crossed the Mississippi River and into the Hawkeye State. Being a University of Michigan loyalist his whole life gave him certain distaste for Iowa. And Illinois, Wisconsin, Indiana, and especially Ohio, home of the evil empire, The Ohio State University. Rivalries aside, Iowa looked like a pretty decent state from the outside looking in.

"It's not much farther. Get off the interstate at the next exit so we can pick up some supplies. Davenport will most likely have the best selection of stores. Clothing is at the top of the list, and we'll have to stop at a hardware store," Noah answered, as puzzling and cryptic as ever.

"Oh yeah, we need blouses and a hammer. I didn't pack either," Jack replied, smiling. He had to admit, the little weirdo was growing on him.

"No, we need one hundred percent natural clothing, made using cotton, hemp, wool, or flax, and if you want shoes, they will have to be made of leather. And I need a rasp or very fine file," Noah countered, evidently not getting Jack's joke. He was serious.

"Whatever you say, buddy. We should get some food too. What do you feel like for dinner?"

Noah had eaten a classic double with everything from Wendy's in four bites for lunch. *Normally breathing your meals must give one quite an appetite for red meat*, Jack thought at the time.

"I think eating at this point would be a bad idea. If everything goes as planned, we'll get all the nourishment we need later on tonight," Noah stated as Jack pulled into a parking space in front of Kohl's. "We need eight pairs of sweat pants and T-shirts, four smalls, three mediums, and one triple extra large. And make sure they are one hundred percent cotton. Also, be certain they don't have metal eyelets around the drawstring holes and make sure they don't have zippers. You should be able to find a sufficient file in the household goods department, but it has to be very fine. And don't look up at the sky. And beware of security cameras."

"Is that all, your majesty?" Jack said, mocking him again. It was especially rewarding when Noah didn't get the joke.

"I'm serious, Jack. You could end up on a foreign planet naked and afraid—or very possibly dead—if you don't do exactly as I say," Noah admonished. He was really serious.

"I'm not going to any planet other than Earth and neither is Jacob, so you can cross off a couple of pairs of those organic sweatsuits, Noah," Jack explained in an authoritative voice as he exited the driver's side door. *It's time to take back control of this situation*, Jack thought. "I will drop you off at your destination, and then Jake and I will be on our way." Jacob was once again staring at him with those big, blue, and incredibly sad-looking eyes, and Jack felt he had little choice but to continue on.

"Fine. Come on, Jacob, let's go get the supplies," Jack acquiesced, and Jacob unbuckled his safety belt and exited the Durango. "Aren't you coming in?" Jack asked, just then remembering Noah's little problem with invitations.

"You know I can't. Jacob is going home, and you can't stop him. You can come along, or you can stay and fight it out with the soldiers. It makes no difference to me. If you don't go, you may not see Jacob for a while. If you do go, it will be a fantastic journey few humans have ever taken. Now go get the supplies!" Noah commanded.

Jack couldn't have known at the time that people had been falling into temporal anomalies and simply disappearing from Earth and arriving on Niburu since humans had been in existence. While it is a fact Anunnakans have the ability to purposely travel between many worlds by controlling when and where the temporal anomalies occur, many actually crop up spontaneously.

In 1521, a Spaniard named Juan Cervantes made just such a trip to Niburu. Señor Cervantes was a hired man in the Florida landing party of Juan Ponce de León. Ponce de León and his men landed near what is now St. Augustine and began a trek inland in search of the native Calusa Indians in an attempt to forge a treaty.

On the third day of the incursion, Señor Cervantes was the last in a line of eight men forging their way through a thicket of scrub brush. One moment he was there, the next moment he was gone, the man directly in front of Cervantes would tell Ponce de León. A search party was formed, and the group fanned out in ever increasing circular paths, but Cervantes was nowhere to be found. Ponce de León was certain Cervantes was kidnapped by the local tribe of Calusas, so he decided to wait patiently for ransom demands.

Later that night, Juan Cervantes simply reappeared, stumbling into camp relating wild tales of hairy monsters and giants. At the ripe old age of fifty-two, Cervantes was considered an old man by modern standards. Before his disappearance, his hair was nearly all gray, his face moderately wrinkled, and his body worn down by a hard life on the open seas.

The man that returned had nary a gray hair, had no age lines, and was as physically fit as a man half his age. The men in the party, especially Juan Ponce de León himself, were awestruck by the transformation and peppered Cervantes with questions about where he had been and how he had gotten there.

He simply did not know. The last thing he remembered was seeing what looked like an enormous wall of water, like a fountain that was simply dangling in mid-air that distorted what stood directly behind it. Curious, Cervantes had crept closer until he reached his right hand out to touch the water of this fountain. The next thing he remembered was waking up in a barren wasteland, and everything was red.

Later that evening, he was miraculously returned very near to the spot he left, and he felt marvelous. The wall of water was nowhere to be found, so he made his way to the camp's fire by following the smoke. The men of the party were extremely doubtful Cervantes was telling the truth about this "dangling wall of water," but his physical appearance was quite convincing. Cervantes looked younger. The men of the party, including Juan Ponce de León and Cervantes himself, would spend the next seven years searching for this incredible wall of water. They were searching for the fabled Fountain of Youth.

Since gold was the key to surviving such a trip, the man's salvation from likely death from hypothermia would be the trace amounts of gold in his system due to contact transfer. Only a very small amount of gold in one's body made all the difference in the world.

CHAPTER 45

Hollis Carrington finally received the call he had been so anxiously awaiting. Unfortunately for him, the results attained by Simon and the Nordic left something to be desired. In fact, they had nothing to show for their very expensive trip to Michigan.

Not that money mattered, though. Hollis had more money than all but a few people on Earth. A smile came to Hollis's face as he remembered the circumstances surrounding his sudden and unexpected windfall.

On August 3rd, 1967, Noah was using the chair in an attempt to manifest unusual objects. The Pentagon was extremely interested and had several representatives present for the demonstration. The first item was the mongrel dog that he had conjured several weeks ago, and Dr. Carrington attempted to exactly replicate the unfortunate characteristics in the same order as before. Those in attendance witnessed mangy mutt after mangy mutt appear at will in Noah's lap, but none of them matched the original dog. Like the first dog, none of them lived very long either.

"Why are we doing this, Dr. Carrington?" Noah asked, sounding a bit perturbed. He didn't like to bring these animals into the world just to see them die a painful death a short time later.

"These men want to see if you can bring back a living thing that has died. I want you to concentrate on bringing back the puppy you brought here last month. It has to be *that* puppy," Hollis explained. Hollis and the men were under the impression that Noah was creating life. Noah knew he wasn't. Once Noah envisioned a puppy, a real puppy would be selected by the alien technology. The sordid characteristics added by Dr. Carrington amounted to nothing less than animal abuse. These puppies would be missed by their human families. Had they tried to manifest an actual person, an unfortunate random soul with similar characteristics would have been transported to Camp Hero. Each of the men thought of experimenting with humans, but none of them had the nerve to step up and recommend it.

"I'm trying, Dr. Carrington. I just don't think I can," Noah pleaded.

"Then let's leave the puppies alone for now. Can you envision a book then? Think about an old book, like *Moby Dick* or something," Carrington asked. *This should be easy for him*, Hollis thought. The question is, will the inks be period and will the pages show any sign of yellowing or oxidation? The book that appeared, a first printing of Melville's *Moby Dick; Or, the Whale*, looked as though it had been printed yesterday. It even smelled new. It raised more questions than it answered. It raised even more questions for Russell Turow of Bethesda, Maryland; he wanted to know where the fuck his Melville first print went.

Impressed beyond words, the guests at Camp Hero clamored for additional demonstrations. One of the men asked if Noah had ever conjured money, and it had never occurred to Carrington to try. *Now is as good a time as ever*, he thought.

"Noah, concentrate on a twenty-dollar bill," Carrington persuaded. Doing as he was asked, Noah promptly produced a crisp, seemingly brand-new twenty-dollar bill to the amazement of everyone in the room. The military applications for the device were limitless. A soldier could imagine a bazooka and moments later have the weapon at his disposal, they contemplated. The art of warfare would be changed forever.

The fact that Noah could produce cash at will was not lost on Hollis, and he intended to use the boy as his own personal ATM at some point in the very near future. Once again, he was unaware that Noah wasn't making money, but rather he was taking money. Someone might not miss a twenty-dollar bill, but they most definitely would miss two grand.

Carrington and the others had no way of knowing that the apparatus was simply a device Anunnakans used in everyday life, especially when off-world, because of its many unique applications.

The most common use of the device was described best by Howard Carter, as a "dream catcher." Any Anunnakan (and some special humans, of course) could access any previous life on demand and relive any portion of it. It was simply entertainment.

The second use was as a communication device. The Anunnakan wearing the device could summon virtually anything, such as food, slaves, or fellow Anunnakans. There was no need for cell phones when one could simply bring the other party to the user's location by picturing who or what they wished to bring forth. At that point, they could "enhance" (positively or negatively) the person or object to their liking. The only drawback was that what could be conjured had to be organic and non-mineral. The Anunnakans would have had no use for slaves had they been able to simply summon the gold they so desperately needed from the ground.

The third and most important use of the relic was as a transporting device. The Anunnakans helped the Egyptians built the pyramids using the device by moving the multi-ton blocks into place with precision that could not be matched even today. They were also able to move their precious gold from Earth to the transport ship. It operated using gravity, or more precisely, antigravity, hence the transport ship had to be within the gravity field of the Earth. The gold transport ship was typically "parked" just within the Earth's outer atmosphere.

On August 6th, 1967, Dr. Carrington placed Noah in the chair and directed him to conjure one million dollars in cash. Noah, having ulterior motives, recommended setting his sights on gold, which would allow for greater value in a smaller space.

"Do you think you can conjure gold, Noah?" Carrington asked his young prodigy. Hollis was thinking doubloons and coins, not quite the scale Noah had in mind.

"I'm sure I can. It might be a good idea to deposit it somewhere other than here, though. It might raise suspicions." It had taken a couple of months, but Noah finally had Dr. Carrington and the US government right where he wanted them. He had come for his gold, and he was about to take it. Once he had the gold in a verifiable (and, more importantly, numerically plottable) location, he could simply move the gold from that location to the space-based transport.

"You're absolutely right. Could you place it in the living room of my house? Would you be able to do that?" Dr. Carrington asked, his mind racing with the liberties a small hoard of gold would allow him.

"Can I put it in your barn? I think I'll be able to visualize that better. I don't want to make a mistake and send it to some random house because I got the color of your sofa wrong in my head," Noah rationalized. The cavernous barn was a remnant from the days the property was a bustling apple farm and was used to store the picking crates in the off months. It was now completely empty.

"Sure. Whatever is easiest for you," Hollis replied, his heart starting to race at the thought of his imminent windfall. He imagined a pirate's treasure chest overflowing with riches. He was getting gold fever.

"Ok, One shipment of gold to your barn!" Noah excitedly shrieked. *This is like taking candy from a baby*, he thought. He smiled to himself when he thought about what he was actually doing: stealing gold from the most secure place on this planet.

Noah placed the device on his head exactly as he had previously, both in this life and in others. Noah pictured the gold and very easily physically moved it from the vault to the apple barn at Dr. Carrington's home. Once that was complete, he would simply envision the space transport, known in biblical times as the Wheel of Ezekiel and in modern times as the Black Knight Satellite, and get it moving so it would be directly over the gold within hours. He would plot the gold's exact location, move the transport to exactly where it needed to be, then use the headpiece one last time to shoot it up, of course leaving a couple of bricks behind for Dr. Carrington's trouble. Carrington would never even know his barn was used as Noah's half-way house for the gold.

But something was wrong. The transport, permanently stationed in space 22,500 miles directly below the magnetic South Pole and dormant now for millennia, was not responding. Noah sat in the chair attempting to access the transport for almost three hours to no avail. It was not responding, and there was absolutely nothing he could do. The mission was a failure. The only other way to power up the transport remotely would be via radio wave in the Sumerian language it was most recently programmed with, the same Sumerian language that had been dead for almost as long as the gold transport had been dormant. Noah could only recall a few key phrases himself, so the language would have to be deciphered and learned by a computer with AI capabilities, he determined. It would be decades before Earth computers would have the hardware and software required to properly communicate with the transport, so Noah had no choice but to wait decades.

Noah, frustrated beyond comparison, removed the device from his head and handed it to Dr. Carrington.

"Take good care of this, Dr. Carrington. I will return someday to use it again," Noah quipped as he walked out the door of the chair room and headed left down the hallway. By the time Dr. Carrington reached the door just moments later, Noah was gone, vanished into thin air.

When Hollis finally arrived home that night (he had searched the Camp Hero grounds in vain for hours for his wonder child), he rushed to his apple barn, unlatched the two by fours, and flung open the double doors. The wall of gold stretched the width and length of the barn and rose nearly to the loft. All told, there were almost three hundred and fifty thousand bars of gold, each weighing four hundred troy ounces and worth nearly five billion dollars.

Dr. Hollis Carrington was rich beyond his wildest dreams.

CHAPTER 46

August 6, 1967, began like most other days for Fort Knox Private First Class Travis Kent. He woke to his alarm clock playing reveille at precisely zero four hundred hours, showered, shit, shaved, and headed to the mess hall where he ate his usual scrambled eggs and a toasted bagel. He relieved the night shift watchman at exactly zero seven hundred hours at the entrance to the vault, and the morning was totally uneventful for the first two hours.

Around zero nine hundred, Travis heard an extremely loud *bang*. He wasn't sure, but it seemed to originate from inside the vault, and it piqued his interest if nothing else. *Probably a sonic boom from an F-22 on maneuvers*, he thought.

Thirty seconds later, there was an equally as loud double *bang*, and it most definitely originated from inside the vault. He decided report the anomaly to his superior officer.

"Good morning, sir. This is PFC Kent at the door of the vault. There seems to be loud noises originating from…" Travis was explaining using the hard-line located just to the north of the vault door when a triple *bang* rang out from inside the vault. Two NCOs and the fort's commanding officer were at the scene within two minutes.

"Open it up, soldiers," the commanding officer instructed. Just as the vault door began to swing open, four loud bursts in immediate succession erupted from inside the vault, and the two-ton door was thrust open an additional foot with each *bang*. The four gold bricks, now having found a way out, continued through the atrium and burst through the main entrance door to the outside.

Moments later, a river of gold bars quickly and quietly glided out of the vault on the same path as the original four. With each passing second, the river grew until gold bars were spewing out of the vault fifty at a time.

"Should I try to close the door?" one of the young soldiers asked the CO. The officer answered the request with one simple word: "No."

Coincidently, the United States would abandon the gold standard just four years later.

CHAPTER 47

"So you're telling me that you are going to walk up to a military base and ask permission to use their state-of-the-art supercomputer? And these are the same people that are chasing you?" Jack asked Noah. The skepticism in his tone was unmistakable.

"Yes. There are some extenuating circumstances, and I may need your help, but I think we can convince them to let us in. We have to."

"There is no 'we' and there is no 'us,' Noah. This is your baby. Leave Jacob and me out of it. We will drop you off and then head back to Michigan," Jack explained. This was the end of the trip. *And what a trip it is*, thought Jack. Whatever beef Noah had with these people, or vice versa, was no business of his.

"Once we arrive you may leave. Jacob is coming with me, just like I explained earlier. There is no need to be afraid, Jack. Neither you nor Jacob will be harmed," Noah argued.

"You know I'm not leaving without Jacob. I just don't get what is so damn special about a thirteen-year-old autistic boy from Michigan. You say he's some Anunnaki

Grand Poohbah or something. I say he's just a boy, and this is most likely scaring him to death."

It wasn't the first time Jack used what he thought Jacob was thinking to make a point. What he didn't realize was that Jacob was fully cognizant of what was going on around him. He simply lacked the ability to speak, thanks to the self-inflicted coma he'd put himself in when he was minutes old.

"A Grand Poohbah exists only in the cartoon world of the *Flintstones*, Jack. Jacob is an Anunnaki god, and he knows it. He knows everything. If Jacob had wanted to rid himself of his human body, he would have done it long ago. Like I said before, I am extremely envious of Jacob, of all humans actually, as I would thoroughly enjoy living a life free of this burden of knowledge."

Jack had always believed that Jacob was cognizant. When Jack looked into Jacob's light blue eyes, he could see a certain sparkle, a certain shine. Jack glanced back at Jacob in the back seat, and their eyes met in the mirror. Jacob was pleading with Jack using his eyes as his words.

"Jesus Christ," Jack muttered under his breath. "What exactly would you like me to do when we get there?" Jack asked Noah in utter resignation. Once again, Noah won a battle. Either Jack was a pushover or Noah was a master manipulator. Jack figured it was a little bit of both.

"Just follow my lead. There are four residents, two males and two females. We will likely be dealing with only the leader, and he is having some serious trust issues. By the way, you will find one of the young ladies particularly attractive, Jack," Noah confided in his trademark cryptic style.

"Now how in the world would you know who I might or might not find attractive?" Jack wondered out loud. The very last thing he was interested at this moment was starting a relationship, even if he was attracted to someone. Deep down, he longed for a girlfriend, and not just a girl friend like Abbie, but it was one of the luxuries he subconsciously deprived himself of due to his self-guilt over Jacob. Abbie, for all her great qualities, simply was not attractive to Jack. His type was sandy haired, blue-eyed, petite but not skinny, and sure of herself. A mental picture of his perfect woman began to form in his mind.

"I know a lot of—" Noah started to explain before Jack cut him off.

"I know, I know. You're a *Watcher* and you know these things. What you don't know is that I'm not looking right now. I probably won't be for a long time. Once Jacob is an adult, *maybe* I will allow myself to date." Just saying the words out loud depressed him, but it was part of the vow he made two years ago after the car crash killed their parents. Jacob came first, period.

"Just keep an open mind, Jack," Noah replied, sporting a little cat-ate-the-canary smile.

"Stop the car!" he exclaimed moments later. Jack slammed on the brakes and pulled the Durango onto the dirt shoulder. Good thing there was no traffic in either direction.

"You have got to stop doing that!" Jack yelled at Noah. "A little warning would go a long way." Just ahead was a gravel two-track that headed south. The field corn growing on the plot was about waist high but still allowed sight all the way down the access road. About a quarter mile away was a small toll booth-looking structure, like the kind they had fed quarters to several times on the turnpike. There were several satellite dishes on the property, so it looked very much like a rural radio station.

"Is that our destination?" Jack asked with fair amount of trepidation. It didn't look very ominous, but Jack's stomach was in knots.

"Yes, we are here."

CHAPTER 48

The mood at the silo was somber to say the least. The adrenaline rush of the past fifteen hours had long worn off. Bass was fearful for their lives, and Mikayla was fearful Bass was starting to crack under the pressure. Steven and Leah were still somewhat unaffected. What they did not know was not hurting them.

"You would think they would have to pass a camera at some point, wouldn't they?" Steven asked out loud. "If I were aware of cameras, I would avoid them. But you're right. My guess is that they are hunkered down somewhere," Bass replied. He *really* wanted to find these guys as it may be the only thing that kept them alive.

Mikayla rose from her work station and approached Bass. "You know that thing you wanted me to work on? I think I have it. I can't lock out the keycards, but I can shut the power off to the elevator independently from the rest of the silo," she explained.

It's better than nothing, thought Bass. Until Baker blew the door off with a grenade, or piped poison gas under the door…

"Great job, Mikki. How long will it take to shut the elevator down once the decision has been made?" he asked. It wouldn't do much good if it took five minutes to power down that portion of the structure. The elevator opened directly into the control room, so they could all be dead in a matter of seconds.

"A couple of key strokes and it's done. You still haven't told me why you would want to lock out General Baker. Please tell me. Let me help," Mikayla whispered as to not alarm the others.

"I can't, Mick. I'm not even sure myself. Hell, I'm not sure of anything anymore after witnessing a boy just appear out of nowhere over a ditch in Michigan. I just wanted to know if a lockout was possible." The last thing he wanted was to worry Mikayla.

"What are you two whispering about over there?" Steven interjected.

He can't stand not being in on everything, thought Bass. Any shrink would give anything to study that inferiority complex.

"Just talking about how you couldn't find your ass with both hands. Where are these kids?" Mikayla shot back, laughing.

"You can kiss what I can't find with both hands, Mikayla. I'm going to reset OSCAR…I don't think he's feeling right," Steven replied. He always talked about the computer as if it were a person. It was probably his best friend.

"Why is that? I think he's been operating properly," Bass asked. He'd never seen OSCAR make a mistake, ever. "If there is a problem, it's surely operator error."

"Ok, get this," Steven said excitedly. He would love to prove Bass wrong. "One of the vehicles that exited the hospital parking garage was a metallic mint-green 2017 Dodge Durango. A few minutes ago I asked OSCAR to locate all of the metallic mint-green 2017 Dodge Durangos within possible driving distance of the last known position, the hospital parking ramp," he explained.

"Great. That was a really good idea, Steven. So what's the problem?"

"Well, the color is evidently pretty uncommon, so there are only twenty-one of them, and they're all properly accounted for except one. OSCAR is saying it is 242 meters from here, but I'm sure he means 242 miles," Steven elucidated.

Bass's heart sank as he ran over to the security panel and pulled up the driveway on monitor four. There it was, parked at the end of the lane—a metallic mint-green 2017 Dodge Durango. Although he couldn't see the people inside, he knew who it was.

"They're here! They have been driving here the whole time!" Bass exclaimed. *Why on Earth would they come here?* Bass thought. Now he was really getting scared for himself and everyone else in the bunker, but especially Mikki. He just got a girlfriend, and now she was in imminent danger.

"How do you know it's them?" Leah asked. She was obviously frightened due to the quivering of her voice.

"It's them. Mikki, cut the power to the elevator. Steven, find a way to barricade the door. We are soldiers, and even though we don't have weapons, we are going to defend our outpost. Each and every one of you is a soldier, don't forget that. We have a duty to protect this installation to the death, though I hope and pray it doesn't come to that." He could see they were all anxious, especially Steven.

"Uh, Bass?" Steven moaned.

"Yes, Steven. What is it?" Bass replied.

"OSCAR is saying the vehicle is moving," Steven whimpered. "And it's getting closer."

CHAPTER 49

"That little adventure is going to cost us at least a half a brick, buddy," Hollis Carrington said to his corgi, Augie. Hollis routinely talked to his best friend like he was a person. If Augie could talk, he would have some wild tales to tell indeed. "Our friends struck out again. Next time, I'll send you!" he quipped as he nuzzled noses with Augie.

"This is just like 1967. Noah is here one minute and gone the next," Hollis lamented. Carrington was desperate to locate Noah, or someone like him, as liver cancer had taken its toll on his whole body. He knew he only had months or maybe even weeks to live. He didn't know how Noah could help him or even what he was exactly, but he knew he could save him.

Not that Noah would want to, though. After he deposited a mountain of gold into Hollis's care and subsequently disappeared, Carrington became desperate. Camp Hero simply could not continue the way it had without Noah. Noah was freely able to time travel and conjure—and who knows what else given the opportunity.

In the aftermath of Noah's disappearance, young Rowland just wasn't producing results the way Noah did and it seemed his abilities were even declining. Every other boy had been released from the program in the weeks before Noah left, so Rowland was it. As Rowland went, so went Camp Hero.

Sure that time travel and conjuring abilities were tied to the youth of the chair occupant, Hollis came up with a brilliant idea two weeks after Noah disappeared. He sought out the only medical doctor in the camp, Dr. Isaiah Conway.

"Hey, doc, I have a procedure for you to perform today," Hollis casually informed Dr. Conway. Hollis had to use a bit of delicacy here.

"It's an orchiectomy. It's a fairly simple procedure, no?" Hollis asked.

"Well, yes. Do you have testicular cancer, Hollis? I'm so sorry. Come down to my office this afternoon so we can discuss your options. There may be another way," Dr. Conway answered. Isaiah was a good man, a good doctor, and he genuinely cared about his patients.

"Sure. Can you explain the procedure to me, though?" Hollis asked, looking for details. He was a doctor, too, goddammit, and if it was easy enough, he would do it himself. He would most likely have to anyway as Conway would never agree to what he was thinking of: removing the healthy testicles from a healthy twelve-year-old boy. Even Carrington thought the idea somewhat insane, but he had no choice. Once Rowland started going through puberty, Carrington would have to start over with new untrained boys, and that would set his work back years.

"Sure. It can be done with local anesthetic on an out-patient basis. It's really quite simple. Make an incision in the scrotum, remove the testicles and spermatic cords, and sew it back up," Dr. Conway explained in a pacifying manner with calm, deliberate hand motions to match. He truly thought Hollis was having a cancer crisis.

"Thanks, doc. You've been a great help," Hollis quipped as he turned and walked away from the doctor. Now he had a way of keeping the only boy with the ability to use the chair young forever. Hollis thought—no, he *knew*—that this is what Rowland would want: the ability to serve his country no matter the cost. His parents, on the other hand, may not be so willing.

Dr. Hollis Carrington committed murder for the first time that very same night. At roughly 2:00 a.m., Hollis broke into the home of Stanley and Mary Baker and slit their throats while they slept. For the next hour, he was euphoric, on a high that he would never quite experience again as he roamed the Baker home picking up items that he felt had value. Once he'd filled his pillow case, he left by the same door he'd entered. On the ride home, he stopped on a bridge spanning the Toms River and deposited the items he had ransacked, pillow case and all, into the roiling water.

Hollis informed the boy of the murder/robbery later the next day and young Rowland was inconsolable. The two people he loved most and had loved him the most in the world were gone.

"What if I can make it so you can stay here forever with me, Rowland?" Dr. Carrington asked, the empathy in his voice overt. "Would you do anything to stay here with me?"

"I guess so. I don't have anywhere else to go," Rowland replied, still sobbing. "What will I have to do?"

"You don't have to do anything. I can make it so you can use the chair forever, and you'll probably get better at it, like Noah," Carrington promised.

"I would like that a lot!" Rowland stated, perking up a bit. He was sick and tired of playing second fiddle to that little shit picker Noah.

"It's settled then! I'll come get you tonight after dinner," Hollis said, his demeanor brightening just as Rowland's had.

That evening Dr. Carrington prepared a special cocktail of sodium thiopental and PCP for little Rowland and had chloroform on hand in case he needed it. He didn't. Dr. Conway was correct; it was an easy procedure. In less than twenty minutes, Hollis removed both of Rowland's testicles, inserted two aluminum ball bearings (somewhat larger than what he had removed so the boy could grow into them), and sewed up the incision. Hollis felt as though he had created a superhuman being that would break down the barriers of space and time for the benefit of all mankind.

What he had actually produced was one pissed off little eunuch. When Rowland discovered what had been done to him, and it didn't take long, he immediately asked to use the chair without any pharmaceutical help.

Dr. Carrington was ecstatic. The first day after fixing his problem, the boy wanted to get back to work. Hollis seated the boy, placed the alien device on his head, and fired up the monitor.

Young Rowland knew what he had to do. He had to destroy Hollis Carrington and this whole damn camp. Fueled by rage, Rowland envisioned the white-haired monster of his recurring nightmares. It was at least eight feet tall. No, make that ten feet tall. With beady bloodshot eyes and yellow fangs. It had long sharp nails on the tips of its fingers.

And it was mad! As the monster took shape in his mind and on the screen, an alien being that had simply been minding its own business was ripped from its home planet and was promptly incarnated at Camp Hero. And yes, it *was* mad. Rowland could hear a commotion outside the closed door. Then he heard gunshots. And screams. An Abominable Snowman was loose in the camp, and it was destroying *everything.* Rowland simply stood up, tossed the device on the floor, and walked out. He would spend the remainder of his childhood in the care of Dr. Conway, who felt truly sorry for the boy. Years later, Dr. Conway would get Rowland into West Point despite the castration Dr. Carrington performed. Camp Hero and the Montauk chair would remain vacant to this day.

Dr. Carrington himself was lucky to live through the ordeal. In fact, now that he was independently wealthy it was the perfect scenario to disappear, so he very effectively faked his own death. Once the stolen gold was secure in his newly purchased Atlanta mansion, Hollis would undergo facial reconstruction surgery in Mexico to alter his identity and would become Dr. Christian

Lomax, an early retiree who would live out his days as an Atlanta suburbanite.

"Yeah, I've done some pretty bad things, boy," Carrington said to the little corgi. "But I did them with the best of intentions," he contended as Augie barked his approval from Carrington's lap.

What Dr. Hollis Carrington, or Dr. Christian Lomax, didn't know right then was that the little boy he had emasculated all those years ago had just discovered his true identity and location, and he was still mad as hell. And he was coming for him.

CHAPTER 50

"I'm going to the bunker, and I'm shutting it down," Rowland stated to the man on the other end of the line. He'd had enough. Keeping one lie running was hard enough, but three? He was lying to his superiors about the second clandestine black site. He was lying to the current occupants of the silo about the nature of their work and the likelihood of them surviving. And he was lying to himself about not wanting revenge for his manhood being taken away. He wanted revenge before, and he still did now.

Despite the castration forced upon him, Rowland had led a pretty good life. He had even been happy at times. Dr. Conway was a good mentor and role model during Rowland's teen years when he suffered from bouts of severe depression. Dr. Conway became one of the leading physicians in developing hormone replacement therapy, and Rowland benefited greatly from it. He even had to shave every other day when he was in his twenties.

Once Rowland reached his mid-thirties, he had solidified his standing in the army and the need for hormone replacement wasn't nearly as necessary. He knew people talked behind his back about his voice and feminine attributes, but he didn't care.

He thought he had gotten over his hatred for Dr. Carrington, but it was a lie. Rowland had to make him pay, and pay he would. Now that he knew where Carrington was and who he had become, he could carry out his revenge with the help of the United States military, regardless of Hollis's advanced age. It was more the point of it. You don't go around cutting off the balls of unknowing little boys and get away with it.

"Are you insane? No, I'm not going to eliminate them. They don't know anything, and who really gives a shit anyway?" Baker tried to reason with the man. "The world is changing, Secretary. Maybe it's time to go public with everything we know. The public is much more intelligent and resilient than you give them credit for." Rowland thought there had been entirely too much denial about UFOs and aliens from the government. He thought he might even go public himself.

"Well, thank you, sir, I appreciate that. I've been in the armed forces for almost forty years and have never betrayed my country, but there comes a point in time where the truth must be told. Lies have to be told over the years to cover up other lies ad infinitum. The American public is ready for disclosure."

There was a long silence as Baker listened to the man on the other end of the line. He directed Baker to head to the silo, stay put, and await further orders. It seemed to Rowland like he had gotten Nastally to see his point of view, and for that he was relieved. The Silo 9 team would be all right after all.

This was it. This was Rowland Baker's endgame, what he had been waiting most of his life for. After tidying things up at the silo, he would head to Atlanta for a date with the butcher of Camp Hero. He could care less that Carrington was almost eighty years old; he still had to die a slow, painful death that lacked any semblance of dignity.

"Yes, sir, will do. Thank you, sir," Baker said into the phone as he wrapped up the call. He was about a half hour from the silo, so he would have plenty of time to catch a flight to Atlanta tomorrow.

The man Baker had been talking to placed another call immediately after hanging up. This time he called Lt. Gumper, who was flying high over Indiana en route to Dobbins Air Force Base near Atlanta. They now had new orders. They were to head west to Iowa. Gump was told there were hostiles at Silo 9 and they were to clear the area. Gump's heart sank as he realized he was being ordered to kill fellow servicemen, on American soil no less. Failure to comply would mean a certain court martial. If he were to carry out the orders, he would be a cold-blooded killer. He didn't know what he was going to do. As the Chinook banked toward the west, he knew he only had forty-five minutes to decide.

CHAPTER 51

"**D**on't come any closer or you will be fired upon. You are trespassing on United States government property!" Bass yelled through the microphone. He had a bad feeling about this. There was no doubt in his mind that the boy talking was the kid that fell out of thin air and into the ditch. The other two must be the residents of the home he walked to, Jackson and Jacob Wheaton. Why would this kid drive from Flint, Michigan, to Iowa?

"We mean you no harm, Sebastian. We are here for one purpose: to gain entry to your complex and use of your computer," the boy explained.

Bass didn't care. No one was coming in, and no one was leaving. Bass saw the older boy lean over to the ditch cannon-baller and speak softly in his ear. *That won't help*, Bass thought. *This system hears everything*.

"That wasn't very convincing, Noah. You can't just walk up here and say you want to come in and expect them to buzz you up, or down in this case. Let me give it a try," the older boy said.

"Look, Sebastian, is it? My name is Jack Wheaton, this is my younger brother Jacob Wheaton, and this is

Noah…just Noah," Jack explained, and he pointed out each individual as he introduced them. He never got Noah's last name, figured he probably didn't even have one. "I just met Noah last night, as you already know, and he has quite a tale to tell. I'm convinced he's here with good intentions. Noah isn't from around here; he's a Seraph, kind of like a guardian angel."

"I don't give a fuck if he's Jesus Christ. You people are not coming in here. You shouldn't even know this place exists. Leave now before you are fired upon," Bass replied. *It's not even up to me*, he thought. *It's protocol*.

"Funny you should say that, Sebastian. I found out earlier today that my baby brother here is the second coming of Jesus Christ, or something like that. They evidently share the same blood," Jack stated. Now he wished he'd asked Noah a few more questions about that fun little fact. Like, could Jacob perform miracles? Could he summon a swarm of locusts? Not that a swarm of locusts would help their chances of entering this bunker right now.

"We know you don't have weapons, Sebastian. You are in there with Steven, Leah, and your recently beloved Mikayla. Now, time is becoming of the essence, so we must enter immediately," Noah reasoned. It wasn't working.

"I don't care! Get out of here!" Bass screamed. Mikki was giving him a look like he was overreacting.

"What? You know I can't let them in," Bass said to Mikki, his shoulders shrugged and hands out to each side, palms up. "And keep the power to the elevator turned off just to be safe."

"What if they're telling the truth? You know the dark-haired boy is from…well, you know he's not from *here*," Mikki expounded as she tapped the power down command into her computer again for good measure. She had a great point, but it still wasn't a reason to let them in. The older boy leaned in to Noah again, and Bass turned the volume back up.

"I think you're going to have to find another way, buddy," Jack surmised. Noah was shaking his head side to side.

"There is no other way. We need Sebastian, and we need the use of that computer. We're almost there, Jack. He is going to let us enter in three minutes and forty-five seconds, but it will get a little dicey first," Noah whispered back. Bass laughed at the thought of him giving these idiots access to the silo and to OSCAR and in so little time. And he was supposedly going to help them! He started the stopwatch on his right wrist anyway to have a little fun with it.

"You know I can hear every word you douche bags are saying. I'm not going to let you in here in any amount of time!" Bass exclaimed, laughing as he said it. Just then, all three of the interlopers at the door turned as something caught their attention. Bass switched cameras and watched as General Baker's car came to a stop next to the Durango.

General Baker exited the vehicle and drew his weapon. The boy named Noah stepped forward in front of the other two boys and began slowly walking toward the general. No words were spoken, and the distance between them narrowed until the muzzle of the gun was nearly touching Noah's forehead. Bass and everyone else inside and outside the silo reflexively held their breath in anticipation of what was to come.

"Is it really you, Noah?" General Baker exclaimed as he holstered his weapon, stepped forward, and gave Noah a stiff but welcoming hug.

"Yes, Rowland, it is I. I'm so very sorry for the way things ended after I left all those years ago. I am here now to rectify those wrongdoings to the best of my ability, but I need access to this silo and the computer it houses."

"I'm not so sure they will even let *me* in, but I can try. What exactly is it you're intending to do?" Baker asked Noah. Bass and the rest of the staff had been watching the reunion unfold and were more confused than anything else. *How could Baker possibly know this kid,* wondered Bass.

"What do you make of that, Bass?" Steven asked Sebastian. "It seems as though they know each other." Before Bass could answer, the attention of the topside contingent was once again interrupted. The reason was the CH-47F Chinook assault helicopter closing quickly on the silo. Once it was four hundred or so yards away, machine gun fire was heard, and the group attempted to take cover. General Baker ran to the entrance and scanned his keycard. The light next to the card reader should have turned green, but it actually did nothing. Not even a beep—Mikayla had succeeded in locking out General Baker. The machine gun fire ceased momentarily as the Chinook backed off slightly to unload its cargo of soldiers.

"Bass, you have to let us in! They are going to kill us all!" General Baker screeched in his unique falsetto voice.

"What do you want me to do, Bass?" Mikayla asked solemnly.

"They're just kids!" Leah cried out. She was nervously pacing behind her console, and Steven was doubled over as if he was about to vomit.

If I let them in, we're probably going to all die. If I don't let them in, we are probably going to all die, thought Bass. It was a proverbial no-win situation.

"Bass?" Mikayla nervously asked again. The soldiers were at the ready to jump down as soon as the Chinook was safely on the ground.

None of us stand a chance against them, Bass thought.

"Let them in!" he exclaimed, and Mikki immediately typed the command to restore power to the elevator and reverse the lockout. "General, use your pass key!" Bass yelled into the microphone, and he watched General Baker swipe again, this time successfully.

Bass happened to look down at his watch, which was still displaying the stopwatch he'd activated earlier. He clicked the button on the right side of the dial, and it stopped at exactly three minutes and forty-five seconds. *Whatever our fate*, Bass thought, *this kid is good*.

CHAPTER 52

No one in the silo knew what to expect when the elevator doors finally opened. Would they storm them and take over the station? Bass and Mikayla stood side by side, and Leah had made her way over toward Steven, instinctively looking to a male for protection. When the doors finally did open, they were all dismayed by what they saw.

"Rowland has been hit!" Noah shouted. Noah was on Baker's right arm and Jack was on his left helping to keep him upright. Baker's girth made that futile, so they allowed him to gently fall to the floor just inside the elevator door.

"Well, don't just stand there! Get me a first aid kit or something!" Jack ordered. Baker was on his back with Noah holding his head up. Jacob had also entered the command center wearing his over-stuffed backpack but just stood by the side as Noah and Jack helped Rowland.

"It's not that bad. I just got winged in the shoulder," General Baker stated. Based on the amount of blood, it was a lot more serious than a wing shot. Noah mentally noted that it appeared to be a through and through wound, and he was thankful for that.

"I'll get the first aid kit," Leah offered as she headed down the corridor to the common room. She wasn't sure how much help it would be for a gunshot wound, but it couldn't hurt.

"I'll get some isopropyl alcohol. More than fifty percent of gunshot wound deaths are attributed to infection and sepsis than the actual damage from the bullet," Steven interjected. His knowledge of gunshot wound statistics went unnoticed.

"General Baker, why are they shooting at us?" Bass asked. It was a legitimate question as they were all part of the same military.

"I'm afraid that's my fault, Sebastian. I believe they were given orders to eradicate the occupants of Silo 9, myself included. I was fed up with the bullshit I was getting from above and said some things about disclosure I probably shouldn't have." Leah returned with the first aid kit, but it of course held nothing of use. Steven returned with a bottle of alcohol and poured a good bit on the wound as General Baker winced in pain.

"Rowland will be fine," Noah surmised. "We need to act fast as we do not have much time. Leah, go put ice and milk in a blender and mix it until it is thick, then fill four small glasses. Sebastian, you and I are going to teach your computer Sumerian. Mikayla, take this gold bar and file it until you have a generous pile of dust. Jack, you stay with Rowland and keep his head elevated," Noah instructed nonchalantly.

Sure, Bass thought, *let's make milkshakes and teach OSCAR a language that's been dead for five thousand years. And what about the gold dust? Is this kid on something?*

Everyone simply stopped what they were doing and stared at Noah. Leah and Mikayla were huddled tightly trying to process the scene in the aftermath of the shooting.

"Look, people. This kid came into my life less than a day ago and I trust him," Jack stated. He went on to divulge the fact that Noah was really a Seraphim and Anunnakan Watcher and could travel between dimensions.

"I've known Noah for…years and I agree. We need to do what he says. Our only way out of this ordeal is through Noah," General Baker agreed.

"Mikki, can you shut down the power to the elevator and lock out all of the pass codes again?" Bass asked. "We also need to bar the elevator doors." He didn't know how long he could keep the US military out, but he could at least make it hard for them.

"Done," Mikayla responded as she tapped the command into her keyboard one last time. She was more into Bass than ever now that he'd taken control of the situation. She couldn't wait to be alone with him.

"Speaking of pass cards, Sebastian, why did you lock mine out?" General Baker asked. He thought he knew the answer but wanted to hear it from Bass himself.

"Because you're a ruthless killer of unarmed misfit and forgotten young technicians, that's why. Does the word 'grooming' mean anything to you? I know you eliminated the last group of techs that were stationed here!" Bass accused. Everyone except Noah stared at General

Baker with looks of disdain and disbelief. Noah continued typing on OSCAR's keyboard, seemingly oblivious to the accusation.

"I have never killed anyone in my life, Sebastian. It was a ruse that had to be done to keep them all alive. Most of the previous crew is at my home doing research for me, and the doctor is laying low at his cabin in Montana. A paintball pellet at short range to the back of the head is very convincing to hidden cameras. Speaking of that, we should disable all of the cameras so they don't know what we're up to. There is one in each light switch," Baker responded as everyone let out a massive sigh of relief.

"Cameras? Where are the cameras?" Steven asked. All of them had done some pretty untoward things to themselves in their bedrooms in what they thought was privacy. Steven blushed with embarrassment as he had been particularly creative with himself lately.

"The cameras and microphones are in the light switches. They're like two-way mirrors: you can't see in, but the camera can see out. If you're worried about what you've done, don't be. This station will probably be shut down after today. I'll see to it that anything that was recorded gets destroyed," Baker promised, even though he had neither the will nor the power to do either.

"Enough about cameras! Sebastian, I need you to help me with the computer," Noah exclaimed. He had already given OSCAR the meaning of several series of key glyphs and now needed to explain the base eight numerical systems. OSCAR was learning the Sumerian language and numbering method at one hundred quadrillion bits per second.

Everyone turned to the outside monitor when the machine gun fire spontaneously erupted and one of the men started screaming obscenities. He was clearly upset.

Whatever plan Noah has, he had better hurry, Jack thought.

CHAPTER 53

Hollis was trying to piece together the meager intelligence Simon and the Nordic had gathered. The boy had appeared in a Michigan alfalfa field, went directly to a home, left a few hours later, and escaped the mighty United States military.

"How old is the retarded boy?" Carrington asked Simon. There was a connection here somewhere; he just had to find it.

"He's not retarded, he's autistic. There's a difference. And you don't say 'retarded' anymore, it's 'cognitively impaired,'" Simon chastised. He didn't care if Hollis was his boss; there were some things you just didn't say anymore. Hollis just stared at him.

"How old is the autistic boy then?" Hollis correctly asked.

"He is thirteen, sir. He was born April 8th, 2006, Easter Sunday, as a matter of fact," Simon replied. Simon knew he was on thin ice by Carrington's tone, so he'd better not correct him again.

"Contact the cabal and see if they have anything on or around that date," Hollis ordered. He seemed to recall a brief incursion around that time in mid-Michigan. Before he could send Simon or the Nordic, it was gone. Hollis waited patiently with a fresh iced Balvenie while Simon inquired. Simon returned ten minutes later with some interesting news

"You were right, Hollis. They did detect something at that very time in Flint. They sent one of their top psychics, but the mark was gone before it was pinpointed," Simon explained.

"So the retar…*autistic* boy is special. I have to have these boys, Simon. You need to do everything in your power to bring them here. Find them!" Carrington ordered. The Michigan boy was the answer to his affliction. His cure. He was born with the knowledge of the universe so, according to the cabal, had to be born with pure blood. Anunnaki blood. The blood of God.

"I'll do what I can. I have our contact at the silo, but other than that we don't have the means to track down anything, let alone a thirteen-year-old boy," Simon muttered as he walked out the door. He was nervous as Carrington seemed desperate. It was time for Simon to break protocol and place a call to the informant, and maybe sweeten the pot a little bit.

Hollis thought back to the "chance" meeting of Noah in the supermarket, Noah's incredible use of the Montauk chair and the alien device, and the manner in which Noah summoned all that gold. Then he abruptly disappears before showing up almost half a century later at the home of a pure-blood Anunnakan? *It seems as though I've been played*, thought Carrington. But what's his angle? What's his new mission?

Hollis was now sure that it was all connected. It seemed even little Rowland Baker was involved, too, now that he headed the paranormal arm of the US intelligence organization. But how?

"The kid is in Iowa! He's at the surveillance site!" Simon blurted out as he stormed through the closed door without knocking. "He's at the fucking surveillance site!" Simon repeated as if Carrington hadn't heard him the first time.

"That's very interesting, Simon. Thank you, you can see yourself out," Carrington responded nonchalantly.

"Ok. I thought you would be ecstatic. We found him!" Simon triumphantly exclaimed. His disposition would not be dampened by Hollis's lack of enthusiasm.

"Well done, Simon. Thank you. See yourself out now." A scenario was developing in Hollis's mind, and it was more than a little unnerving. There would be no need to continue chasing Noah or this Anunnaki boy because he was pretty sure where they were headed.

They are coming here, Hollis thought. But he would be ready.

CHAPTER 54

"We need to call the press. That's the only way we're going to get out of this alive. My phone is not working. They have either jammed the cell signal or I'm just not getting reception, so I'll need Steven's sat-phone," General Baker gasped.

He's right, Jack thought. And without some kind of intervention, the soldiers would get in eventually.

"Well, go get it, Steven!" the general ordered. Steven had been trying to process how Baker knew about the phone, and then he remembered the cameras.

"Right on it, sir," Steven replied. He ran to the bathroom, and as he was removing the cover of the toilet paper holder in the only stall, it startled him when it started ringing. He finally had all of the screws out, retrieved the phone, and pressed the green button.

"Hello?" Steven asked sheepishly and then listened to the response. There was only one person with the number, so he knew who it was. However, Steven had demanded that he never call. Steven would call when he had information.

"We know exactly where he is. The weird kid is here," Steven replied to the caller's question. One second later, the phone went dead. "That was odd," Steven muttered to himself as he walked out the door and back down the hallway toward the command center. Leah was ahead of him holding four glasses of slushy milk, and they entered the control room together.

"I have the milkshakes ready, Noah," Leah stated as she set the glasses down on a cart used for holding satellite trajectory maps. Jack looked at her, really looked at her, and couldn't believe his eyes. It was the girl he had thought about in the car, just as Noah had predicted. Leah could feel his stare and stared back for several seconds.

"Oh, Jesus Christ," Steven mumbled as he saw the two of them staring at each other. He knew the look. He had hoped Leah would look at him this way since the day she arrived. *What the fuck does he have that I don't?* Steven thought. "Here's your phone, General. It works," he muttered dejectedly as he handed the phone to Baker.

"Your gold dust is ready too," Mikayla stated. She had a feeling what was going to come next, and she was right.

"Split the dust piles exactly four ways, pour one pile into each glass, and then stir them up." Noah directed. "Then Jack, Mikayla, Sebastian, and Leah, drink one of the milkshakes. All of it. You will optimally need exactly three and a half grams of gold in your system, and the sooner you ingest it the better."

Steven was obviously feeling left out. "I don't get one of your shitty milkshakes? All you've done is make colloidal gold. People have been drinking it for centuries for a variety of afflictions," Steven cockily surmised.

"Unfortunately, you can't travel with us, Steven, due to the metal rod in your back. And Rowland, you can't go because of your—" Noah was explaining before General Baker cut him off.

"It's ok, Noah. There's no need for you to describe my situation," General Baker interjected. These people didn't need to know about his prosthetics, although they technically could be easily removed. He needed to stay here anyway to deal with the SEALs. They would shoot Steven just to shut him up. "Help me stand up, Jack," Baker urged.

"You know I'm not going anywhere without Jacob," Jack complained to Noah as he shifted General Baker to one side so he could free the arm that had been pinned between Baker's body and the wall while it supported him.

"Jacob's blood is different, remember? It's pure. He doesn't need the gold infusion, and neither do I. The rest of you will travel a good deal safer with gold in your system," Noah clarified. Jack didn't understand why it mattered, and he didn't argue.

"Where are we going, and how in the world are we going to get there? Do you not see the death squad up there?" Leah asked. She couldn't take her eyes off Jack for some reason. It's almost as if she knew him from somewhere.

"Our ultimate goal is to remove a menace to society, a man named Hollis Carrington. First, we're going to travel to my home planet of Niburu through a type of worm-hole, Leah. It's perfectly safe, and we will all be together the whole time," Noah promised. She shrugged her approval and even offered a small smile as she thought about going anywhere with Jack. She had never been so smitten so fast before in her life.

"Wormhole? Wormholes are theoretical, dipshit. Einstein couldn't prove them, and he was a whole lot smarter than you. Even if they were real, do you think one would just carry you away from here like Dorothy and Toto in *The Wizard of Oz*?" Steven said sarcastically. "Are you going to listen to this you guys? We're all about to die, and this little brat thinks he's going to fly out of here through a wormhole."

Everyone in the room looked at each other and simply shrugged their shoulders.

"I know a lot more than you think, Steven. Take the aether, which Einstein was correct about. Add in quantum entanglement, reduce everything to the Planck Scale, and correctly predict a rogue gravitational wave to hitch a ride on, and you have a mode of transportation that will take you anywhere in—" Noah was explaining as an explosion rocked the bunker.

"Holy shit! They just took out the upper elevator doors. Whatever you need to get done, do it fast, Noah," Jack blurted out. He was glad the argument between Steven and Noah was over, at least for now.

"The program is ready. OSCAR has the language and the math. Now we need to aim the dish. Sebastian, here are the coordinates," Noah stated as he wrote three sets of numbers down on a legal pad.

"There isn't anything there, Noah. I can see that it is in geosync, but this spot would be way out of a typical satellite path," Bass protested. A satellite's path had to be approved prior to deployment now that the space above the Earth was getting so crowded.

"It's there," Noah stated. "It's directly below the South Pole, and it hasn't moved in almost six thousand years. We're going to move it."

Jack looked at the monitor connected to the outside camera and saw two of the men fitting themselves with repelling gear.

"If you say so. Ok, the dish is lined up with your coordinates. What exactly are we aiming the dish at?" Bass asked as a green bulb lit on the dish display.

"It's a gold transport. It's our means of moving gold from Earth to my planet," Noah explained.

Noah was furiously typing and getting frustrated when he didn't get the results he'd hoped for. Nobody had noticed Jacob making his way toward the control panel shared by Noah and Sebastian.

Jacob surveyed the data they had inputted and stopped scrolling after ten or so screens of Sumerian cuneiform had passed. One glyph caught Jacob's eye, and he stopped the scroll and pulled up the image and its translation. Noah thought deeply, and a light bulb of sorts went off in his head.

"You're right, Jacob! That translation is incorrect. It should be *phleth*, not *phleph*," Noah exclaimed as he corrected the mistake. "Let's try this again…there!" A beep was heard, and the screen changed to a language not spoken or written for millennia. Green cuneiform symbols were scrolling down the monitor. The satellite was active.

"Ok, Sebastian, input the destination coordinates and then lock out all access. Did everyone drink their milkshake? It's time to go!" Noah exclaimed and motioned for all the travelers to come together. "Jacob, open your backpack. Everyone, take your shoes and socks off and put the moccasins on. Ladies, take a top and bottom and go change. No bras or undergarments, no earrings or other metallic body hardware. The boys will change out here. Hurry!" he pleaded as they could all hear clinking noises coming from the elevator shaft. The girls grabbed the new clothes and scurried down the hallway to the bathroom.

"Rowland, there is clothing in here for you, too," Noah stated succinctly. Their eyes met, and Rowland gave Noah a slight nod of acknowledgement. Rowland didn't quite know exactly what he was acknowledging yet, but figured he would in time.

"Why can't we wear our underwear, Noah?" Jack asked. He was more nervous than curious, but really wanted the answer.

"The elastic bands won't make it. I think I mentioned only organic items will travel between dimensions. There are wires in bras. If one of the girls were to wear a typical bra, it would act like a garrote on the other end. She would most likely be in two pieces, or the melted wire would be embedded in her body," Noah explained. Jack was correct; he didn't want to know. The thought of Leah being cut in half made him shudder.

"Ok, Noah, we're ready," Leah cautiously stated as she and Mikayla returned. Jack thought Leah looked amazing in the simple cotton outfit she had donned, and her beautiful auburn hair flowed over her neck and back in waves without her elastic scrunchie holding it up. The pounding at the elevator door shook Jack from his daydream.

"Make it easy on yourselves and open the door!" one of the men yelled. It was just a matter of time before they would get the door open. Nobody in the silo responded.

"Everyone gather around me," Noah said as he raised his arms straight up into the air. "Jack, Leah, come to this side and interlock arms. Sebastian, Mikayla, do the same over here. Jacob, come to my front."

"This is ridiculous. You guys aren't going anywhere!" Steven exclaimed as he laughed out loud.

"All right, hold on tight," Noah instructed. Jack tightened his grip on Leah, and she reciprocated. They were looking into each other's eyes and both thinking the same thing. Mikki tightened her grip on Bass, and he gave her a reassuring smile. They were all scared yet excited. "When we get there remember to breathe," Noah reminded them.

"See, what did I—" Steven smugly snorted and then stopped midsentence.

They were gone. One second they were there, and the next they were simply gone.

CHAPTER 55

W hen Jack woke up, he felt as if someone or something was sitting on his chest. And his legs. And his head. He tried to open his eyes, but the reddish light burned like lasers. He gradually opened them anyways and realized it wasn't so bad. He could actually see pretty well, but everything was red.

He looked to his left and saw that his arm was pinned under Leah. She was the most beautiful girl he had ever seen. He lifted his body up and leaned on his left elbow. As a result, his face was inches from hers. He wanted to kiss her so badly. *What is going on with me?* he wondered. *I have never felt this deeply attached to anyone, Jacob included.* Leah started stirring and rapidly blinking her eyes so he thought he'd best not act on his urge at this time.

As he leaned over her, he realized he wasn't breathing, and neither was she. He couldn't breathe. As his mind began to fuzz over, he thought he was about to die, and then…*whap!* Someone or something just blasted him in the back. Jack sucked in air, putrid, stinking air, for what seemed like an eternity.

It was Noah. Noah grabbed Jack under each armpit and moved him a couple of feet away from Leah. Noah rolled her over on her side and…*whap!* That did the trick because she inhaled an enormous amount of air just as Jack had. Jack and Leah both coughed a couple of times and then their breathing became more regular.

"Breathe in and out normally. You'll be used to it in a couple of minutes," Noah encouraged as he walked away. The air was thick. It felt like breathing water vapor in an intense fog. Jack tried not to breathe through his nose so the putrid stench wouldn't make him vomit. He attempted to stand up but fell over on all fours. His legs simply weren't working.

Jack stayed motionless on his hands and knees and started checking off a mental checklist of sorts. His eyes were fine, but everything was red. He could hear, but there wasn't much noise at all. Overall, he actually felt awesome. Another attempt at standing up was successful, and he helped Leah to her feet after she offered her hand to him.

"Are you all right, Leah?" Jack asked. His voice sounded different, but he didn't know how or why. It almost sounded like he was talking into a paper lunch bag.

"Yeah, I think so. Yeah, actually, I feel pretty good. Where is your brother?" Leah asked, and it was like a punch to the stomach. Jack was so concerned about himself and his new crush he had forgotten all about Jacob.

Jack looked frantically in every direction and was about to yell Jacob's name when he saw him. Tears rolled down Jack's face instantly when he realized Jacob was free of his affliction. He was normal. Jacob was walking steadily toward him. Jack was frozen in his place.

"Jacob?" was all Jack could say, and even that one word was a strain with the enormous lump in Jack's throat.

"Hello, Jackson," Jacob whispered in the sweetest, most angelic voice Jack had ever heard. It was exactly the voice Jack envisioned him having in the dream. "Welcome to Niburu." Jacob seemed at ease here, at *home*.

"Hello, Jacob. I've dreamed of this day since I was five," Jack whimpered. "Since the day I was holding you and you almost died." The tears were steadily streaming now. His crying likely didn't win him points with his dream girl, but he didn't care. Jack glanced at Leah, and she was crying harder than he was.

"You know that wasn't your fault. If I could replay that day, I wouldn't have done what I had to do when you were holding me. When I was in your arms, I felt the immense love you had for me, and I knew that if I survived, I would be in good hands with you as a big brother," Jacob explained, and Jack choked up all over again. He loved this boy so much. He would give any-thing, even his life, for him. Jack wiped his tears as Noah, Sebastian, and Mikayla made their way over to the group.

"How's everyone feeling, pretty good?" Noah asked. They all took their own mental inventory and nodded in unison.

"Why is it so hard to walk?" Mikayla asked. Everyone was thinking the same thing. Jack remembered his dream of running in the goo, and that was exactly what it felt like.

"The gravity here is more than double that of Earth. Mikayla, you weigh the equivalent of about two hundred and sixty pounds here. You'll get used to it. It's important now that you breathe deeply to feed your body…it's been through a lot in the past two minutes."

"Just exactly what *did* we go through, and how far away is Earth?" Bass asked. They all leaned in to hear the answer.

"In a nutshell, you were vaporized and put back together element by element, atom by atom, cell by cell. Your soul holds your memories and personal history, even your DNA sequences, so you are basically a whole new and improved you," Noah explained. Jack nodded his head slightly as Noah spoke. He was fully on board now, and would believe anything Noah said or did.

"Earth is a couple of trillion miles away. That is your sun right there," Noah continued, pointing to the sky. They were in a kind of twilight, so they could see a couple of stars. The one Noah pointed to looked like Venus would at twilight on Earth, except this sun looked red. Hell, everything looked red.

"Is this sun setting or rising? And why is everything so red?" Leah asked. Everyone looked in the direction of the light, but had no sense of direction. The star had been just below the horizon since they arrived.

"Neither. Niburu is in a static orbit with the red dwarf sister star of your sun. Ninety-nine percent of this world is uninhabitable. The above-ground Anunnakans live in a roughly five-mile wide swatch of land that encircles the planet. Direct starlight would deliver a lethal dose of radiation, and darkness is close to absolute zero. Niburu is actually only a couple of hundred thousand miles from the star, about as far as your moon is from Earth," Noah explained.

They all looked around in amazement, but no one said a word. They didn't have to. The enormity of what they had just accomplished, traveling to another planet, was not lost on any of them.

"Don't be alarmed at some of the idiosyncrasies you may find on and about your body. You were put back together as your best self. Scars will be gone, your teeth will be straight and perfect, and your hair is how you picture it at its best. But you are still you," Noah reassured them.

Jack was thinking about the return trip home and what it meant for Jacob. "When we go back will Jacob… change back?" he asked. He wasn't sure if he wanted to know the answer.

"Jackson, I will be like this for the rest of my life," Jacob promised in his sweet and pure voice. Jack turned his head to the side and started bawling all over again.

CHAPTER 56

"Could you please turn that thing off, Steven?" General Baker asked. *Icarus* had sounded its alarm no more than a couple of seconds after the group disappeared. It was truly amazing. The scene reminded him of the cloaking device the Predator used in the movie to avoid detection. It was like you could see them for a few moments, but you could also see through them. Then they were gone.

"I guess that answers the question of whether *Icarus* can detect anomalies originating in buildings. We're a hundred feet underground, and it still spotted it," Steven replied as he turned off the alarm and reset the satellite. Steven transferred the data to a monitor and sure enough, the anomaly originated from Silo 9. They had other issues, however, like armed SEALs wanting to destroy them and the bunker.

"Gump! You need to do the right thing here! We are not the enemy!" General Baker yelled in the direction of the elevator. It had been quiet on the other side of the door for several minutes.

"I have my orders, General! You of all people should be able to respect that!" Gump yelled back.

Where the fuck was the press? Baker wondered. He'd called Tom almost a half hour ago.

"It's an unlawful order, Gump! Matthew Nastally is a psychopath! You'll be court martialed and sent to prison for life!" Baker countered. Their only chance was to convince Gump he was doing the wrong thing by following this order because it seemed the press wasn't going to show. "The kid is gone! It's just me and a tech, and we're unarmed! Don't do this!"

"You're lying! We saw you and that group of kids go in there and we know there's only one way out!" Gump yelled, his voice seeming to be a bit farther away than before.

"We need to get behind that panel, Steven. Could you give me a hand? They're about to blow the door," Baker surmised, and he was correct. Just as they reached the safety of the bank of computer monitors, a small explosion blew both doors from their hinges. "Steven, get your hands up and don't say a word," he advised. On the monitor in front of them, he could see a news van crawling up the dirt two-track to the silo. *The cavalry*, Baker thought to himself. Lieutenant Gumper appeared in the doorway with his weapon raised and ready to fire.

"Gump, stop. The kids aren't here. The one you are looking for jumped dimensions with the two he rode with and took three of my people as hostages," Baker explained. "But I think I know where he's going next." If the truth couldn't save him, maybe lies could.

"I'm listening, Baker," Gump answered. The original mission was to capture the kid after all, Gump remembered.

"They're going to Atlanta. Take a look at this monitor and it will explain everything," Baker admitted. Baker explained the silo's purpose and showed Gumper the *Icarus* alarms, especially the one that originated from the silo a few minutes ago. "It can give you their exact location when they return. They will drop, and two minutes later the alarm will go off," Baker continued, staring at Steven as he said *drop* and *two minutes*. Steven knew the alarm would sound immediately, and he easily deciphered Baker's code. He would drop two minutes of latitude from the location of the next anomaly.

"Sounds like a bunch of sci-fi bullshit if you ask me," Gump stated. "Fine, Baker, but you're coming with me." To Gump this was the best and likely only chance to catch the little shit.

"Sorry about the media. You left me no choice," Baker apologized. "I'll tell them we're running a war games exercise." He smiled as he talked, very happy with himself. Not only did he save Steven's life and his own, but he also found a free ride to Atlanta. General Rowland Baker could not wait to get to Atlanta.

CHAPTER 57

Hollis sat in his study mentally kicking himself for not realizing Noah was from another world all those years ago. He would have run more tests. He probably would have dissected Noah to see what made him tick. At the time, Hollis thought Noah was just the typical street orphan who had some amazing parapsychological abilities.

He could understand why the Baker boy would have issue with him, but not Noah. Hollis believed they left on good terms. Noah summoned all that gold and Hollis had been more than willing to cut him in, but he just disappeared, literally. So why was Noah back now?

Hollis had pulled the headpiece out of the rubble shortly after that thing had torn the camp apart. No such luck with the chair and monitor, though. It was likely still in that room, sealed off for all of eternity under the several feet of concrete poured over the site a week later. Hollis tried out the headpiece several times in the ensuing years with no success. He even took acid a couple of times to see if that would help, and it did not. Hollis figured he was simply too old. Chopping off his own family jewels like he had with the little Baker boy was certainly out of the question, even if it would work. He had to draw the line somewhere.

Hollis knew Baker had been searching for him for years, and he came really close once. Baker had flown to Mexico in the summer of 1969 to interview a plastic surgeon, the very same plastic surgeon that performed Hollis's facial reconstruction surgery a year earlier. It didn't matter to Hollis if the doctor had anything meaningful to divulge, as he had sent a young Nordic gentleman to silence him and destroy any evidence.

What Hollis really needed now was a number of new internal organs. The cancer had started in the pancreas, metastasized, and spread to his lungs, liver, and stomach. It was only a matter of time as all the mainstream doctors could do was prescribe narcotics to ease the pain. He even tried holistic medicine and found it so horrific he ordered the cabal to thin their ranks. The Nordic had been very busy lately.

If Noah was truly from another world, perhaps he could offer a cure for Hollis's cancer. If he had the ability to travel interdimensionally, his people certainly would have found a cure for cancer. Noah could name his price, and Hollis would be able to pay it. At current value, he had ten times more gold than the day he'd acquired it despite his penchant for spending money frivolously.

Yes, Hollis would get his cure one way or another. He could kidnap the little brat and the misfits he'd been traveling with. *Even the retarded boy could fetch a handsome price from the right buyer*, he thought. He could torture all of them in ways to cause unimaginable pain. If a cure was out there, they would provide it.

What Hollis really wanted was to force Noah to provide one last thing: answers. Who was he and why was he here? Where was he from? How was he able to freely travel through space and time? Why did he leave so abruptly? The answers to these questions and others had been plaguing Hollis for decades. Yes, Hollis would demand a cure, and he would demand answers in exchange for their lives. The Nordic could make defiance especially painful, so Hollis was sure Noah and his posse would comply.

Hollis would force his will through pain, just as he had his whole life. The trap was set; now he would simply wait for the mice.

CHAPTER 58

"So what's the plan, Noah?" Bass asked as the group started toward the only building in sight. It seemed logical that it was Noah's home. As houses went, it wasn't much to look at. It was a rectangular one-story building with square windows that wrapped around the dwelling about two thirds of the way up to the flat roof, and it had only one door. The door lacked a handle and latch, and it swung easily when Noah tapped it. Upon closer inspection, the windows held neither glass nor screen.

"We're going to stay here for a day and then travel back to Earth," Noah answered as he entered his home and motioned for the others to follow. The main room lacked furnishing of any kind save one high-backed chair and a plain desk made of a type of wood Bass had never seen before. And everything seemed red. There were three rooms off the main room that had the same type of doors with swinging mechanisms that the front door had.

"Aren't you afraid someone will break in?" Mikayla asked, astonished at the utter lack of security.

"No, we don't have that problem here, Mikayla," Noah explained, with a wry smile on his face. "There is no crime here. Look around you…what would someone steal anyway?"

Jack noticed there wasn't a kitchen or dining room, just a plain red desk and a chair.

"Is this where you watch from?" Jack asked.

Sebastian, Mikayla, and Leah looked at Jack and then at each other with a puzzled stare.

"Noah claims he is a Seraph, or a watcher angel, like in the Bible," Jack tried to explain, but it seemed to put them deeper into the abyss of bewilderment.

Jacob spoke next, and there was a certain tension in his voice. "We all need to rest. It is much more taxing to jump from Niburu to Earth than vice versa due to the available trace minerals on Earth. There are three rooms, and the arrangements are flexible as you are all adults. Noah and I will stay in this room as we have much to discuss."

Jack had to remind himself that his brother had the knowledge of the universe in that adorable little head of his. He had a myriad of questions, but would give him some space for now. The girls looked at each other, and the boys did likewise.

"Sebastian and I will take the room on the left, then," Mikayla offered as she took Bass's hand and led him away. The touch of her skin on his sent a fresh wave of chill down his spine and once again started the blood pumping below his belt.

This might be the night I've dreamed about, Bass thought as a whole new set of worries entered his mind. *Would I do it right? Would she like it? Would I last long enough? Oh my God, I can't do this!* he thought. Bass followed her lead, regardless of his misgivings concerning being an adequate lover.

"Maybe we could go for a walk?" Jack asked Leah, hoping he could get to know her better. He was more mesmerized by Leah as he was of the new Jacob, and that felt inherently wrong, but he couldn't change how he felt, and he didn't want to.

"I would really like that, Jack," Leah replied while looking directly into his eyes.

God, she's beautiful, Jack thought. Jack tenderly took Leah's hand in his, and they headed for the door.

"Don't stray too far," Noah warned. "You may not be able to find your way back, and this can be a scary place for the uninitiated." They promised they would remain close and walked out the door together.

"They make a cute couple," Noah said to Jacob. "It's fortunate they are attracted to each other. It will make it a lot easier for Jack to kill Hollis Carrington if he thinks he is protecting Leah."

"Yes, very fortunate indeed," Jacob replied sarcastically. "You and I both know you had a hand in their mutual attraction. I know Jack, and the *real* Jack would never be smitten this way, and so soon. The Jack I know would be fawning over *me* right now, not a girl he just met."

"It was necessary for the mission, Jacob. You do realize that, don't you?" Noah asked.

"If you say so."

CHAPTER 59

"I can tell you love your brother very much, and he just adores you," Leah offered, finally breaking the silence that had almost gotten to the point of becoming awkward.

"He is my whole life, the reason I get up in the morning. Ever since our parents died, I have been his sole caretaker," Jack explained. *It really was like having a full-time job*, he thought.

"You should win an award or something. There aren't many teenagers who would make that sacrifice, Jack. I don't know if I could. Surely a handsome guy like you has a significant other back in Michigan to ease the burden," she asked, fishing for clues concerning his love life.

"There is a girl that helps me a lot with Jacob, but she is definitely not a significant other. I never had time to pursue a relationship," Jack clarified as they slowly walked toward the source of the red light. Leah's heart sank when Jack mentioned the girl in his life and then leaped when he stated he wasn't interested in her romantically.

"Well, now that Jacob is…*cured*, or whatever he is, you can find time to find some happiness for yourself."

"I don't know where I would even start to look," Jack joked, sporting a wry smile.

Leah squeezed his hand and spun herself into Jack's arms. He didn't resist.

"I've never felt this way about anyone, Jack. It's almost as if I'm under a spell or something, or in a dream."

"I feel the same way. When we were driving to Iowa, Noah asked me to picture my 'perfect woman,' and an image of you popped in my head. When I saw you for the first time at the silo, I couldn't believe my eyes," Jack confessed. They were both thinking Noah may have had an influence on their sudden and mutual attraction.

"Well, I for one don't really care. Maybe that's part of his watcher job, you know, helping people fall in love. Not that I'm in love with you. I mean…" Leah sputtered before Jack thankfully cut her off.

"I know what you mean, Leah. Why don't we head back? Let's just take this slow, you know, and see what happens," Jack advised, Leah still in his arms. He wanted to kiss her so badly. It was Leah who leaned in and kissed Jack firmly on the lips and then open mouthed.

"If you say so…" Leah whispered.

CHAPTER 60

Bass was a bundle of nerves as Mikki led him to the privacy of the room on the left. She could sense his apprehension and tried to set him at ease.

"Sweetie? You're working yourself up over absolutely nothing. Even if nothing happens here, I am committed to you, Sebastian. Nothing you say, do, or don't do will change the way I feel about you," Mikayla promised.

Bass finally started breathing normally again but was still extremely anxious.

"Thank you, Mick. I think I'm just putting a lot of pressure on myself," Bass explained as the door swung back and shut behind them. There were two of the square windows in this room, and they faced the light source so they could see fairly well.

It'd probably be better if it were dark, Bass thought.

"Their windows don't even have glass in them, Mikki. Anyone could stick their head in here and see what's going on," Bass exclaimed. He was a nervous wreck again. "What if we make noise? Everyone will know what we're doing," he worried, obviously out of sorts, even for Bass.

"Then let's just lie down and get some rest then, Bass. I want to fall asleep in your arms, though," Mikayla conceded. She didn't want to force Sebastian into anything he wasn't ready for. Maybe it would take some time to get him comfortable around her sexually, but it would be worth it in the long run, she thought. He was worth it.

"Ok. There isn't even a bed. What kind of accommodations are these, anyway?" Bass asked as they both laughed at the sparseness of the room. There was nothing in the room, not even a lamp.

"I'm not going to leave the maid a tip!" Mikki promised as they both continued to chuckle at the thought of Noah in a maid's uniform. Once the laughter subsided, Mikayla sat down with her back to the wall with a window directly above her and motioned for Sebastian to join her. She spread her legs outward so he could sit between them, his back to her.

"Take your shirt off. I'll try to rub some of the tension out of your neck. These fingers can do magic, you know," Mikki promised as Bass removed his one hundred percent cotton tee. The warmth of her hands and the strength of her fingers melted the stress from Bass's back and neck. He put one hand on each of her thighs and began to gently massage them.

"That feels great, Mikki. You're right, you have magic fingers," Sebastian whispered, his eyes closed. Mikayla removed her own shirt and leaned him back into her bosom. She reached around him and began to massage his chest and stomach. Bass did not resist.

The feeling of Mikki's bare skin against his back was more than Bass could stand. He could feel her firm breasts pressing against him, and he had to see them. Sebastian slowly turned until they were sitting knee to knee. Her breasts were beautiful, her nipples rosy and taut. He raised his hand slowly.

"May I?" Bass asked.

"Please," Mikki sighed. "I want you, Sebastian, right here and now," she whispered into his ear as she nibbled on his left ear lobe. Sebastian cupped her breasts and began gently rubbing his thumbs across her nipples. She leaned in for a kiss that started at his lips and trailed down to his neck.

"I want you too." He was ready. He was in a strange red world in a barren room with no privacy, but he was ready. "You'll have to help me." Mikayla turned and lay on her back, removed her sweatpants with one hand, dispatched Bass's bottoms with the other, and pulled him on top of her.

Mikki guided Bass's manhood into her, but something wasn't right.

"Stop!" Mikki blurted out, alarmed and deeply concerned about something.

"What? Am I hurting you?" Bass asked. He knew he was above average in size when comparing in the locker room, but he didn't think he was so big that he would hurt a girl with it.

"No. You're great. It's me. I think I…I think I'm…" Mikki stuttered. "I think I'm a virgin again!" she exclaimed. She checked down there and sure enough, she once again had an intact hymen.

"Remember what Noah said? We were put back together as the best and likely original version of ourselves," Bass remembered. A quick check of his own equipment filled him with more curiosity than surprise. "It seems I'm not circumcised any longer, not that it really matters to me." It was just something he would have to get used to, he guessed.

"This *is* going to be special," Mikki whispered as she guided Bass back into her. Bass took her newly recovered virginity with an initial thrust, and Mikki gasped at the familiar sting. Sebastian hesitated, but Mikki pulled him in deeper and ground her hips against him. Within seconds, his mind and member exploded.

"Oh, no. I'm so sorry, Mikki. I ruined it," Bass mumbled dejectedly. Mikki put her finger to his lips.

"Shhhh," Mikki whispered. "It was perfect because I lost my virginity to you, and that means everything to me. My *first* first time was nothing special, and I've always regretted it. This time it is real, because this time it is with you," she said with heartfelt emotion and tears in her eyes. Mikki kissed him deeply, and they were lost in each other again, mouths and hands exploring. To his astonishment, Sebastian realized he was hard again. Mikki smiled.

"Let me do all the work, Bass. You just enjoy the ride," she whispered as she straddled him and gave him a little wink. "Try distracting yourself by counting backward from one hundred, or recite pi to triple digits…it should help." As she leaned in for a kiss, she drove back into him and found the right rhythm.

Both of them did indeed enjoy the ride.

CHAPTER 61

Wen Jack and Leah returned to Noah's "house,"
they found Noah and Jacob where they had left
them, though now they were sitting cross-legged and facing each other, their eyes closed. It looked as if they were
sleeping, or at least in a deep trance, so they decided not
to bother them.

"I can sleep in this room if you would be more comfortable," Jack said, motioning toward the middle of the
three rooms.

"That's nonsense, Jack. I'm in a strange red world. I
would be much more comfortable with you in the same
room with me. And I want to say something we both are
thinking: I want to get to know you better before anything sexual happens. I'm *really* into you, and my body
says 'jump your bones,' but my brain is saying, 'Whoa,
slow down, girl.' You know what I mean?"

"Thank you." Jack let out an audible sigh of relief.
"Yes, I feel the exact same way, but I don't think we
should rush into anything. I want to take the route that
leads to a relationship, not a one-nighter." Jack almost
told her he was a virgin but decided it wasn't the right

time. The closest he'd come to intercourse was the "high school handie" Lisa Covington gave him last year. His pecker hurt like hell for a week, but he enjoyed it at the time.

"Well, you really know how to say the right thing, don't you Jack?" Leah replied as she took his hand and led him to their sleeping quarters. As the door swung shut, they were shocked by the lack of furnishings, the lack of *anything*.

"What the hell? Where is the bed? Maybe we should try the other room?"

"I'm sure it's just as empty as this one. Let's just lie on the floor," Leah offered as she squatted down and tugged on Jack's arm as an invitation to join her. Just thinking about sleeping next to the most beautiful girl he had ever met was getting him excited, which was extremely difficult to hide given the sweatpants with no underwear. He sat down but kept his knees bent.

"Whatever you say, but I'm talking to the manager in the morning and demanding my money back," Jack replied as he lay down on his back, offering his right arm for Leah to rest her head on. He continued to keep his knees bent out of necessity.

"You're a funny man, Jackson Wheaton, and I like that about you," Leah stated as she rested her head on Jack's arm. They lay there for some time in total peace enjoying each other's company before Jack broke the silence.

"I'm scared. I'm scared for Jacob. He's just a thirteen-year-old boy, and I think something bad is going to happen," Jack confessed, tears welling up in both of his eyes.

Leah turned her head to look at Jack and saw the anguish on his face.

"I don't think you have anything to worry about, Jack. Look at it this way: Noah has gone to some pretty fantastical extremes to go after this Carrington guy. I think he has found a way to take care of his business with Carrington, so the only person getting hurt is Carrington himself."

"I guess you have a point. But why does he need Jacob? Of all the people in the world, he has to go after this piece of shit with my baby brother?"

"I think Jacob will surprise you, Jack. I think he can take care of himself," Leah explained. That brought up a whole new round of worries for Jack.

"So you don't think he will need me anymore? I've taken care of him and protected him his whole life."

"That's not what I meant. Jacob will always need you, and you will always need Jacob. It's the way brotherhood works." Leah wanted to kick herself for saying Jacob could take care of himself.

"If anyone tries to harm Jacob, or you, or *anyone*, I will definitely take care of them, I promise you that," Jack replied as anger welled up inside of him.

"I'm sure you will, Jack. Now let's get some sleep. It's going to be a big day tomorrow," Leah stated as she lay her head back down on Jack's arm.

Jack and Leah fell asleep at the exact same time. As a matter fact, Jack, Leah, Sebastian, and Mikayla *all* fell asleep at exactly the same time.

CHAPTER 62

The light was white and blinding, a sharp contrast to the meager red aura of Niburu. But where was he? The last thing Jack remembered was lying next to Leah and closing his eyes. Was he dreaming? A quick pinch to the thigh felt like a hornet's sting. No, he didn't seem to be dreaming.

"Hello, Jack," a voice came from behind him. Although he had heard this voice only twice in his life, he knew exactly who it was: Jacob.

"Hi, Jacob," Jack sighed. The fact that Jacob was free of his self-imposed prison still hadn't completely sunk in. "Where are we?"

"The world of the subconscious is limitless. Your body is technically asleep, but your soul is always active, and on Niburu even more so," Jacob explained. Due to the events of the past twenty-four hours, Jack couldn't doubt anything anymore.

"So I'm dreaming?" Jack asked.

"More like an out-of-body experience, Jack. You will remember this just as you would any waking memory, and that will be very important. Follow me. The others are this way," Jacob explained as he motioned for Jack to follow him. Sure enough, the whole group was there: Sebastian, Mikayla, Leah, and Noah. They seemed to be waiting for them.

"Is anyone else weirded out about this?" Jack asked to no one in particular. Everyone except Noah and Jacob nodded and shrugged in unison. Jack walked over to Leah and took her hand in his. "Hello, Leah," Jack whispered. She was just as beautiful in this dream as she was in real life.

"Hi, Jack," Leah whispered in his ear as she gave him a peck on the cheek.

"Jacob and I are going to acquaint all of you with our target, Dr. Hollis Carrington. We will accomplish this by using a technique called 'remote viewing' on Earth," Noah explained as the intensely bright light dimmed to the point of almost total darkness. Planets started whizzing by at dizzying speeds, first Pluto, Uranus and Neptune, then Saturn and Jupiter, and finally Venus. As the Earth appeared, the breakneck speed slowed considerably. It was almost as if a movie were playing all around them.

"Is this how you do your job as a Watcher?" Mikayla asked.

"Yeah, I guess you could say that," Noah replied matter-of-factly.

"How is this even working?" Sebastian asked.

"Jacob is controlling the session," Noah replied. The group looked at Jacob and saw that his eyes were closed and he seemed to be asleep. The image of the Earth rotated so the United States was visible, and the image continued to enlarge. The Deep South became Georgia, and then the city of Atlanta appeared.

"Dr. Hollis Carrington, or Dr. Christian Lomax, as he is known now, is one of the evilest individuals ever to walk the Earth. Over the course of Earth's history, we have occasionally felt the need to intervene for the benefit of humankind," Noah explained. "The most notable times being what the Bible would describe as Great Flood and the Tower of Babel, and also during the infancy of the United States of America. We have never removed an individual human from Earth until now."

Jack had so many questions he didn't know where to start. "What exactly did he do to deserve the death penalty, and is he really worse than Hitler? The man took out millions of Jews and you didn't touch him?" he asked. Jack was thinking about all the evil humans over the course of history that the world would have been better off without. People like Nero, Genghis Khan, Ivan the Terrible, and Pol Pot.

"It's interesting you would mention Hitler. Carrington is much like Adolph Hitler. The man's soul is rotten, so extremely corrupted it is now considered unsalvageable. He is to be entombed forever with the other degenerate." Noah explained.

"And who might that be?" Bass asked.

"You know him as Satan. Satan is an Anunnakan, like us," Noah replied, motioning to himself and Jacob.

"Oh…*Satan*. The devil. So you are going to send Carrington straight to hell?" Bass asked. As an avowed atheist, Bass didn't believe a single word of the Bible before today. In light of recent events, his paradigm has shifted considerably, though.

"There is no such place as hell, Sebastian. Satan has been confined to the gold transport we started moving back at the silo, and he will stay there forever. Tomorrow, he will have company. There is no escape. He would have to be the closest Anunnaki soul to a fertilized Anunnaki egg *and* the transport would have to be powered up. Since all babies are manufactured here on Niburu as needed, that would be impossible, and the transport hasn't been powered up for over two thousand years. Even if he did, we would realize it and simply confine him here for his natural life, then send his soul back into exile," Noah explained.

"Isn't Jacob's soul Anunnakan?" Jack asked Noah somberly.

"That was a fluke. It won't happen again," Noah replied sharply, sounding irritated at the question.

"So what has this Dr. Carrington done that is so evil?" Mikayla asked.

"He is the leader and chief financier of a cabal that is assassinating homeopathic doctors across the world. The next major breakthrough in medicine will come from a doctor in this field, and we find it necessary to remove Carrington to protect her. The cabal will subsequently die with the death of Dr. Carrington," Noah promised. The room was darkening as the focus was now on a mansion somewhere north of downtown Atlanta. The image magnified until the setting stabilized and the group was standing in the front yard of 16 Parkside Lane.

"That was incredible!" Leah exclaimed. They were all in awe concerning how real this mirage seemed.

"Let's go inside," Noah said as he led them toward the home. Instead of knocking on the front door, Noah simply walked through it, and the others followed.

"So…is this an image of the house inside Jacob's head?" Jack asked Noah incredulously. Jack knew Jacob had never been to this place, but the details were unbelievable.

"No, Jack. We are actually here at this place, at this time. Jacob has simply led us here. Our souls can travel without our bodies, Jack. In your dream last night you actually visited Jacob on Niburu, and then your soul was returned immediately when the lightning struck. If any of your bodies were to wake up on Niburu right now, your souls would zip back in an instant," Noah explained. "Have you ever heard of ghosts? Right now, you are all like ghosts: souls without bodies."

The entryway was empty, but a voice could be heard nearby. Noah led them toward the conversation.

"This is Dr. Hollis Carrington, the man who has been condemned to death for all of eternity," Noah announced, sounding like he was reading a guilty verdict at a murder trial. The man Noah motioned toward was talking on the phone. Although the group was no more than five feet from Carrington, none of his words could be deciphered. He sounded like the teacher in the old Charlie Brown cartoons.

"Is he talking in a foreign language or something?" Bass asked. They were all thinking the same thing.

"No. When you are remotely viewing scenes, all noise is simply that: noise. This is not a perfect system. Think of it this way: your actual ears aren't here to properly decipher the sound waves," Noah explained. At that moment, Carrington abruptly stopped his conversation and looked directly at the group.

"Can he see us?" Leah asked, slightly freaked out. Jack held her hand a little tighter and pulled her to his side.

"Not likely, but different people are able to see different ghosts. Carrington most likely feels our presence," Noah explained as he walked over to Carrington and abruptly swung his foot upward into Carrington's crotch. "That's for Rowland, you piece of shit," he continued as the others chuckled at the childish act. Noah's foot simply went right through Carrington's body without connecting with anything.

"Why didn't you simply take this guy out when you were here in the sixties?" Jack asked. Bass, Mikayla, and Leah looked puzzled. "Oh yeah, Noah claims he is over a hundred years old, by the way." That didn't help the group's confusion. Carrington, meanwhile, continued on with his conversation.

"When I was here in the sixties, I was on a reconnaissance mission. I was to secure the transportation device, secure our gold, and dispatch it up to the cargo ship. The problem arose when the ship would not respond. I decided to leave the gold and the device in Carrington's possession until human technology would allow me start up the ship and deliver the gold."

"Well, you should have taken out Carrington at that time if you knew he was so evil," Bass chided.

"I can't kill a human, even a despicable one, and neither can Jacob. At the time he wasn't about to set back human medicine, and humanity itself, by decades, either." Noah explained. "The girls will be able to handle Hollis Carrington." Leak and Mikayla, suddenly with loathsome looks on their faces, spoke up at the same time.

"I'm not going to kill him!" they said in unison. They were sweet and innocent, incapable of murder, Jack thought.

"Neither of you will actually kill him. You will hopefully lead him to make decisions that cause his own death. I will explain your parts in detail later. I just wanted to bring you here to see the house and to get a look at Carrington," Noah made clear. The expression on Mikki and Leah's faces was one of distrust.

"Can we see the gold? How much is there? Several thousand ounces at least, right?" Bass asked. Growing up poor, he'd always dreamed of treasure chests at the end of rainbows.

"Hah! Try over a *hundred million* ounces. Noah stole all of the gold in Fort Knox, Sebastian." Jack proclaimed.

Bass did some quick multiplication in his head and figured there were about a quarter million bars of gold worth upwards of two hundred billion dollars.

"I want to see it," Bass demanded. He thought of all the things one bar of gold could purchase, not to mention hundreds of thousands of bars.

"Follow me," Noah advised as he began walking toward the back of the home and then simply disappeared through the far wall. The others followed single file and exited in the same manner, following Noah to a barn-like outbuilding.

"This is why Jacob is here, Jack. Jacob will secure the gold while I am dealing with Carrington. The wild card in the equation is your government and how they feel about getting what they may think is theirs back," Noah explained.

"Pretty good idea, hiding the gold in plain sight," Jack commended. Upon closer inspection, the "barn" was made of at least one-inch thick steel panels held in place by one-inch rivets every six inches. It looked like the side of an ocean liner. The entrance was a swinging vault door controlled by both fingerprint and retinal scan. "How are you going to get the gold out? This looks harder to get into than Fort Knox itself. Carrington would have to open the door, and you know he won't do that," Jack asked.

"The gold isn't going out. The gold is going up, Jack," Noah explained. They all looked at each other and then remembered the device Noah was talking about. "Well, if you want to see it, walk on in!" Noah exclaimed. Jack, Leah, Bass, and Mikayla walked through the steel wall and were amazed by what they saw: a veritable mountain of gold.

"Holy shit!" Bass exclaimed. The mountain was thirty feet long by twenty feet wide and almost twenty feet high. The group could see where Carrington made withdrawals, but if that was all he'd used, he hadn't even made a dent in the pile. "Each one of those bars is worth about six hundred grand," Bass stated in awe.

"It's time to go," Noah said solemnly, breaking them all out of their gold-induced trance. In a matter of seconds, the group backtracked through space, past all of the planets, and back to Niburu where they were sleeping. And almost immediately thereafter, each of them woke at the same time thinking the same thing: that was a *shitload* of gold.

CHAPTER 63

"You know, Brady, you don't have to follow illegal orders," Baker stated. He wanted to get Gumper talking and thinking about how idiotic his boss was.

"Do you want me to throw you out of this helicopter?" Gumper replied. Baker didn't think he was kidding.

"I'm just saying, think about what you are doing and what you are being told to do. It's not right, and you know it." Rowland looked out the window. Cars looked like crawling ants, so it would be a rather long drop should Gump indeed give him a nudge.

"There is nothing you can say that is going to save your hide, Baker. The only reason you are still alive is the fact that you can find the kid when he comes back. And you better not be fucking with me!" Lt. Gumper was getting agitated, and that was not what Baker had intended.

"Settle down, Gump. I'm on your side. I want the kid too. Christ, he took most of my crew from the silo. I'm just saying that killing him, or me, or any of us is not the answer. It's not what the United States military does. We serve our country and protect her freedom, not shoot and kill kids."

"These are not normal times, though. There are bad people out there, General, and you know it. We are now in a 'shoot first and ask questions later' age, unfortunately. *And,* you and I both know that is not a normal kid," Gump responded.

At least he's calmed down a bit, thought Baker.

"I get it, but not in this case. Nastally has it wrong. The kid is not the enemy we think he is, and he means us no harm. He is here to fight the real enemy, his and ours," Baker suggested, trying not to be too specific. Rowland really needed to keep Gumper from shooting everything in sight if there was a confrontation.

"All I know is that Nastally is adamant about stopping this kid and I have been given the green light for the use of lethal force on anyone or anything that gets in the way, including you."

"Well, I want to talk to Nastally when we get to Dobbins," Baker replied. Talking sense into that man would be like talking to a wall, but he had to give it a try. "Just promise me you will keep an open mind and really *think* before you pull that trigger, would you please?"

Gump just stared at him without blinking for what seemed like an eternity before replying. "*If* there is a way to contain the boy without using lethal force, I will consider it. If I feel he is any threat at all, he's going down along with anyone else that stands in the way."

At least I got him to think about it, Baker thought. "That is all I ask. And I want the opportunity to talk him down and bring him in peacefully," he said, pressing the issue.

"That's not going to happen. You're going in the brig at Dobbins until I figure out what to do with you. You're going to give me the coordinates when your boy in Iowa calls and then both of you are out of the loop. Period. You have nothing to bargain with here, Baker." Gump was getting himself all worked up all over again.

"Yeah, fine. I told you I'm on your side, Brady. I'll do exactly what you want me to do," Baker replied, trying to defuse the situation one more time. The fact of the matter was this: one way or another, Rowland had to break out of Dobbins.

CHAPTER 64

When Jack woke up for the second time, he was where he expected: lying next to the most beautiful girl he had ever seen. No remote viewing mind trips this time, just good old-fashioned reality.

"Good morning, sunshine," Jack whispered excitedly as Leah opened her eyes. "Did you sleep all right?" He could definitely see himself waking up with her at his side every morning.

"Miraculously well. I feel completely rested," Leah replied. Even the increased gravity seemed to have less effect on her, and she felt lighter. In the adjacent room, Bass and Mikayla woke up together as well.

"I had a great time last night, Sebastian," Mikayla said as she rolled to her side and put her left hand on Bass's cheek.

"I did too. Wasn't that remote viewing trip amazing?" Bass replied, smiling. Mikki gave his face a little slap and backed away. "I'm kidding, Mikki! You know that was the best night of my life so far." Bass sat up and placed his hand on her bare stomach. "I don't know the correct protocol for this, but I think I love you, Mikayla," he blurted out. Mikayla took his hand in hers and squeezed it.

"No one has ever told me that before, not a foster parent, not a friend, no one. I think I love you too, Sebastian." She had tears welling up in her eyes.

"Hey, it's ok. Look, we'll always have each other," Bass reassured her. "I won't let anything happen to you, or us, or Leah, or even Jack and Jacob. Tomorrow, we'll be able to start the rest of our lives together."

"I'm just afraid. I finally have someone great in my life, and I'm afraid I'm going to lose you," she explained as Bass tenderly wiped her tears, her sobs subsiding.

"Look, don't ask me why, but I think these kids are going to keep us safe. We just have to help them any way we can. Come on, let's get dressed and get this over with."

Bass and Mikki walked into the main room just as Jack and Leah appeared. Leah looked at Mikki and raised her eyebrows. Mikki stuck her hand behind Sebastian's back and held up two fingers, and they both started giggling.

"Good morning, all. I trust you slept well?" Jacob asked. They all nodded in agreement that they had indeed slept well. Jack wasn't sure who exactly was in charge here, Noah or Jacob, but he supposed it didn't really matter.

"We're going to leave soon, so gather around. It's time to go over the plan," Noah stated emphatically. Jack got his answer: it looked like Noah was still in charge.

CHAPTER 65

"Here we go! It's game time!" Steven exclaimed to no one. The light started its circular travels about ten seconds before the siren went this time, but Steven didn't think much of it.

"Let's find out where they are…" he said out loud to himself. Steven treated OSCAR like a real person, so he didn't find it odd at all that he talked to him. "Ok, OSCAR, where are they?" he asked, tapping on the keyboard of the main control panel. An image of the earth came up on the main viewing screen and began to enlarge the Deep South.

"You guys are in Georgia, huh?" All right, let's get the exact coordinates, OSCAR." Steven switched to street maps for the moment because he was utterly unfamiliar with the area.

"Holy shit, they're practically in downtown Atlanta!" The red *X* finally appeared on his map, and he studied it for almost two minutes. They were in a neighborhood called Tuxedo Park, and a quick Google search told him that it was the wealthiest area in Atlanta. The red *X* was entirely enclosed by a swimming pool in the backyard of a rather swanky home.

"What to do…what to do…" Steven said to himself. He would have to call within the next couple of minutes. Then he saw it! The governor's mansion was almost directly south of the landing spot. Steven made a couple of quick calculations and picked up the phone.

"This is General Baker, Steven. You are on speaker-phone," Baker explained from the other end of the line.

"Yes, sir. An alarm came *up* exactly one minute and thirty-five seconds ago, sir. There really is no need to give you coordinates because they landed at the governor's mansion in North Atlanta. Tuxedo Park, actually." He hoped he hadn't stressed the word "up" too long. He didn't. General Baker knew the landing site was actually one minute and thirty-five seconds of latitude north of the mansion, or approximately a mile and a half.

"Great work, Steven. Now don't go anywhere. We will need you at the bunker to provide updates. Get satellite coverage and try to track the group," Baker ordered, stressing the word "don't" exactly as Steven had stressed the word "up." Steven knew exactly what to do: get the hell out of Dodge.

"Thank you, sir. I'll do exactly that. You can count on me." He didn't know where he would go, but west sounded good. Baker and Jack had the satellite phone number, so he would take that with him, powered down for now, of course. Steven had never hitchhiked before, but he was actually looking forward to the adventure.

"Adios, OSCAR!" Steven exclaimed as he took the stairs two by two to the top of the silo.

CHAPTER 66

"You have to take me now, Gump. Even you won't be able to fly the Chinook over downtown Atlanta and land on the governor's front lawn," General Baker advised Lt. Gumper.

He's right, Gump thought. *That would be out of the question.*

"Fine, Baker. Get suited up. We leave in five minutes."

"I'll just wear what I have on now," Rowland replied, alluding to the sweatsuit he had changed into at the silo. "But I'm going to need a sidearm and a pack, too." A pack would contain the survival gear that Rowland would need if he had an opportunity to put *his* plan into action. He knew Gump would never give him a gun, but it was worth a try.

"Wear what you want, but a sidearm is not gonna happen, old man. And let me tell you another thing: one false move and a bullet will be deposited into your head to match the one in your shoulder, and I mean it," Gump warned. Even taking Baker with them was risky, but if things went south, he could simply eliminate all of them at once and then send someone back for the little loud-mouth prick at the silo, Gump thought. Problem solved.

"Then at least give me a knife and a pack. You just said yourself that I was an old man. I'm no match for you or your team, but if I get close to your perp, I can take him out with a knife." Baker countered. Gumper thought for a moment and conceded.

"I'll give you a pack, that's all. There is a jackknife in it. If you think you can stick the kid with it, you be my guest. If you try to stick me or one of my men with it, that will be the last thing you ever do on this earth, do you understand me?" Gump warned. *Baker is about as little of a threat as there can be*, Gumper thought as he grabbed a survival pack from under the front seat of the Chinook. He tossed it to Baker reluctantly.

"Thank you, Gump. You won't regret this. I'm going to hit the head before we leave," Baker said as he stuck each arm through the corded loops attached to the pack and wore the survival gear like a backpack. Once in the bathroom, he locked the door and rifled through the gear until he found what he needed.

"I hope I'm doing the right thing here…" Baker whispered to himself. Part of him thought he was, and the other part thought he was crazy as he opened the largest blade of the jackknife. The two-inch incision he made in his scrotum didn't hurt much, but it bled a lot. Baker calmly removed the aluminum ball bearings Dr. Carrington had implanted all those years ago and dropped them in the toilet. "Bye-bye, balls," he whispered as he flushed the commode and watched them get whisked away by the whirlpool of water and blood.

"Come on, Baker!" Lt. Gumper screamed from just outside the door, making Rowland flinch.

"I'm taking a dump, Gump! Just like a thoroughbred before a big race!" The iodine he applied stung something fierce, but it actually helped with the bleeding. A half a roll of gauze and several pieces of tape later and Baker thought he could manage to walk and not bleed to death. He exited the bathroom and joined the rest of the group in an unmarked black SUV.

"You feel better, Baker?" Gump asked.

"You know what? Yes, I do. I feel like a weight…no, make that *two* weights have been lifted," Rowland replied as the van started toward the governor's house.

CHAPTER 67

Noah had warned them that the trip back could be very difficult, and he was correct. Jack could feel that he was himself but could not see, talk, touch, or smell anything. This state continued for what seemed like an eternity, and then finally he was just there, ten feet above a pool in some unsuspecting person's backyard, just hovering, oblivious to the laws of physics. He was holding Jacob's hand on his left and Leah's hand on his right. Noah, Sebastian, and Mikayla were across from him.

And then…*sploosh!* They all fell at the same time into the swimming pool, and Mikayla missed the edge by mere inches. They were all thankfully in the deep end, so no one rammed into the bottom. Jack stayed under for several seconds and then surfaced. One by one, the others appeared. Noah shot up first, then Sebastian, then finally Jacob and Mikayla. Leah was nowhere to be found.

"Where is Leah?" Jack frantically asked. The group looked at each other and then down into the water. Leah was lying on the bottom.

"No!" Jack yelled as he took a deep breath and dove beneath the surface. A good swimmer, he had no problem getting to Leah, scooped her up, and kicked off of the bottom to surface. Sebastian was already out of the water.

"Bring her over here, Jack!" Sebastian shouted as he reached out to grab Leah's motionless body from Jack. Jack handed her off and pulled himself out of the water.

"No, no, no, no…" Jack stammered. He was shaking and tears had started to stream down his face. *I can't lose her now*, he thought. "Does anyone know CPR?" Jack asked frantically, looking around at the group with the hope that someone would step forward.

"I do, Jack. Just give me a moment," Bass answered as he checked her carotid for a pulse. There wasn't one.

"Move aside, Sebastian, and let Jacob take a look at her," Noah stated in his trademark calm and serene manner. Bass released his fingers from Leah's neck and stood up. Jacob went to his knees next to Leah and looked up at Noah, who nodded some sort of approval. Jacob next placed his forefinger and middle finger just beneath Leah's left breast, directly over her heart.

"That's not how you do it, Jacob!" Jack bawled. Jack didn't know much about CPR but knew more than two fingers were used while administering chest compressions.

Jacob was undeterred by Jack's lack of confidence. While his two fingers were over Leah's heart, he leaned over and blew one large breath into her mouth. The others watched as Leah's chest rose as he blew. When her chest was fully expanded, her whole body jerked as if by electrical stimulation. Leah immediately clenched her fists, turned on her left side, and coughed up a great deal of water. Everyone let out an audible sigh of relief.

"You're a pretty good kisser, Jacob," Leah said, her voice still raspy from the coughing. Jacob smiled and backed off so Jack could take his place by her side.

"Are you all right? Oh, thank God, you are all right," Jack moaned, still teary-eyed.

"Yeah, I'm fine. That was one hell of a trip!" Leah exclaimed as she attempted to stand up and get her sea legs back. A quick survey of the yard revealed a girl, maybe seven or eight years of age, sitting on a swing overlooking the pool. She had apparently seen everything.

"How's that for a magic trick, darling!" Bass shouted out to the girl. They all stared at the little girl awaiting her reply, each hoping she wouldn't run away screaming for her parents.

"I've seen better, but what is wrong with your eyes?" the girl replied nonchalantly. The group looked at each other and just then realized all of their eyes were completely black.

CHAPTER 68

The route to the governor's mansion from Dobbins was a straight shot down I-75, fifteen miles at the most. Daylight had faded to dusk, and Gumper was driving like a bat out of hell.

"We'll be there in less than ten minutes," Gump announced. "Any word from the squirrely kid at the silo about where they went after they arrived?"

"There's no answer, sir," one of the team members informed Gump. "But I'll keep trying."

"You wouldn't have anything to do with him not answering, would you, Baker?" Gump asked.

Of course I did, you piece of crap, thought Rowland. *The more pressing issue will be escaping the SEALs and somehow traveling a mile and a half north.*

"You're paranoid, Gump. How many times do I have to tell you that we're on the same team?" Steven was miles from the silo by now, or so he hoped. Baker thought Nastally might possibly call in an air strike, but that would be pretty risky given the civilians in close proximity to the silo. No, if they intended to take Steven out, they would send a team.

"The mansion is just ahead. Ready your coms and prepare to execute a standard perimeter search," Gump announced. "Baker, you come with me."

"It would be my pleasure, Lieutenant Gumper!" Rowland exclaimed, feigning interest in helping him in any way. *How do I escape from a highly trained and trigger-happy soldier?* Baker thought.

The SUV came to a stop in front of the house, and security met them to check credentials. Of course, Gump lied about the real reason they were there.

"We have a report of heavily armed and dangerous fugitives in the area. My men and I will handle the search ourselves, so please go in the house and stay there," Gump ordered. "Fan out, men!" he exclaimed, and his men jumped out of the SUV and began the search. Baker noticed the keys were unbelievably still in the ignition. "Come on, Baker!" Gump shouted as he scurried toward the west side of the mansion.

Minutes into the manhunt, a sound could be heard in the distance, an ominous low rumble that was getting increasingly though rather slowly louder. Gump's men stopped their search and gathered in a clearing about fifty yards behind the residence.

"You've gotta see this, Gump!" one of the men shouted, pointing up into the darkening sky. The rumble was still increasing, and Gump could feel it as well as hear it.

"Come on, Baker, double time!" Gump said as he started running to the clearing where his men stood gawking at the sky. When he got there, Brady couldn't believe his eyes. Something seemed to be entering Earth's atmosphere from the south. Billowing clouds of smoke were backlit by the object's entry burn. Gump and his men just stared in amazement as the object seemed to be coming right toward them.

If my men and I can see this, so can everyone else, and that could present a huge problem, Gump thought.

"What do you make of that, Baker? Baker? *Baker!*" Gump called out. Rowland Baker was nowhere to be seen. "Goddammit! Fan out and find Baker!" Gump ordered. Moments later, Gump and his men could hear the engine of the SUV gunning and its tires squealing as it obviously sped out the driveway with General Baker presumably at the wheel. Gump raised his Glock to the firing position but unfortunately didn't have a clear shot.

The aerial anomaly had thankfully ceased its rumbling, but it was too dark and too high in the sky to see anything. Whatever it was, it was now in Earth's atmosphere. Gump had a feeling this UFO, or whatever it was, had something to do with the group of kids he was after, and he was absolutely right.

CHAPTER 69

"Yeah, Noah, what's wrong with our eyes?" Jack asked sarcastically. Noah never did explain why his eyes were completely black when he arrived at the house.

"We're not entirely sure, Jack. It only occurs when traveling from Niburu, though. The eyes are a miraculous organ made up of very specialized cells. They will gradually return to normal within a couple of hours. We need to get moving. The sooner we get this over with, the better." They all said their goodbyes to their new friend on the swing and started toward the front yard.

"Where are we?" Mikki asked. The pool and accompanying home they arrived at was simply spectacular, easily in the two-million-dollar price range, she surmised.

"I'm not sure. North of Atlanta, Buckhead maybe? We're close," Noah replied. They all knew the target lived in Tuxedo Park, but none of them knew which way it was from there. When they arrived at the road, they had a decision to make: left or right. There were more cars traveling east, so they decided to head west, as Carrington lived in a cul-de-sac that branched off of another dead-end road.

"What time is it, and how long have we been gone?" Leah asked, simply trying to ease the nervous tension they were all feeling.

"We have been away for one day, Leah," Jacob replied.

Jack still couldn't get over Jacob's transformation. Simply looking at him caused tears to well up in his eyes. A vehicle approaching from behind slowed to the speed at which they were walking instead of passing, even though there was no other traffic in either lane.

"Go around, numb-nuts!" Bass turned and yelled at the driver to no avail. The vehicle then stopped, and a man exited from the driver's side.

"Is that any way to talk to a superior officer, Sebastian?" the man asked. The voice was unmistakable: it was General Baker. "Jesus, you guys look like shit! And what's wrong with your eyes?" Baker asked. They all just looked at each other and then at Noah because they weren't sure this man could be trusted.

"Hello, General Baker," Jacob said as he stepped forward and moved in front of the group. The last and only time Baker had seen Jacob, he was what Baker would have described as severely and profoundly handicapped. Now he looked like any other thirteen-year-old boy. Baker couldn't believe his eyes, and it gave him hope in regards to his own delicate situation.

"You're…*fixed*. How did you do that, Noah?" Baker asked, more than slightly perturbed. *If Noah can make a mute talk, he can definitely help me with my problem,*

Rowland thought, *but he also could have fixed my problem fifty years ago and decided not to*.

"Rowland, at the time there were things I was allowed to do and not allowed to do. I was not allowed to help you, and for that I am truly sorry," Noah explained, though Jack, Sebastian, Leah, and Mikayla had no idea what he was talking about. "At this time, I am allowed to make it up to you, if you can help us." That sounded like a pretty good deal to Baker. All he really wanted out of the rest of his life was to see Carrington die a very painful death.

"I'm going to kill him when I see him. You do know that, right?" Rowland promised. First, he would shoot his kneecaps out so he couldn't run away, and then he would shoot him in the nuts with the remainder of the clip and watch him writhe in pain before he ultimately bled out.

"You can't, Rowland. It has to be done my way, and if you are going to come, you have to promise me that," Noah countered.

"I want to be there when he dies then," Baker replied. Rowland didn't just want to be there, he had to be there.

"It's a deal," Noah responded promptly, as though that was the plan all along.

"All right then. What can I do to help?"

"Can you give us a ride?" Jacob asked. It was the only thing Jacob and the rest of the group needed.

CHAPTER 70

"**D**oes that fireball in the sky have anything to do with you guys?" Rowland inquired of no one in particular. He was sure it was more than a decoy to help him elude the SEALs, but it was definitely effective. *The air force is no doubt involved by now, and the powers that be are surely huddling to devise an appropriate cover story*, he thought.

"It's a transport ship, among other things, that we dialed up from the silo, Rowland. Take a right at the light," Noah replied.

"What other things?" Leah asked. They were all just as curious.

"Well, let's see…first and foremost, it is a gold transport from here to Niburu. Gold can't be transported the way people can. It's also a prison for the nefarious soul, as I had mentioned earlier," Noah replied from the back seat.

Baker looked quizzically at Jack sitting in the front passenger seat, so Jack mouthed "the devil." Rowland simply shrugged his shoulders in acknowledgement.

"It has also been a beacon. If its reflective panels are aligned with the sun properly, it has a greater luminosity than the moon, but of course it is much smaller. It led the three clairvoyants, or wise men, as King James decided to call them in 1611, to Bethlehem to protect the baby Jesus, but that is a whole other story. Oh, and it's been known as the Wheel of Ezekiel, of course, and it was the manna machine and Red Sea divider used during the Exodus," Noah continued to explain.

"So the devil lives there, huh?" Baker asked with genuine interest.

"Nobody *lives* there, Rowland. The soul of the outcast Anunnakan known to humans as Satan is imprisoned on the transport, yes. Due to its extreme distance from Niburu, Satan will never incarnate again. Ever. An Anunnakan would have to be conceived on Earth for—" Noah was elaborating before Jack cut him off.

"Like Jacob. You say it can never happen, but Jacob happened, didn't he?" Jack sniped.

"It's not going to happen again, Jack! Stop doubting me!" The subject was obviously a sore spot for Noah. "The transport would have to be powered up too. Until today it hasn't been turned on in thousands of years. Take another right at the stop sign, then a quick left on the next cross street, Rowland," Noah instructed.

Jack wondered if Noah was responsible or culpable in some way concerning Jacob based on his hostile reaction, and he was correct.

The children of Jesus and Mary Magdalene, one boy and one girl, each inherited half of the Anunnaki-soul gene from their father and passed it down through their generations, unbeknownst to all. Noah was the sole Anunnakan responsible for ensuring none of the progeny united, as the consequences could be dire. Jesus was the product of artificial insemination on Niburu, which also explained his mother's virgin birth, but the eggs and sperm of Jesus' descendents were just as viable as any other human's. Jack and Jacob's father was a descendant of Jesus' son, and Noah knew that, but how the boys' mother ended up with the gene was still a mystery to him.

The only explanation Noah could legitimately consider was somewhere along the line, DNA was intentionally taken, mishandled, or misplaced, and possibly twice, because none of the descendants had ever had relations or even knew each other. This would imply that another party, unbeknownst to Noah and the Anunnaki, may have created a complete bloodline separate from the two Noah was following.

"Whatever. It's just that *never* is a very long time. You should say it's extremely unlikely that Satan will incarnate again," Jack chided. *Might as well have a little fun with him*, Jack thought.

"How are you going to get the gold on the transport ship?" Mikki asked, thankfully changing the subject.

"Jacob is going to do it the same way I took it from Fort Knox, with the device Carrington still has. The Egyptians used it to move blocks weighing thousands of tons, so a little gold will be no problem," Noah explained. "Everyone knows their role in the plan, correct?" They all nodded their heads in agreement.

"How do you know everything will go so smoothly?" Bass asked. "From what you told us, he knows we are coming." *The plan is sound, but we're dealing with a psychopath*, Bass thought.

"Because I know Carrington. He will jump at the opportunity to save himself, and then his narcissism will force him to do exactly what the girls say, Sebastian," Noah replied. The group had come to the end of the road, and the only way to continue would be the driveway that veered to the right.

"We're here," Jacob announced. Rowland slowly pulled the van up the tree lined driveway at 16 Parkside Lane, and a veritable mansion appeared before them. They immediately recognized it from the remote viewing session taken earlier from Niburu. Everyone was nervously holding their breath as the vehicle came to a stop.

"Let's go get him," Noah stated as he opened his door and got out. The rest of the group followed suit, and they walked hand in hand up to the front door.

CHAPTER 71

"Should I knock?" Mikayla asked after they'd traveled the twenty yards from the driveway to the front door. There would be no need as the door opened and a man with strikingly odd features appeared. He reminded Mikki of Lurch from *The Addams Family*, complete with an extremely long face and odd indentations at each temple.

"Can I help you kids?" the man asked.

He seems harmless, Mikki thought. *How did a meek and mild middle-aged man get tangled up with a monster?*

"We're here to see Dr. Carrington, Mr. Dobbs. Could you please let him know we are here?" Noah asked. The man was taken aback at the sound of his own name. He was either a very good actor or truly didn't know they were coming.

"There's nobody here by that name, son," Dobbs replied.

This cat and mouse game could go on forever, Bass thought. It was time to take the bull by the horns.

"You go tell Dr. Carrington, or Christian Lomax, or whatever you want to call him, that we're here to see him, and we have something he so desperately needs," Bass explained. The man told them to wait there and he would return momentarily. He returned as promised a couple of minutes later.

"Dr. Lomax claims you have nothing he needs and expressly informed me to forbid, *forbid*, any of you from entering his home," Dobbs informed them. Noah looked genuinely nervous to Jack. Getting in the home was integral to their plan.

"As Sebastian said, we have something he so desperately needs," Noah stressed while pointing at Jacob. Dobbs looked at Jacob and did a double take, obviously surprised he was no longer handicapped. "This boy is Carrington's cure. Go get him or we're leaving. I'll give you one minute."

Jack was impressed that Noah turned the tables so quickly. Once again, the door closed and they waited in silence. There was no doubt Carrington was watching and listening.

It took only thirty seconds for a balding elderly man to come to the door holding a brown colored drink with one large ice cube in it. Despite the plastic surgery, Noah recognized him immediately.

"Hello, Hollis," Noah said quietly and somberly.

"What is he doing here?" Carrington sniped while pointing at General Baker.

"He's with us. He helped us get here. May we come in and discuss terms?" Noah said, changing the subject. Jack was once again very impressed.

"No. There is nothing to discuss. You're *not* coming in, and you're *not* taking my gold," Carrington explained.

"But just for shits and giggles, what is it that you have and I so desperately need, may I ask?" Carrington's verbatim recantation of what Noah said to Dobbs was proof that Hollis had indeed been listening earlier.

"Your health. This boy can cure you, Hollis. All I ask in payment is the return of my gold," Noah said in reply. Hollis was deep in thought for several seconds before replying to the offer.

"Go fuck yourself, Noah. It's my gold. I have faith that my doctors can cure me!" Carrington vehemently replied. Hollis backed away from the door with the intention of slamming it in their faces when Mikki spoke up.

"What if you can live for centuries?" she blurted out. The door stopped mid-slam.

"No! That is not part of the offer, Mikayla. Our apologies for wasting your time, Hollis," Noah said hurriedly as he turned to leave. The door quickly reopened, and Hollis appeared with a very muscular man with white hair. The goon also had a gun.

"Grab that one, Sven," Carrington said, pointing at Mikki. Mikki tried to escape the brute's clutches but was unsuccessful.

"You have a deal, sweetmeat!" Carrington said to Mikki. "You cure me, you answer *all* of my questions, and you make good on her deal of immortality, and I'll give you some gold," Carrington said, this time to Noah. Noah simply stood there with his eyes closed for several seconds, seemingly mulling it over before he replied.

"Fine, Hollis. You win," Noah stated resignedly. "Now may we enter your home?" Noah had been adamant when discussing the plan that no one was to enter the house before Hollis answered affirmatively to this specific question.

"Come on in!" Hollis replied.

CHAPTER 72

"Did he take the bait?" Matthew Nastally asked lieutenant Gumper. He and Gump both knew Baker would never give up the location of the group, so they had hoped he would lead Gump and his crew to them. They were correct.

"Yes. He drove around for about five minutes then stopped and picked them up. I don't think he knew exactly where they were, but he had a pretty good idea. It's likely the boy in Iowa used some sort of code for the landing site. They are now at the Buckhead home of a Dr. Christian Lomax," Gump replied. He could wring that little shit's neck in Iowa for deceiving him, but he probably would have done the same if the roles had been reversed.

"Good, good. I want you to get over there and cleanse the scene, Gump. This Christian Lomax character is probably some sort of ringleader. I want him delivered to me personally, do you understand that?" Nastally asked.

"Absolutely, sir. Everyone is to be eliminated except Lomax, correct?" Gump asked. He wanted to be sure he was killing the right people, of course.

"Correct. Then bring Lomax directly to me. Great job today, Gump. Now go finish this thing. Goodbye, Lieutenant." Gump heard a distinct click on the other end.

"Did you hear all that, sir?" Gump asked. Nastally had no idea he was on a three-party call that Gump had arranged behind his back.

"Yes, Brady. You were right in your decision to bring me in on this. There are entities in play here, as you most likely know, that are beyond your pay grade. Some are even above mine," the president of the United States stated. "Nastally is a traitor, likely in cahoots with Lomax, and he is trying to use you to do his bidding for him."

"So I am the patsy, like Oswald?" Gump asked, somewhat bewildered. Gump thought back to all the missions he'd been on the past two years at the direction of Matthew Nastally and wondered how many of them were bogus.

"Don't beat yourself up, Lieutenant Gumper. You were following direct orders. I will have Matthew Nastally detained and you will only take orders directly from me now, do you understand?" the president asked.

"Yes, sir. How do I proceed?" Gump asked.

"For now, you will stand down. This group is actually on our side," the president revealed. Gump felt like he had been punched in the stomach. He had treated these people, especially Baker, so poorly, and he felt ashamed.

"The boy is here to collect payment, so he will need some time. I want you to get to the scene and monitor the proceedings from the sidelines. If you feel the group is in imminent danger, then take action to protect them from Lomax. Otherwise, stay out of it," the president explained.

"I don't understand, sir. What is he collecting a payment for?" Gump asked, even though it was technically none of his business.

"It's a debt owed from the infancy of our country, Brady. These aliens helped our forefathers win the American Revolution and establish this great country of ours. I'll just leave it at that," the president explained, and that was good enough for Gump.

He would protect this group with his life.

CHAPTER 73

"You don't have to squeeze my arm so hard!" Mikki sniped at the white-haired goon. He let up on his grip of her arm, but not much. Bass wanted to rip his head off.

"Sven, these are our guests!" Carrington said sarcastically. He didn't care if his fixer tore her arm off. "Everyone into the den, and if you try anything, everyone dies!"

"Hollis, there is no need for hostility. As you will see, there will be an equitable trade. Let's cure your cancer, then we can talk," Noah said, attempting to deescalate the scene. "I'm sure you have an IV so we can get the transfusion started." This piqued Carrington's interest.

"How are you going to cure me with a simple blood transfusion? I've had stem cell therapy already, and it didn't help," Carrington explained, nodding to Simon to get what Noah had asked for.

"This blood is special," Noah replied, pointing to Jacob. "Have you ever heard of golden blood, or the blood of Christ? Well, it flows through Jacob's veins," Noah continued. Simon returned with the kit and prepped both Jacob and Hollis's arms with an alcohol swab.

"Sounds like voodoo to me. How will I know that it worked? It will take weeks to eliminate the cancer, if not longer," Carrington countered. The blood started to fill from Jacob's end, filled the line, and then flowed into Carrington's arm. The jolt Hollis felt caused him to sit up straight on the sofa he had been reclined on.

"What the…" was all Carrington could say. His arm went numb and then began flexing uncontrollably. When the blood hit Hollis's heart, it was like an explosion in his chest. "I don't know what is happening!" Carrington screamed. Sven lurched forward to help, but Carrington waved him off.

"I'm all right," Hollis said to Sven. Noah was right. Hollis knew at that moment that his cancer, if not already gone, would be soon. Carrington's mind was racing with ideas about how he could exploit this kid with the Golden Blood. *People would pay millions for a pint of this*, he thought. What he really wanted to do was open this kid up and see what made him tick.

"Stop the transfusion, Mr. Dobbs. He only really needed a few drops. Any more and his heart might explode," Noah directed. Dobbs turned the dial on the tube, and the blood stopped flowing. "You say you want answers. What are your questions? We don't have all day," Noah asked, sounding annoyed.

"Who the hell *are* you people?" was all Hollis could come up with. His whole body was numb now but in a good way. He could feel his body healing from the inside out.

"Jacob and I are Anunnakan Seraphs, or Watchers, as described in the Bible. We are from a planet called Niburu, which is in a static orbit with your sun's sister star, a small red dwarf we call Regalis. Eons ago, we constructed a Dyson's Sphere around Regalis to harness power, and as a bonus, it safeguards our position from earthly detection," Noah explained. The girls were both paying attention as much as Hollis and Simon as they hadn't heard Noah's origin story before. Sven couldn't care less and continued to squeeze Mikki's arm.

"How does the Montauk device work?" Carrington asked. This one had been eating at him for decades, and he had to know the truth.

"It is simply a transportation device. When we were at Camp Hero, Rowland, the other boys, and I were travelling through time via our memories, replaying memories of previous lives. It was also used in ancient times to transport stone blocks to build temples and pyramids. It's an Anunnaki device, so most humans cannot operate it," Noah explained.

"So why could he use it so effectively? He's not an Anunnaki, is he?" Hollis asked, motioning toward Baker.

"No, he's a regular-old human like you. Rowland had success with the device because his memories of past lives were still partly accessible. For most humans they are not. The only reason the device is less effective for older humans is because they are farther away from their previous lives. It has nothing to do with maturing into adulthood," Noah explained.

Hollis looked at Rowland and shrugged his shoulders while mouthing the word "Oops." Baker wanted to throttle the old man with every fiber of his being but decided against it. Noah had warned him that Hollis would try to get under his skin.

"Why are you still a kid? Are you a time traveler?" Hollis asked. Time travel had always interested Hollis, and he hoped Noah would be able to help him accomplish it.

"No, I cannot travel in time. No race that I know of can. We can see into our own past, but not our future, using the device," Noah replied. "I am not a child, and I am actually older than you are. My life expectancy is about nine hundred years, like humans of the pre-Flood Old Testament."

"I want to live for nine hundred years, Noah! Make that happen, and you can have some of my gold," Hollis exclaimed. This is what Hollis really wanted: immortality, or the next best thing. *Living for almost one millennium would do for now*, he thought.

"I can't do that. You got the transfusion, and that will increase your life span by twenty years or so. That's the best I can do."

"Not good enough!" Carrington screamed as he stood up. The strength in his legs he never thought he would regain was amazing. That boy's blood was truly incredible. Hollis nodded to Sven, and the brute drew Mikki toward him and placed his gun at her temple. "You're taking me to your planet and making me immortal, godammit, or sweetmeat gets it, do you understand me, boy?"

"That's not how it works, Hollis," Noah stated in his calmest, most soothing voice. "Simply going to Niburu will make you the best version of yourself, but you will still be old and will age accordingly."

"You let me worry about that. You take me there, and I will convince your people to use gene therapy or something. You have a leader, right? I'll put a bullet in his ass if he doesn't do it. *Capisce?* Get ready. We leave in ten minutes."

"You're the boss. We need to start transporting the gold now though, Hollis," Noah said, still calm and collected.

"Your golden-blood buddy can do that. You, my friend, are coming with me. Simon, go get the bowl for them," Carrington commanded. He had one thing on his mind right now: getting to Niburu and becoming a god, and *nothing* would stop him. Simon returned with the transporting device moments later.

"Can you do this, Jacob?" Noah asked. At least this part of the plan was coming to fruition. They would just have to improvise everything else.

"Of course I can. I've used it many times. I believe the transport is in place, so I will get started," Jacob replied, and he set the device on his head and closed his eyes.

"Allright! Noah, you are going, of course. Sven and sweetmeat, you two are going. Baker, you're going, and Dobbs, you are going," Carrington stated as if he were Oprah handing out new cars at Christmas. "And you are going too. Leah, is it?"

"That's too many, Hollis. The most I've transported is five people, and you want to take six. Leave the girls." Once Carrington's mind was made up there was no changing it, and Noah knew that.

"Screw you, Noah. The girls are coming as hostages. If your boss doesn't give me what I want, then they will get it. Sven, pack a couple of extra clips. We may need them." Sven patted his jacket pocket, acknowledging he had plenty of ammo.

"You should take a gift for their leader, Dr. Carrington. Maybe a little diplomacy will get you farther than threats," Mikki offered. Hollis stared at her as if she was tricking him somehow, but either way he thought it was a good idea.

"That's a good idea, missy," Hollis said. *Now what to give the god who has everything?* he pondered. Gold, and he had just the piece. "Dobbs, get my necklace, the new one on my nightstand. And hurry!" Hollis wanted to get there right now.

Dobbs returned moments later with a gaudy half-inch thick rope with a 1978 Krugerrand attached to it. The rope was worth ten times the amount of the coin, but Hollis loved the coin for its intrinsic beauty. If this wouldn't entice a gold-hungry Anunnakan leader, nothing would. Hollis slipped it around his own neck.

"Are you ok, Rowland?" Noah asked. This was not specifically part of the plan, and Rowland could possibly be killed by any metallic objects in his body.

"Yes, Noah. I had a slurp of milkshake at the silo, and I took out the nuts," Rowland stated as he gave Noah a wink with his left eye. Noah breathed a sigh of relief that Rowland had both ingested some gold and removed his prosthetics.

"Enough yapping about milkshakes and nuts! Speaking of nuts, you're welcome for the impressive pair

I gave you back in New York, Rowland…how are they hanging, by the way? Now let's go!" Hollis exclaimed through a coughing fit of laughter. He was giddy, seemingly drunk on golden blood, and ready to claim his destiny: eternal life. Rowland's fists were clenched, and he fought the urge to beat the old man senseless right then and there.

"Gather around in a circle and interlock arms around me," Noah said as he drew them in closer, lowered his head, and closed his eyes.

"Could you at least holster that thing?" Mikki pleaded with Sven. The Nordic gave her a stern look but stuck his weapon between his jeans and his waist anyways.

"All right, here we go…" Noah whispered.

And they were gone.

CHAPTER 74

"I hope the girls are all right. I should have gone with them," Jack lamented. Simply being separated from Leah was eating him up inside.

"They are more than capable of taking care of themselves, Jack. I know either one could take me, but that isn't saying much," Bass replied, getting Jack to laugh a little bit.

"Tell me about it. They are both badasses. I don't know what it is about Leah, but she is all I can think about. Did she ever hook up with that other guy there, or talk about previous boyfriends?" Jack asked, fishing for information. If there was a possible other suitor, he wanted to know what he was going up against.

"Hah! Steven tried to get in her pants every day, but it definitely never happened. It's kind of funny, though. It appears Baker picked us and the girls with the intention of us coupling off to keep us happy. I was too intimidated to ask Mikki out, and Leah was too repulsed by Steven. I think I've been in love with Mikki since the day I met her," Bass explained. *So much has changed in the last two days*, he thought. *I asked the love of my life out, subsequently lost my virginity to her, and now I'm talking about it all with someone I barely know.*

"That's good to know. I just don't want to mess it up, you know?" Jack sighed. He had never felt this way either.

"I don't think you can. I know Leah pretty well, and she is really into you," Bass responded, and Jack let out an audible sigh of relief. Jacob then entered the den.

"I'm ready to get started. Can you guys give me a hand?" Jacob asked.

"Of course!" Jack and Bass replied in unison. They walked outside to the three-season deck, and Jacob sat down in a chair facing the outbuilding.

"What do you need me to do, buddy?" Jack asked, realizing he'd probably asked Jacob that exact question a thousand times without ever getting a response. This time he would.

"I have to keep my eyes closed, so I can't see what's happening. I need you guys to warn me if things get out of hand. It's been a while since I've done this," Jacob explained. It was a clear night and the moon was only a couple of days past full, so the visibility was pretty good.

"You got it, but I don't really know what I'm looking for," Jack responded.

"If things get out of hand, you'll know it," Jacob said, smiling as he put the device back on his head and closed his eyes. Several minutes passed with absolutely nothing happening, but both Jack and Sebastian stayed silent so Jacob could concentrate. Then, all of a sudden, there was a deafening *bang* as loud as any gunshot either of them had ever heard.

"Holy shit! What was that?" Bass asked. Before Jack could answer, they saw a steady stream of gold bars flying out of the outbuilding straight up into the sky. They gleamed in the ambient light.

"You have got to be kidding me! That is incredible!" Bass exclaimed. The river of gold bricks gleaming in the moonlight was seemingly endless.

"He must be sending them to the transport," Jack observed.

Even after twenty minutes, the river of gold was still going strong.

"That transport ship has to be almost full," Bass observed, and he was correct. "Isn't that the same place they're holding the devil?" he asked.

"Yes, but Noah claims that Satan has no way to escape," Jack replied, and he was also correct. The Anunnaki soul marooned on the transport ship also knew there was no escape. The only way it would ever get out of there was by being the closest Anunnaki soul to an Anunnaki egg fertilized by an Anunnaki sperm while the transport was powered up. All Anunnaki egg fertilization takes place on Niburu when a new soul host is needed, and only when needed, so there were never any accidents. Noah was correct; it seemed impossible. Now it appeared it would be taking the twenty-six-year trip to Niburu with a horde of gold. It did have a plan should it ever escape, though, and it refused to give up hope.

Never say never, it thought.

"Hey, look. The gold has stopped flying!" Bass exclaimed. The river of gold bricks had indeed stopped. Jacob had either filled the transport or depleted the supply. Both Jack and Bass felt the former was correct. That was a *lot* of gold. In fact, it was enough pure gold to properly seed the atmosphere of Niburu for another five thousand years.

"That was fun!" Jacob exclaimed, sounding exactly like a little boy who had just finished his first run on a giant roller coaster. *His eyes are different from before*, Jack thought. *They almost sparkle.*

"Jack and I have a bet. Did you fill the transport to capacity or did you run out of gold?" Bass asked. They didn't wager any money, but they were both curious.

"I ran out of gold. That's a really big ship," Jacob replied, still smiling. What he didn't tell them was that not all the gold went to the ship. Three bricks smashed through the rear window of the car Tom and Angela had just rented. Three bars also fell at the feet of Steven as he was hitchhiking on westbound US-30, and he quickly stuffed them in his backpack. The remainder, exactly thirty-three bars, fell from the sky and stacked themselves neatly just outside the porch door. Almost twenty million dollars, Bass figured.

It seemed each of them was now independently wealthy, but all Jack and Bass could think about were their girls.

CHAPTER 75

This trip to Niburu was completely different for Leah and Mikki, just as Noah had warned them it would be. It seemed to take forever. Leah was cognizant of her surroundings yet unable to see. Mikki, also awake and aware, tried to move but was unable to. Then, all of a sudden, they were there on the ground near the spot they had arrived at yesterday.

As they became aware of their surroundings, they were horrified. The gold necklace Hollis had been wearing was a white-hot pool of liquid metal. Carrington's head had been severed by the heat of the gold and had fallen to the ground and rolled several feet from his lifeless body. Mikki was staring at the severed head and noticed several holes and burns in Carrington's jaw and neck.

"His gold fillings burned right through his head and neck," Noah commented soothingly when he noticed Mikki was clearly disturbed by what she was seeing. "He was dead the moment we left, so he didn't suffer, if that's what you are worried about," Noah assured her.

"I know he had it coming, and he was an awful man, but this is pretty extreme," Mikki said. "What about this guy?" She asked, pointing at the Nordic man.

"Pretty much the same. The full clips he was carrying melted and embedded in his chest cavity, and you can see what happened to the gun," Noah offered, pointing at a pool of metal, bone, and blood next to Sven's body.

"I don't understand. The gold Carrington had around his neck killed him, but we ingested gold, and we are fine," Leah said.

"This mode of travel is designed specifically for Anunnakans, Leah. We have a good deal of gold in our system because of our seeded atmosphere. The gold in your body and my body heated up just enough to stave off hypothermia, which is the main cause of death for traveling humans," Noah explained.

Leah simply shrugged as if that was as good of an explanation as any.

Rowland calmly walked over to where Mikki, Leah, and Noah were standing and promptly kicked Carrington's deformed head with all his might. "That's for my parents!" Rowland exclaimed as he booted Carrington's head so far it landed at the entrance of Noah's house. "And this is for me!" he said as he kicked Carrington in the groin so hard the body raised up in the air a couple of inches despite the increased gravity. Rowland then turned away from the girls and put his hand down his own pants.

"How is this possible?" Rowland asked Noah when he realized he now had *real* testicles hanging from his midsection. His voice startled him as it was lower and much more authoritative than it was previously

"You guessed correctly when you self-operated, and now you have been made whole, Rowland. It's one of the side effects of traveling this way. You are now how you should be," Noah explained. Rowland had tears in his eyes as he gave Noah a big bear hug.

"You look great, General Baker!" Leah exclaimed. His "moobs" had been replaced by much more muscular and appealing pectoral muscles. His previously soft and pudgy midsection was now flat, and his saddlebag hips were replaced by more strapping and masculine thighs.

"I suppose I am going to face the same fate as my friends," Simon Dobbs uttered somberly. Everyone had forgotten about Dobbs because he wasn't a very threatening man.

"No, Mr. Dobbs. We mean you no harm," Noah answered. "You are a beautiful human being who has been corrupted by an evil entity. You will be returned to Earth to live out your remaining days as you wish. I believe you will find your appearance has changed dramatically for the better, too," Noah explained.

"But I don't understand…" Simon uttered as he felt the differences in the shape of his face and head with his hands.

"Your birth was complicated. The doctor improperly used a forceps and other tools attempting to extricate you from your mother's womb. Your appearance was due mostly to these errors, not genetics. You are now as you were meant to be," Noah explained.

Simon was now crying along with Rowland, and then the girls started crying because they were crying. Noah shook his head and smiled. This was a splendid outcome, he thought.

"What are you going to do with the bodies?" Simon asked. He didn't want to be implicated in their deaths and spend the rest of his life in prison.

"They will be set in the direct light of our star, which will effectively cremate them. The Gulfstream G650 is currently thirty thousand feet over Bermuda and will soon run out of fuel, presumably with Carrington and Sven on board, and it will crash into the ocean and be lost forever. The last will and testament of Dr. Christian Lomax will leave everything to General Rowland Baker," Noah stated. Leah's eyes lit up when she heard Rowland had inherited the mansion. She deduced some of the horrors Carrington had inflicted on him and felt the general deserved it.

"I don't want it. I don't want anything from that man," General Baker stated solemnly. He really wanted to forget what happened to him at the hands of Carrington, and he surely couldn't forgive, at least not yet.

"Maybe you could try to track down some of the other Montauk Boys and make reparations. If Carrington is as bad as you say, there are likely a slew of middle-aged men out there with physical and psychological issues," Leah offered. Baker's eyes lit up at the thought.

"That is an excellent idea, Leah! I've always wondered what happened to some of them," Baker exclaimed. His whole mood brightened as he had discovered a whole new opportunity to explore.

"You all can do whatever pleases you. I have reserved twelve hundred ounces of gold for each of you. That's about two million dollars apiece to do with as you wish as a gift from my people."

"What is Jacob going to do?" Leah asked. If Jacob had to come back to Niburu or be separated from Jack for any reason, Jack would be devastated.

"My good friend Jacob is a thirteen-year-old human boy about to enter the eighth grade at Bad Axe Middle school. He's going to play soccer in the fall and basketball in the winter for his school team and act in the school play. He'll be popular, and the girls will surely be fawning all over him. If you ask me, he is the luckiest little boy in the world because he has a brother who loves him unconditionally. It gives me great hope for the human race," Noah explained, fighting back tears. It was the first time any of them had seen Noah get emotional.

"So this is all over now?" Mikki asked. She was ready to start her life with Bass.

"Yes, it is over," Noah replied as he released a long sigh. "The good guys won, and the bad guys lost. Now who wants to go home?" They all raised their hands.

CHAPTER 76

The trip back to Earth was much less eventful. The girls warned Rowland and Simon that they might get wet, and they were correct. Splashdown was in another family pool, this one roughly half a mile north of Carrington's estate.

"Wow! That was exhilarating!" Rowland exclaimed upon surfacing. He immediately reached into his sweats to take an inventory, and he was not disappointed.

"Are you all right, Simon?" Mikki asked. Simon had been mostly silent and withdrawn since they had arrived on Niburu. Mikki really couldn't blame him as he had witnessed the gruesome death of his only companions in the world.

"I just don't know what I'm going to do. I have no friends and no family. My only reason to live was to serve Dr. Carrington, and now he's gone, too," Simon replied. Mikayla felt sorry for him.

"That settles it then. We are going to stay at the mansion for a couple of weeks, and you are going to stay with us. You know the house and grounds better than anyone. You can continue as the caretaker until General

Baker sells the house," Mikayla offered. She felt it was the least she could do, and Noah guaranteed that Simon was harmless and could be trusted.

"Thank you, Mikayla, you are too kind," Simon replied. "I will be the best butler you have ever had," he said, smiling.

"Can you stay in Atlanta for a while, General Baker?

"Thank you for the offer, but I have a lady friend in Des Moines that I would like to visit, so I will be leaving tomorrow," Rowland replied as he climbed out of the pool. Mikki and Leah didn't know exactly what atrocities Carrington had inflicted upon Rowland as a child, but they surmised it had something to do with his genitals. Neither of them really wanted to know the whole story.

"I understand," Leah replied. She was actually somewhat relieved as it would have been weird living with their former military boss.

"All of you will be formally honorably discharged, by the way, and when the smoke clears, I will personally see to that," Rowland added as they made their way around the house and to the road. They had no idea what time it was but figured it was between 2:00 a.m. and 4:00 a.m. as the sky was pitch back and the traffic was practically non-existent. They headed toward the brighter lights to the right and walked briskly without talking, each of them thinking about their own future and how bright it was.

Ten minutes into their walk, a black van passed and abruptly did a U-turn and pulled up behind them.

"What the hell is this?" Mikki wondered out loud. The driver's side door opened, and a man exited the vehicle.

"Well, look what we have here!" the man shouted. It was a voice Rowland recognized immediately.

"Oh, shit," Rowland whispered. "Is that you, Brady?" he yelled to the man. It was indeed Lt. Gumper and his death squad. The girls and Simon tried to huddle behind General Baker.

"It's all right, Baker! I was hoping I would run into you guys. Secretary Nastally has been exposed as a traitor and I have new orders to help you any way I can. Hop in, and I'll take you to the house," Gump replied. Gumper and his team had already been to Carrington's house and spoken with Sebastian and Jack, informing them of their order to stand down from none other than the president himself. The group looked at each other and shrugged their shoulders.

"Ok. Let's go," Baker responded. They didn't know where they were anyway, and they were actually walking in the wrong direction. The group piled in the van, and they were on their way.

"How far is it? Can you call them? What time is it? What *day* is it?" Leah asked in such rapid succession Gump didn't have time to answer any of them. She was excited to see Jack again even though they had only been apart for less than four hours.

"Slow down, lady!" Gump replied as he started tapping numbers on his phone. "It's just up the road. You must have a hot date or something. Here, tell him you will be there in five minutes. Give the phone to Baker after you're done. Someone wants to talk to you on speed dial number one, Rowland," Gump said as he handed Leah the phone and gave a wink and nod to Rowland.

Sebastian answered and was excited they were back so soon. Leah told him they would be there shortly. When the van pulled up the long driveway, Jack, Sebastian, and Jacob were out front waiting for them. Leah and Mikayla exited before the van even stopped and ran into the arms of their respective men.

"Oh my God, Jack, it was incredible! And disgusting!" Leah said as she held him tight to her bosom and nuzzled his neck. Even though they had met just two days ago, she was ready to take the next step in the relationship. Mikki, thrilled to see Sebastian again, gave him a big hug and then reminded Leah to give Jack the message Noah had sent.

"Hey, Jack, this house belongs to General Baker now. I want all of us to stay here for a while before you, me and Jacob go back to your farm in Michigan," Leah pleaded. She wasn't sure how Jack would respond.

"I want what you want, Leah. If that makes you happy, it makes me happy," Jack replied, and Leah could feel tears welling up in her eyes. She loved him so much.

The teary reunion was broken up by the whir of a helicopter's rotor increasing in volume until it was right in front of them: a Boeing AH-6 Little Bird attack helicopter and it was so close Gumper recognized one of the men immediately. It was the secretary himself, Matthew Nastally, and it seemed he meant to take care of some unfinished business. Unsure of what to do, the group, including the SEALs, just stood there staring at it, dumbfounded. The moment the gunfire erupted from the Little Bird, Jacob stretched his arms out into a crucifixion position, closed his eyes, swung his arms forward until his hands clapped together, and then swung them back out to their original outstretched position. At that point, something very peculiar happened.

Jacob disappeared.

CHAPTER 77

On July 9th, 1755, General Braddock's men were attacked by French and Native American forces while clearing land near the Monongahela River, thus starting what would become known as the French and Indian War. The battle itself was a sound defeat of the British forces, and General Braddock would die a few days later from a wound received in battle. The British army was saved from complete annihilation by the heroic efforts of a young aide-de-camp: George Washington.

Most historians believe it was pure luck that Washington survived the battle, as he had two horses shot out from under him, and later it was discovered that his jacket had four bullet holes in it. Christians would claim divine intervention, which would be much closer to the truth.

The battle was attended by an unassuming Anunnakan masquerading as a British soldier tasked with keeping Washington from harm. The method he used would also be employed by Jacob in this reprehensible attack on his friends. The Anunnakan controls time by speeding himself up, so the action before him in real time is slowed considerably. The Anunnakan in 1755 diverted six musket balls that most likely would have claimed Washington's life, effectively changing the course of American history. Jacob would be much busier, altering the trajectory of at least fifty high-powered slugs that would have hit a human target.

Once Jacob sped up his body, he moved quickly over to the group, who, of course, could not see him. The semiautomatic weapons of this era kept him busy. A simple tap of a bullet while in flight, which he could very easily see, would send it harmlessly on another path. The speed at which they were being fired was another issue, as the bullets were flying, in his time, at about one foot per second, so he literally had to run back and forth between each of the members of his group.

He had one chance—and one chance only—to end the "turkey shoot," as Nastally had called it. Rush the helicopter, create a diversion, and rush back to continue redirecting bullets.

"Now is as good of time as any," Jacob muttered out loud, as there seemed to be a momentary lull in the firing. He rushed the helicopter, which was now hovering just a few of feet off the ground, and saw his opportunity. One of the men firing clip after clip had two hand grenades hanging from a jacket pocket. Jacob quickly pulled the pin of the one on the left and hurried back to divert bullets.

Thankfully, by now most of the group had taken cover in real time. The three SEALs, who would have all surely died without Jacob's intervention, were at their weapons but not yet prepared to fire back. Jack, Sebastian, and Mikayla were behind the van. General Baker, Leah, and Simon were scurrying, but still in harm's way, and all of the bullets were now directed at them. It seemed Simon had purposely put his body between the gunfire and Leah.

Instead of tapping the bullets to one side as he had been doing, he began sending them up into the air by sticking his middle finger behind his thumb and then flicking it at them. He found this to be much more effective, but the sheer volume of bullets was taking its toll. One bullet was a mere inch from Leah's temple before he flicked it out of the way.

"That was close," Jacob said to himself. *Had that bullet struck its target, Jack would have been devastated*, he thought. Jacob redoubled his efforts to clear the path. "Why isn't that grenade going off?" he whispered to himself.

And then he saw it. A bright orange flash began at the soldier's pocket and started spreading rapidly within the helicopter. Jacob cleared the final bullets and determined he had an even larger problem.

"Oh shit," was all Jacob could say. The helicopter was in the process of exploding and shedding pieces of itself in all directions. Diverting bullets was one thing, but diverting a fifty-pound piece of metal, or perhaps one of the rotors, was quite another. Thankfully, nothing too large made its way toward the group, and after flicking away several small bits of shrapnel, he determined that they were finally safe.

Jacob surveyed the scene before returning to real time and saw that he had unfortunately missed at least one bullet.

CHAPTER 78

"Why aren't we hitting anything?" one of the soldiers in the Little Bird yelled seconds before the helicopter exploded. Jack knew. He didn't know how, but he knew Jacob was protecting them. The explosion shook the van, and Jack could hear bullets and shrapnel embedding in the other side. Gump and his boys had finally gotten to their weapons, but the shooting stopped when the helicopter exploded.

"Is everyone all right?" Baker screamed. *Based on the distance from the target and the amount of shots fired, everyone on both sides of the van should be dead right now*, he thought, as he slipped away to place that phone call to speed dial number one.

"Simon has been hit!" Leah screeched. Simon was sitting with his back against the passenger side rear wheel of the van and had a large red splotch in the middle of his chest.

"Hang in there, buddy," Jack said to him as he started to apply pressure to the wound. Simon winced in pain and he knew, as did the rest of the group, that this was a mortal wound. "I saw what you did, and that was the most heroic, unselfish act I have ever witnessed. Thank you," Jack added, referencing Simon's shielding of Leah. Simon acknowledged Jack's thanks by nodding slightly.

"Can I get a mirror?" Simon croaked. The bullet had pierced his right lung, and it was difficult for him to speak.

"What was that? Did you say you want a mirror?" Jack asked, uncertain if Simon was in his right mind. Jack looked closely at Simon and understood. Traveling to and from Niburu had changed Simon. The rest of the group had gathered around the wounded man. Both of the girls were crying.

"Give me your gun, Brady," Jack blurted, quickly grabbing Gumper's Uzi. With the butt of the gun Jack broke off the van's passenger side wing mirror and took it over to Simon, who studied the image intently for several seconds.

"I look good, don't I?" Simon asked Mikayla, a tear falling down his right cheek. Mikayla nodded in agreement.

"You look great, Simon. You are a very handsome man," Mikayla responded. And he did, she thought. Simon smiled at Mikayla, exhaled loudly, closed his eyes, and peacefully died. "Where's Jacob?" she screamed.

"Right here. Mikayla, I'm sorry, but I cannot help him. It doesn't work that way," Jacob stated somberly after appearing out of nowhere. "Electrically stimulating a heart into rhythm is completely different than healing the catastrophic damage caused by a bullet. Once again, I'm sorry."

"We have to get out of here," Gump stated. He knew this would be a huge story and he had to initiate full damage control immediately. "Put the body in the van, boys," Gump directed his two men.

"I'm sure the media will be here soon as that was quite an explosion. The story from the Pentagon will be an urban terrorism training mission gone south. Do you understand?" Gump asked the group.

"I'll handle the news crews, Brady," General Baker assured, as he ended his phone call by pressing the red button. "I've done it before. They'll believe anything if you make it sensational enough."

"Thank you, Rowland. And I'm…I'm sorry. For everything," Gump said not to just Rowland, but to the whole group.

"Don't mention it. You were following orders, but at the end of the day you did the right thing, so we should thank you," Sebastian said. Thanks to the intervention of the president, Gump, and his men, no one in the group was wanted by the government any longer, and no one was in trouble with the law.

"Ok. Stay safe!" Gump yelled as the van started down the driveway. Sirens could be heard in the distance but were getting steadily closer.

"How is the Pentagon going to explain a helicopter crash in Buckhead of all places?" Mikayla wondered out loud.

"It's what they do," Rowland answered.

CHAPTER 79

"That was something else, wasn't it?" Jack asked the group. When the National Guard had pushed the media back to the road, they pretty much disbanded, off to the next sensational story.

"It's been a very crazy day—make that couple of days," Sebastian answered. Two days ago, he hadn't even asked Mikki out yet, let alone made love to her. *The future is bright for Sebastian Parker*, he thought.

"What do we do now, though? Noah told us the house belongs to General Baker, and we have all the money we will ever need, but what do we *do*?" Leah asked.

Jacob stood up and thought carefully before speaking. "Incursions such as these are literally once in a lifetime. We just don't do it unless absolutely necessary, and in this situation, action was absolutely necessary. Our atmosphere was failing due to lack of gold, and Carrington was killing doctors for reasons still unknown to us," Jacob explained. "That said, now we simply live our lives. I would like all of us to be together here, at least for a short time. Traveling the way you did can have side effects that may not manifest right away, and I can help if

302

you develop symptoms," he warned. "Then I'm going to start middle school in Michigan, and work on the farm. I consider myself the luckiest Anunnakan in the universe."

"But won't you already know all the answers?" Leah asked, smiling. She had only known this little boy for a couple of days, but she already loved him to death.

"That's not the point," Jacob replied, also smiling widely. "The last Anunnakan to live as a human on Earth was two thousand years ago, so I have an opportunity to enjoy something few of my people ever have."

"The last one ended in a crucifixion, though, didn't it?" Bass asked. He didn't want to be a buzzkill, but life could be dangerous for Jacob. "What I mean is there are people out there that would kill to get to you. Some have already tried. You are going to have to be extremely careful."

"He's right, Jacob. What kind of danger are you in right now?" Jack asked. "What about being tracked like when you were born? Can you still be tracked that way?"

"I can control it now. It's like excreting waste. When I was a baby, I could not control urinating or…you know, and now I can. It's the same with my soul. I promise you, no one else will discover my true identity," Jacob explained.

It makes sense, Jack thought. But he wasn't entirely sure it was true. Evil people could be very resourceful when motivated properly.

"There are still members of the cabal out there, right? They know who you are now, don't they?" Mikki added.

Jacob seemed deep in thought. "Apparently, the head of the cabal was Nastally, and the number two was

Carrington. The rest, I'm sure, were simply foot soldiers who didn't even know the true identity of their leaders. Like most nefarious organizations, the foot soldiers don't know who is in charge or even the true plan in case they get caught. They can't squeal about what they don't know," Jacob explained. They were all hoping that the whole cabal had been squashed like a bug on a windshield.

"Do we have anything to fear from the government?" Leah asked. Being in the armed forces, she knew how persistent the military could be.

"Let me tell you all a story," General Baker interjected. "You have all heard of the Book of Secrets, right? It's the book that the president has with all the answers to all the questions, right? Wrong. There *is* a book, but it is held by a normal anonymous American family, passed down from generation to generation. A president can only add to the book for future presidents. The keeper of the book determines if a sitting president needs any of the information from previous presidents," he explained.

"I was told by the president himself that George Washington authored an entry describing in great detail all of the aid given by 'otherworldly beings' during our nation's infancy and that the debt would be collected in gold in approximately two hundred years. Kennedy was the first to hear of it, as the keeper felt the number may be slightly less than two hundred. When Johnson took office after the assassination of Kennedy, he was also given the information. When Fort Knox was 'robbed' in broad daylight during his term in office, he felt the debt had been paid in full." Rowland explained.

"Well, this family is either well connected or it has people monitoring everything, because the president was informed yesterday about the presence of an Anunnakan and that it was imperative that no harm come to him. It's how that traitor Nastally was flushed out," Rowland explained.

"I would love to get my hands on that book!" Leah exclaimed. She always wondered who really shot JFK and what had really happened in Roswell in 1947.

"No, you wouldn't," Jacob warned, shaking his head. "Knowledge burdens you, believe me. For the first time in a very long time, I am not burdened by knowledge, and it is unbelievably refreshing. You can't worry about what you don't know about, Leah."

Leah shook her head in agreement. She hadn't thought about it that way.

"Jacob, we are all going to see to it that you have a normal American teenager experience. You will have a ten o'clock curfew, and there will be no dating until you are fifteen…no sixteen," Leah stated, smiling. "You better watch what you wish for, Jacob!"

"It is what I want, believe me. I'm truly hoping I…*we* can put all this behind us and just be a family. Jack is a better father than most fathers, and you, Leah, are going to be a great mother," Jacob replied as he was choking up and had tears welling up in his eyes. "And I have Uncle Bass and Aunt Mikki to run to when my parents make the mistake of grounding me!" he exclaimed, smiling brightly again. Jack was also overcome with emotion just watching Jacob interact with the others. He looked so *happy.* Jack had dreamed of the day Jacob would be free of his affliction, and today was that day.

"I hate to rain on your parade here, kids, but how are you going to explain the fact that Jacob isn't autistic any longer? Not only is he not autistic, but he will likely be the smartest eighth grader at his school, correct?" General Baker asked. Everyone's smiles turned to frowns as they stared at Jacob. The mesmerizing boy even *looked* smart now.

"I can explain that," Jacob interjected. "There has been at least one case of rapid spontaneous recovery from autism, and we can tell people we were in Atlanta seeking treatment. Uncle Pete will be the hard one to convince, but leave that to me. Since I was homeschooled by Mom and later by Abbie and Jack, there really isn't anyone else to convince otherwise."

"See? He's already the smartest person in the room!" Mikki exclaimed.

"I don't know about all of you, but this old man is tired. It's past 2:00 a.m., and I am going to bed," Rowland announced. The rest of them decided not much else could be accomplished at this point and decided to join him. Leah took Jack's hand and squeezed it tight.

"I'm ready, Jack," Leah whispered in his ear. Just the thought of being with her sent blood coursing to his extremities. Their pact to take things slow just wasn't humanly possible.

"So am I, Leah. I don't have protection, though," he whispered back as they climbed the spiral staircase. Leah felt as though she was in a fairy tale and this was the happy ending.

"I'm on the pill," she replied. She was on the pill, but not *totally* on the pill. Since she wasn't sexually active at this point of her life, a couple of missed tablets here or there didn't concern her too much. As they crossed the threshold of their chosen room, they both noticed the walk-in shower in their private bathroom.

"Do you want to take a shower?" Leah asked coyly. Jack removed his shirt, started the water, and all three heads erupted with a fine mist.

His upper body and washboard stomach are fabulous, Leah thought. Jack would credit hard work on the farm, but in actuality, traveling to and from Niburu had more of an impact.

"I'm not a virgin, but I'm a virgin. Does that make sense to you?" Leah asked. She didn't want to have a conversation about her number but wanted Jack to be aware.

"Yes. Sebastian mentioned the strange side effects that traveling has on women," Jack replied. He was also uncircumcised now, but Leah probably already knew that, so he decided not to mention it.

"So you and Bass were talking about us, huh?" Leah said, smiling. She and Mikayla talked at length, and *about* length, concerning the boys earlier, so she really couldn't say much.

"Just about that," Jack said, smiling sheepishly. Leah removed her clothes, and Jack was stunned. Not only was she was the most beautiful girl he had ever met, but her body was also *perfect*. "You look amazing, Leah," Jack whispered in her ear while water fell over them from all sides. The walk-in shower had a bench, so Jack took a seat and pulled Leah toward him. His hands and mouth disrupted the water beads coursing down her body.

Leah felt a tension in her belly, and she throbbed with an urgency that needed to be sated. She straddled Jack and eased herself down, hesitating as he took her reclaimed virginity. They became one as she moved in delicious circles, grinding until they both exploded into simultaneous full-body orgasms. They sat motionless as the water poured over them, gazing into each other's eyes. Leah was still shaking when Jack picked her up and carried her to the king-size bed, grabbing towels along the way.

"That was amazing," Jack whispered in Leah's ear as he patted her back and extremities dry.

"Yes, it was. It's almost as if we were meant to be together, Jack, like we were *made* for each other," Leah said sleepily. Having been up for almost twenty-four hours straight, she was physically, emotionally, and mentally exhausted. Jack lifted her to the right side of the bed and pulled the covers up to her midsection before crawling in himself. He leaned over and kissed her one more time on the forehead.

"I love you, Leah," Jack whispered as he gently stroked her cheek with the index finger of his right hand. She didn't reply, but that was all right with Jack.

She was sound asleep.

EPILOGUE

Two Days Later

During its time in captivity, it had been practicing for the day it would be set free. Controlling one's soul was crucial for avoiding detection. They would never know it was gone.

It was curious when the transport's main engines fired. The last time that happened was just over two thousand Earth years ago, when the spacecraft directed those meddlers to the baby. Now it would be possible, though still highly improbable, that it could escape the confines of the transport ship. It would never give up hope, because never was not a valid length of time for an immortal being.

When the feeling of embryo implantation hit, it immediately went into what it thought of as a sort of mental hibernation, exactly what it had been practicing for so many millennia. It completely shut down its thoughts. It had to act human.

Jack knew he most likely carried the recessive Anunnakan gene, because Jacob did. Leah did not know that she was the granddaughter seventy-seven times removed from Jesus and Mary's daughter and also had the gene. Together, they had a twenty-five percent chance of creating a receptacle for an Anunnaki soul.

The odds were not in its favor, but it hit the jackpot. Jack and Leah were pregnant…with the *Antichrist.*

Nearly two trillion miles away in a bare home bathed in crimson light, a little black-haired boy sat in the middle of the dwelling with his legs crossed and his eyes closed. As he opened his eyes, the corners of his mouth began to turn upward, and soon his pursed lips separated and his teeth began to show. Before long, he was grinning ear to ear, for the little boy had just completed the longest of the long cons, many centuries in construction. This little boy's father was finally free, and he was *smiling.*

Two Weeks Later

"Where is the boy now?" asked the man wearing the scarlet ferraiolo. His mind returned to the day thirteen years ago when the psychic alerted them to the child's presence. "I knew the seer was right. There was a divine birth, and we missed our opportunity. It will be a hundred times harder to get to this boy now."

"He left Atlanta Wednesday and is back at the family farm with his brother and the brother's girlfriend," the mercenary divulged. "They aren't going anywhere, cardinal. He's already enrolled in the local middle school. And you know what we're dealing with here… the Anunnakans can be clever little buggers."

"What's done is done, gentlemen," the only woman in the room declared. "What matters now is what we do from this point forward. The Bilderbergs have deep pockets, so whatever it takes, you have our financial support."

"What are our options? How can we even get close to the boy without his knowing? How in the hell are we going to trick him?" the cardinal asked of no one in particular. "Remember, he is the embodiment of our savior, Jesus Christ, and I believe Jesus would have sussed out a common kidnapping. You all saw the satellite footage of the helicopter attack by that idiot, Nastally. The kid disappeared."

"Matthew Nastally served his purpose and our cover is still intact. We believe the black-haired Anunnaki boy baited Lomax and his henchman somehow and then crashed the empty plane in the ocean," the mercenary replied. "Pretty ingenious plan, really."

"I think I can help," the elderly man representing the Illuminati interjected. "The boy must be befriended. We have a young girl in mind and have already enrolled her in the same school as the boy."

"He'll see right through her, Lyle," the cardinal interjected. "I don't see any way to get close to him."

"She can do it. She won't know what she's doing or why she's doing it, so there won't be anything for the boy to find out," Lyle explained. "She's a cute little thing, and she'll have him eating out of her hand in no time."

"I'll believe it when I see it, but I pray you're right. The rest of the plan must go exactly as outlined in the prophecy," the cardinal countered. "The boy must be crucified, and I want it done before his fourteenth birthday. At that momentous occasion, my friends, we will usher in our new world order."

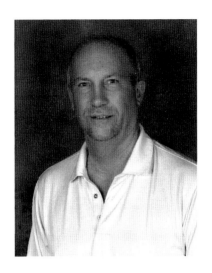

ABOUT THE AUTHOR

Michael Klug was born and raised in Michigan, where he still resides. He attended Berry College in Rome, Georgia, on a baseball scholarship, and graduated with a BS in accounting. He currently works as a night shift team leader in the automotive industry. Michael has been married to wife Kristin for 30 years, and together they have two sons. His interests include hunting, fishing, and sports card collecting.

Visit blackeyedseraph.com